KINGDOM OF THE DEAD | BOOK TWO

QUEEN OF THE DEAD

A ZOMBIE ROMANCE

RYANA HUNTER

Black Rose Writing | Texas

ISBN: 978-1-68513-621-5
PUBLISHED BY BLACK ROSE WRITING
www.blackrosewriting.com

Printed in the United States of America
Suggested Retail Price (SRP) $21.95

Queen of the Dead is printed in Garamond Premier Pro

*As a planet-friendly publisher, Black Rose Writing does its best to eliminate unnecessary waste to reduce paper usage and energy costs, while never compromising the reading experience. As a result, the final word count vs. page count may not meet common expectations.

For those that find hope in the darkest of places.

Hierarchy of the Horde

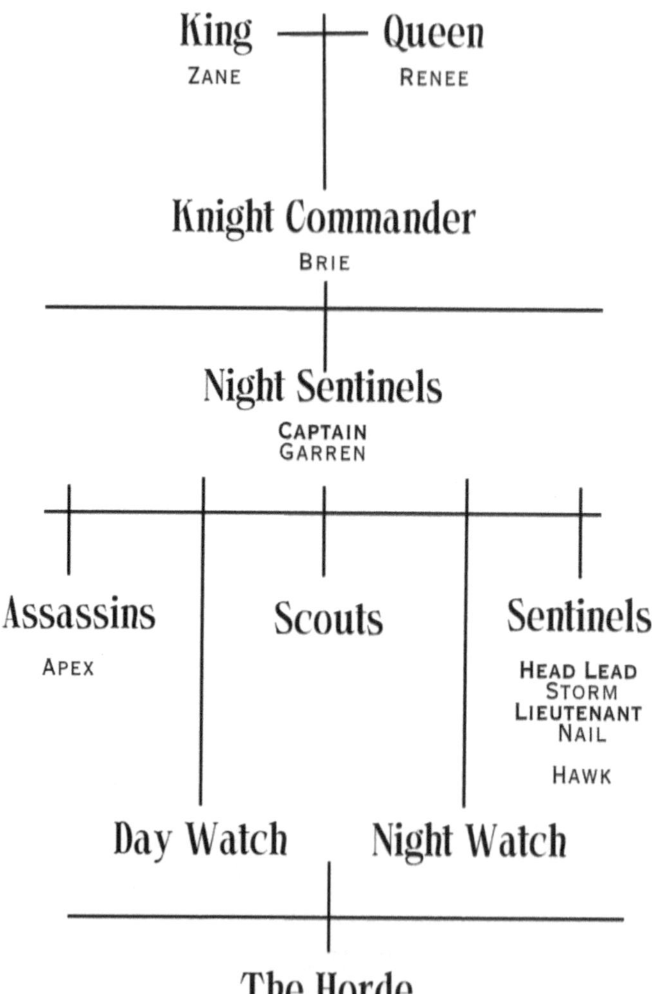

New York
Massachusetts
Connecticut
Pennsylvania
Maryland
Worcester
Boston
New Haven
Albany
New York
Philadelphia
Baltimore
Boston Necropolis
Horde
?????
Survivors
Ander
N
E
W
S

QUEEN OF
THE DEAD

Prologue

Miles smirked as his minions herded the humans back into their cages. They wanted to devour them. Hell, he wanted to devour them, but that wasn't the plan. Landry wanted them for his experiments, which, for now, he'd go along with. But he wasn't as stupid as Landry thought.

Landry believed he was using him to control the others, but the truth was Miles was using Landry to get what he wanted. Endless food. When he first turned into *this*, he was too stupid to understand what would happen as he continued to make more and more undead to follow him.

Sure, he finally had the army he'd always deserved, but after a while, when he got smarter, he realized how bad things were going to be for him if he didn't figure something out. Miles wasn't a scientist or doctor, but after he'd gotten sick when he was still alive, he'd spent enough time around them to pick up a few things. When he was human, his family didn't have a lot of money but they had influence with the military and because of that, he was approved to be part of a program he technically didn't qualify for. That put him around a bunch of smart people that hadn't always been total dicks to him and sometimes indulged his questions.

He wouldn't give up his army, they were *his*. His and no one else's, but it was hard to keep them all from wasting away without fresh meat. Over the years, they had devoured most of the Midwest, and they were now consuming most of the east coast, but that wasn't a solution. Plus, he was tired of moving around all the time.

They'd taken other territories from other hordes because he didn't want to leave the east coast. He liked it. Being close to the water felt peaceful. Miles enjoyed waking up to the smell of the sea, its tangy salt odor tugged on his memories of things he used to like to eat. He'd tried to eat something other than meat, but it always came back up or something acidic burned his mouth.

Other zombies tasted like garbage compared to fresh humans, but tough times, and his lack of motivation to move, demanded it. When his horde found Boston, he knew he had to take it for his own. The idiot humans had spent too much time there, getting many luxuries put into place, like they were preparing for their new ruler — him. Too weak to fight off his horde, they took the territory easily and then started capturing humans for his and Landry's purposes.

Miles liked having running water and electricity again. He was finally getting the luxuries he'd deserved his entire life. Plus, he had Landry to help figure out how to make food so they could stay. At least that was the deal between them. Landry would figure out the food situation and all Miles had to do was keep the territory, destroying everything that came near them.

As much as he indulged in the comforts of civilization, the beast inside that craved death and violence never slept. It wanted blood and flesh all the time. He'd managed it by thinning his own horde, but those who remained were restless because they wanted fresh, human meat. Landry swore he was close, but if he didn't provide a solution soon, he was probably on the menu next.

The only source of amusement, other than tormenting the captive humans, was poking at his rival, Kendrick. He had that prick on the run and it made Miles happy, except that meant he would be bored all winter. Miles had recalled some of his troops that planned to attack his horde because he knew it would only drive them further north. He hoped Kendrick would start fighting back. They hadn't fought in years, both of them had much smaller hordes then, but it'd been the most fun Miles had since he turned into a zombie.

Miles rubbed his leg. It still fucking ached, even after turning undead. It should have healed like his arm, but it hadn't which only infuriated him more toward Kendrick. Bastard had known exactly where to hit him when they fought. But now Miles had learned where to hit him back and, unlike his injuries, they wouldn't be skin deep. He was going to destroy Kendrick. Strike where it hurt the most — take his pride and more.

Patience had never been his strong suit, but for Kendrick, Miles would make an exception. Nothing would stop him from eradicating him and his horde off the map.

Chapter 1 - Renee

"There. Better," Brie sat back, admiring her work.

"Do you have a mirror?" Renee asked.

Garren hovered near them since Renee and Brie paused during the march to sit on a fallen tree so Brie could tame Renee's hair. Garren handed Renee a small, compact mirror that he had been carrying in his pocket since the last city. As always, he was careful when their fingers brushed against each other's, keeping his sharp claws away from her skin. She flashed him a grateful smile and raised the mirror up to see the braids Brie put in.

Renee's heart squeezed in her chest. Not multiple braids, it was only one, and it was so pretty — *she* was pretty because of it. She looked like a princess about to attend court.

"*Queen* Renny. You look like a queen," Liam corrected her just out of her eyesight, which only made her smile broaden.

"See? I know what the fuck I'm doing. You didn't want it all back, and it's not. That's called a waterfall braid. It's not as practical, but it looks nice," Brie said with pride. "At least this way it will stay out of your face with this wind."

Renee bolted up and grabbed Brie into a hug. She knew Brie didn't like physical affection, but she was happy Brie spent the time to make her as elegant as she was, or at least by appearance. She'd never have Brie's poise, style, or mannerisms, but she was grateful she appeared less frumpy.

"Okay. Okay, you like it. Fuck, I think you're stronger than you used to be," Brie grumbled.

Renee loosened her arms just a tad. "Will you do it like this again later?"

"Yes, I'll do it like that as often as you want if you let me go."

Renee's cheeks heated as she released Brie. "Sorry. I always wanted friends who got me. I didn't even tell you I wanted it like this. I look so regal." Her fingers glided over the braid that wrapped around the back of her head. Even after looking in the mirror, she didn't know how Brie put a braid around her hair, also weaving it into her loose strands.

Brie chuckled. "If you like that style so much, I have a bunch I could try out on you as long as you're willing to sit there for a while."

Renee tried to be an adult but failed when she squealed with joy. Maybe part of her would never grow up. But she hadn't lied. It had taken her actual demise to find a genuine friend who understood her, and that cared what she did or didn't like. Even with the day-to-day difficulties of existing at the end of the world, Renee still felt like the luckiest zombie. She had a boyfriend who was crazy in love with her, who completed her soul, and a best friend who was amazing in every way possible. And while their friendship was unorthodox, given the whole world-ending-thing, they each cherished their newfound friendship with one another.

Garren let out a small laugh, drawing Renee's attention. His red irises were filled with admiration. Renee grinned back at him, but unease dampened her mood. She wasn't sure why he had affection for her — he'd accepted her. He'd immediately seemed to like her, and no one really *liked* Renee when they met her. Individuals needed time to see past her annoying traits, her overly-dramatic words and actions, before they could accept her. But Garren didn't seem bothered by her in the least.

"It's because you're his queen. You should make him the Captain of the Night Sentinels or at the very least Head Sentinel. I don't think anyone else is as loyal as he is other than Brie," her brother piped up.

Tempted to turn her head and address him, Renee didn't. She understood he wasn't truly there, but more and more often, his voice didn't sound like it originated in her head. It sounded like he was standing right there, next to Brie. Unsure what that meant, probably nothing good, she refused to dwell on it for the moment. She was happy.

"We should get moving. We're falling behind." Brie nudged her shoulder against Renee's.

"Oh right. Do you think this will hold up until tonight?" Renee asked as they hurried toward the mass of the horde.

"To impress your boyfriend?" Brie snickered.

"No." Renee lied.

"We're going to be at the next... stop in a couple of days," Brie's voice tightened.

"Okay," Renee said quietly. The pattern hadn't changed from when she'd first started traveling with the horde, but she had. Taking a city or settlement still bothered her. It still terrified her, but part of her was slowly getting desensitized to it. At least the idea of taking a city, the violence involved with it.

"Are we shopping for the horde again?" Brie asked.

Garren edged closer, listening. Both were her partners in crime. She didn't want to keep things from Zane, but he was such an ass when it came to the horde. She didn't feel like she had a choice. Every populated area that had stores. After it was deemed safe, she, Brie, and Garren would scavenge to find coats, wraps, or blankets for the horde.

Often, the chosen received some kind of interior dwellings until they moved on, but the bulk of the horde just wandered around outside all hours of the night. Each day, the temperature dropped just a little, and she knew the horde was cold. No, they had never spoken the words to tell her, but she noticed when they shivered and more than that, there was this strange sensation that "told" her they were chilly.

Renee took that as a sign she was doing her job, that she was being a good queen. "Yes, unless there isn't time. We are, and we'll keep doing it until winter is over or he finds out."

Whenever they distributed the clothing and blankets, the horde members were so grateful and kind. They didn't necessarily say anything to her, but they took the offerings and gave her what she chose to believe were positive expressions—although some of their features were so distorted, it was hard to tell. The longer she continued her quest to make them more comfortable, that odd nagging inside her lessened until it was more like a whisper in her soul.

She was unsure how angry Zane would be from her actions, but she was ready to go to battle with him about it. If he wouldn't do thoughtful things for them, then she would. He was so stubborn — he wouldn't acknowledge that they weren't people, and perhaps they weren't, but they weren't empty husks either. Certainly, basic kindness wouldn't hurt. Didn't even the most repulsive creatures deserve at least one person to see them as something other than gross and unworthy?

"You're not supposed to be sympathizing with the villain Renny," Liam said with a snicker.

"You don't understand Liam. He's not a villain, he's misunderstood. Fae court politics are harsh and he was villainized for trying to change the oppressive structure. They're using him as an example and it's wrong," Renee fired back with fury. Liam always thought she was too attached to her books and the characters in them, but he didn't get it. They were more her friends than the ones from school. The characters made so much more sense to her than her peers.

Liam continued to chuckle. "I swear you would have sympathy for the worst person in the world if they had even a shred of remorse or decency in them." He stopped and frowned.

Crap, he was remembering the attack. Thankfully, according to her therapist, because of trauma, she couldn't recall the night of the attack at all. The last memory she had was feeling annoyed that Liam hadn't messaged her back, and he was supposed to pick her up. He blamed himself for her near-death experience, which wasn't his fault.

He wasn't the one who was supposed to drive her around or take care of her all the time. He was only twenty-one, barely an adult. But he'd been saddled with her since she was born because of their crappy parents. He'd never said it, but she thought he believed her being too nice, or perhaps naïve, was the reason she was targeted by the thugs.

Liam grumbled as he fiddled with the controls on the dashboard to turn on the air. Seconds later, a pleasant citrus scent filled the car as the air conditioning kicked on. The car was still new to him. His friend, Zack or something like that, had given him the car because Liam needed to get to work, as well as take Renee to all her follow-up doctor appointments and therapy sessions.

She wished for a friend like that. Not because Liam's had given him an expensive gift, but he had someone who cared enough to want to help him out. Most of her "friends" had faded into the background after the attack. If she was fair, it was partly her fault. She'd withdrawn from everyone but Liam. Admittedly, she sometimes turned the volume of her implants down so she wouldn't hear anything. She hated being alone with her thoughts, but she preferred silence over the uncomfortable exchanges with people who didn't know what to say and usually made the discomfort worse.

Renee liked the way Liam's new car smelled. It always made her less anxious after her therapy sessions. No clue what type of car it was, she could tell it was luxurious, with all kinds of buttons, dials, and computerized parts on the dash. Liam swore he wasn't keeping it even though his friend told him to. She hoped he would. The seats could be heated or cooled and the driver's seat even had a massage feature.

"I'll be back at five. Try to open up a little Renny, she's trying to help. And remember, you can say anything you want, even if it's about mom and dad. Hell, you can tell her how I boss you around all the time," he offered.

"I'll try. Are you sure you won't get into trouble for bringing me?"

Liam clasped her hand. "Princess, part of the reason I'm working there is because of the flexible schedule. It's fine, I swear. And even if it wasn't, it wouldn't change anything except I'd get a new job."

Tears made his image blurry. "I'm ruining so much for you. You wanted to go to college full-time, and now you can't."

"Stop. That was my choice. I finished two years and I'll finish the rest too. It will just take longer. You are not *a burden Renee. You are* never *a burden to me. I told you—you're a miracle."*

Tears dropped down her cheeks. Renee was positive she would never meet another person as perfect and wonderful as her brother. No one would love her as much as he did. He'd sworn since she could remember, she was his little miracle because she'd been so sick when she was younger. He promised her when she came home from the hospital weeks ago, he'd never leave her side and he hadn't.

"Don't cry, Princess. Remember, this is just the prologue. Your story hasn't started yet."

Renee's steps slowed as she reflected on the memory. Part of it urged her to contemplate the memory more, but his words, "Remember, this is just the prologue. Your story hasn't started yet." repeated in her mind. Had her whole life only been the backstory? The set up for this? Her eyes darted to Brie, Garren, the horde, and then as far to the front of the mass as she could see. She'd just been thinking how grateful and happy she was.

She pressed her lips together because she wanted to talk to Liam about it, but didn't believe he'd still be around. Seconds later, she spotted him on the other side of Garren, a mischievous grin on his face. Her eyes widened because he didn't disappear when she saw him. He continued to march next to Garren like he belonged there. When her mouth gaped open, he shook his head and put a finger over his lips.

Renee shut her mouth. If her silence would keep him near, then she wouldn't speak a word. She'd gone years without speaking when she was younger. For Liam, she'd do almost anything to keep him close.

Chapter 2 - Renee

Renee waited in a bland living room of an abandoned apartment and once again wished there was electricity. Zane never involved her when the horde took a city. He'd had Garren escort her to the apartment so she would be safe, as well as not witness the carnage. If electricity still existed, she would have drowned out the terror with music or at least had more light than a few candles. In the past, she'd always turned up the bass in music so she felt it as she listened. She adored the vibrations of music.

The screams and gunshots from outside were muffled, but every time another one happened, she shuddered. Each pop made her twitch. She curled up on the couch and covered her head with a pillow to deaden the noise. Renee pushed the pillow down on the side of her head, her mind drifting to when Garren dropped her off. He'd bowed as he left, making Renee giggle. She liked that he played along with her antics, even if his general acceptance of her took her by surprise and made her question herself and her actions with different members of the horde.

She bolted and locked the door once she was alone, as she had promised Zane. No telling where humans would run to when chased. Hell, when the zombies found her, she'd run into a hotel trying to escape her death. At the time, she was already dying from her head wound but wasn't aware. Zane might still have lingering guilt about turning her undead, but in reality, he'd saved her. That night she'd been ready to die—too exhausted and couldn't find a reason to go on.

"No more of that Princess," her brother's ghostly voice whispered.

Her brother Liam had been her everything before the end of the world, but after he was gone, early at the fall of man, she'd spent years burying the memory of his death, making herself forget. It was too painful to remember what happened, what had been her fault. During her lowest points, he'd return because he'd promised never to leave her side. If she slipped and thought negatively, he'd pop up and remind her not to think that way.

Since her breakdown, when she realized she was a zombie, he was never far. Of course, when she thought about it, maybe he'd been showing up more often even before that. Damn it. Things were so jumbled in her head. It was hard before keeping track of the days as they passed, the months. Without routine, the days of the week didn't matter or even months, except in relation to the seasons. And the only real reason that mattered was because of the weather.

"I told you before, time only matters if you measure it. If you don't, then you have an infinite amount," Liam said as his fingers glided over her back to comfort her.

Liam had told her that whenever she would get frustrated, if she wasn't learning school subjects fast enough, or was impatient with how long it took her to speak. She grumbled under the pillow but didn't answer him.

Renee frowned. She didn't *feel* his voice, though, ruining the illusion he was with her. Regardless of how often he talked to her or what volume he used, she never felt it. Which meant it was in her head. Renee hadn't told Zane because she didn't want him to think she was nuts and she was worried if she verbalized it, Liam might disappear forever.

She had spent many years deaf, and even after her cochlear implants, she still focused on the physical cues and sensations when someone spoke. One of her favorite things was talking to Zane because when they were touching, his deep voice resonated in her body with each word. It was amazing.

A loud sound that reminded her of an explosion made her flinch against the cushions. Her aversion to violence was a pain in the ass, considering her existence now relied on blood and violence. Her eyes burned, but she refused to cry. She detested the brutality, but was happy to be with Zane. Being with him made everything better. He pampered her by bringing her food and always made sure it was cooked, so it was less like she was eating things she shouldn't. She didn't ask him anymore what it was because it was better she didn't know. He let her exist in blissful ignorance and if that wasn't love, she didn't know what was.

It annoyed Brie, who kept asking her to go on hunts, but she didn't want to. Renee thought Brie would understand because despite her nagging about hunting, she was the least zombie-like of all the horde. Always clean and well-groomed, Brie took pride in her appearance and consequently, was the most elegant and fashionable zombie Renee had ever been around. Of course, Zane's horde were the only zombies Renee had spent any time with.

But that wasn't the only difference between Brie and the others. Although Renee now knew many chosen by their names, Brie was more *alive* than the others. Not just because she was smarter, more graceful, or a badass fighter. It wasn't because she could pivot a plan at a moment's notice or come up with a backup plan to save the horde — it was their relationship, complex and layered as it would be between humans. Brie cared about Renee and expressed it by putting up with her quirks and sometimes even opening up a little about her past. Brie still wasn't comfortable talking about her past, but occasionally she did, and rarely confided in Renee. Renee treasured those moments.

It got colder every night as they traveled. She was lucky because she got to cuddle with Zane every night, but still worried about the horde out in the cold. The chosen decided to secure shelter, presumably to get out of the elements. The mass of the horde though... they almost never had cover of any type, which is why she insisted on helping them. If she didn't, who would?

When she suggested blankets for them, Zane laughed at her and told her she was silly. It infuriated her. Just because they were dead didn't mean they didn't feel things. Brie, through her actions, had confirmed that zombies had some level of cognition, some level of understanding, of emotional intelligence. Renee had witnessed enough to see they were, at the very least, aware of their surroundings. Not only because of her intuition, but she'd noticed they were more focused on getting the fires started each night and sat closer to the flames, huddling together more tightly.

One of the packs called themselves 'Crows,' which had around fifteen members. They had been collecting pliable branches, paper scraps, fragments of twine or yarn, feathers and whatever else they found to make round-shaped pieces. At night, they would connect them together and all pile into what reminded her of a nest. They literally took their group's name to heart. But it also pointed out a level of intelligence that Zane refused to acknowledge.

A soft knock at the door broke her thoughts and made her heart speed up. She recognized it as his knock, the special one only he used to signal it was him. Renee jumped up, racing to the door. She smoothed her wild, loose hair back and unlocked the door.

His bloodshot amber irises brightened as soon as she opened the door. He was still covered in the blood and bits and pieces of his victims, but Renee almost didn't notice. She wrapped her arms around his torso as he tugged her mouth to his. Citrus and sunshine every time. It didn't make sense, but Renee wouldn't complain.

He backed her into the room, kicking the door shut behind him as his mouth devoured hers. Her skin tingled from his nearness and his kiss. He lifted her onto the kitchen counter that was near the door as she wrapped her legs around his waist. His lips traced her jawline and then lowered to her neck.

"I missed you," he told her, before he captured her earlobe in his mouth.

"I missed you," she breathed. "Is everyone okay?"

He let her ear go and pulled back to peer at her. "No. But they're fed. Why do you always ask me that?"

She frowned. He was such a bastard with his horde. Her fingers touched his gaunt face, tracing beside his eye to his sharp jawline.

"Because they're your horde, you should care."

"Not this again Renee. There's always risk and death when we take a city. Brie's fine," he finished.

"I know she is. She always is because she's a badass, but this isn't about her." Renee tugged him closer, with her legs still around his waist.

"I don't want to debate this. I want to clean up and remind myself how lucky I am to have you with me." He smiled his genuine smile that rarely showed itself.

Shit. Shit. That bastard knew when he smiled like that, she couldn't resist him. He wasn't playing fair.

His hand slid to her neck and drew her mouth to his. "We can talk about it later," he said against her lips. "Unless you'd rather not have me" — he peppered tiny kisses on her throat before nibbling on her earlobe — "show you how much I love you."

Zane's other hand slid down, caressing her breast. She arched into his touch. Renee moaned, melting against him. The scent of fresh blood reached her nostrils, surprising her when it didn't turn her off. It made her lightheaded and crave him all the more. She didn't protest when he picked her up and carried her into the bathroom.

Chapter 3 - Renee

"You done playing house for now?" Brie asked as she finished the braid on the side of her head. Her hair was still damp from bathing.

Renee blushed, embarrassed that Brie was familiar with where Zane immediately went after things were secure. "Yeah, he's just finishing cleaning up."

"So, fucking weird you guys are constantly making out." Brie took out her red lipstick and applied it with expertise.

Renee didn't respond because Zane told her not to tell Brie they were having sex. He'd explained it was very unusual. Apparently, zombies had no sexual urges and the fact she and Zane could have sex was not only strange but also a bit of a miracle, because zombies' reproductive parts didn't work. Or rather, they were in a weird "stasis" mode. Renee tried to ask Zane more about it, but he refused to get into details and seemed embarrassed by the conversation.

Then she tried to get him to explain why they were the exception and he changed the subject. When she brought it up again, he distracted her and said it was because they were in love. Finally, when she pressed, he got angry and told her to drop it.

"Yeah," Renee said in a small voice, without looking at her friend. She hated lying, she was no good at it.

"Your secret's safe with me. 'Course, it's not like anyone would believe me if I told them." Brie stashed her lipstick away. "So, are we trying to warm the masses today?" she asked with a smirk.

"Don't make fun of me." Renee's eyes darted to the bathroom door. "It's helped keep them comfortable."

"You know, eventually he's going to find out."

"He's a crap head when it comes to them. He knows they can feel cold and... other stuff."

"Yeah, he just doesn't give a shit. Technically, they can take care of themselves if they wanted," Brie reminded her.

Renee's lips flattened. Perhaps they could, but they wouldn't. They only lived to serve him and what he wanted. Wait. Her mind raced to the awful night they had broken up and Zane's words: *I'm only here to serve its needs.* The words echoed in her mind. Shit. Shit. Did he realize? She stood up and paced the room.

Brie cocked her head to the side. "You, okay?"

"Yeah, I just — he said he was going to tell us where we are headed next. I'm nervous is all," Renee lied and kept moving.

The bathroom door opened. Zane's large frame, clad in all black as usual, stepped into the living room. His irises, still bright from feasting earlier, contrasted against his dark hair and pale skin.

He scanned the room before his gaze rested on Brie. "Where is her food?"

"Garren insisted on cooking it. He'll be here soon," Brie answered, not quite able to disguise her annoyance.

Renee's eating habits reflected her inability to accept her new existence. Brie tried to ignore it because they were friends, but every reminder made her face tight.

Zane's eyes narrowed. "Garren, again?"

"Jealous there, stud?" Brie quipped.

Zane gnashed his teeth. "Don't, Brie."

Brie glared at Zane. "You're lucky he isn't shitty because of all the favoritism you show her."

Before Renee thought of a response to calm things, Zane was across the room and had Brie by the throat.

"Is that so? I own them. *All of them*, including *you*."

"Fuck you, Zane," Brie bit out.

Zane choked Brie, but her reaction was all wrong. She should've cried out, tried to stop him or been scared. Instead, a slow smile crept over her lips.

"It's like old times," she rasped.

Zane let her go, stumbling back, looking like she'd struck him. "Get out of my sight. If you pull something like that again, I'll make you submit."

Brie's face almost had color as her nostrils flared. She stepped toward Zane and bared her teeth at him. "I would rather die."

"Stop! Please stop!" Renee finally found her voice. She moved her body in front of Brie and turned her friend's face to hers. "Please, I need you," she whispered.

Brie's expression softened. She pulled Renee into a brief hug. "I know. I'm just in a shitty mood. We lost some good… troops taking the city. I'll talk to you tomorrow." She squeezed Renee's arm and left.

Renee took several breaths to calm her racing heart. She'd never dealt with conflict well and if people she cared about started fighting, it was all she could do to keep herself from a full-blown panic attack. In that situation, she knew it didn't matter how the argument was resolved, everyone would lose. Or at the very least, if people she cared about argued with one another, she would have to choose, because they would make her and she couldn't handle that.

She pushed her shoulders back and set her jaw, refusing to let that happen with Brie and Zane. She needed both of them.

"What the hell was that?" Renee demanded.

Zane rubbed the rear of his neck as he spoke. "That was Brie being a bitch."

"Maybe, but you were being an asshole," she shot back.

He pinched his brow. "She was out of line."

"Because she poked fun at you? You overreacted."

"She knew exactly what she was doing, and she knew how'd I react. She was lucky you were here. Otherwise, she'd be dead." His hand traveled to his forehead, rubbing it like he had a headache.

Renee stopped breathing and stared at Zane. Her Zane wouldn't do that. But this wasn't her Zane, or rather, it was who Zane was when he wasn't around her.

The zombie king.

Shit. He would have killed Brie, and Brie knew it. Brie had told her more than once she was afraid of Zane. Had Brie smarted off in front of Zane because she was there? Did Brie think Renee's presence would control Zane's actions? Damn it. Now Renee was irritated with both of them.

"She shouldn't have pushed you, but everything can't end in death with you. There are other ways to handle problems."

"Not anymore. Not in this world. I told you I lead them because I'm the strongest. That means I can't allow insubordination. They follow orders or die."

Renee flinched. "I hate when you say things like that."

"It's why you're safe!" Zane's tone was exasperated as he raised his voice and stepped in front of her. "Don't question how I rule the horde."

She pinched her lips together. She should have never called him a king. It had gone to his head. He was using her words to pacify her, but it was only making her angrier. The vibrations from his loud words were pleasant, but she ignored the sensation.

"Does the horde really think you're treating me better?" she asked in a small voice.

"It doesn't matter what they think."

"Yes, it does."

"No, it doesn't! Half of them can't think. Not like you want them to. They're undead. Mindless murdering machines, right?" Zane's tone was cruel at the end and made her stomach knot up.

Renee straightened her spine. She didn't like him throwing her words in her face. She'd already admitted that she was wrong about that. Sure, shamblers were basically walking bags of decay, but even the feral zombies had some semblance of intelligence. He was being a dick. They had been arguing on and off about the horde for weeks.

"I'm going out," she announced and picked up her light jacket.

His heavy footsteps moved behind her. "Where do you think you're going?"

"Away from you. I don't want to argue and you're being a jerk. It's better I go shopping." Renee headed to the door.

"Don't leave like that," Zane's tone switched to how he always sounded when they were alone.

With a sigh, she faced him, hesitating at the door.

He crossed the space in a long stride and smoothed her hair back. "I don't want to argue either. I just want to be with you."

"I know." She hugged him. "But our life isn't that simple. It's our job to look out for the horde. I'm supposed to be queen, remember?"

"You are." He tilted her chin up. "I didn't mean to raise my voice."

"I know. It's why I'm going out. Gives you time to calm down."

He put his forehead against hers and closed his eyes. "All I think about is you. I don't want to be king."

Renee blinked to keep her tears at bay. His words were almost like a plea, but she couldn't help him with his internal struggles. He hated the responsibility so much, but he couldn't walk away. She drew his mouth to hers and gave him a tender kiss. "I'll be back soon, okay?"

He nodded and let her go. With a heavy heart, Renee turned the knob and set out into the city.

Chapter 4 - Renee

Since the city had been deemed safe, Renee explored any store that caught her eye. She hadn't gone far when Garren approached with her meal. It sort of looked like an animal, but because she'd made a joke about "all meat on a stick was the best," any time Garren brought her food, he'd put it on some type of stick. She laughed as she thanked him.

Renee assumed it was Brie's doing because she and Garren got along, but he always shadowed her when she wasn't with Brie or Zane. She chatted to him as she ate; he strolled beside her, attentive but also on guard. He took his sentinel duties seriously.

Renee's steps slowed as she approached a clothing store. "Hey, do you mind carrying things?"

He grinned and shook his head. He'd helped her gather, and take jackets and blankets to the horde before. When Brie showed up at the apartment, she thought it would be the two of them today, but after that weird argument, she didn't know where Brie went.

"Gotta remember to get something for me this time or he'll figure out what I'm doing," she mumbled to herself and stepped into the ransacked store.

It was a disaster as most places were in cities but many winter coats were scattered on the ground. Some were in better shape than others but as long as they were intact, she picked them up. The horde wouldn't care if they were dirty. Even the ones that smelled of mildew would be a pleasant change than the general odor of the horde.

Renee loaded Garren down several times with random jackets and blankets. When both their arms were full, they wandered around finding any horde member who was calm enough to approach. Over the months spent with the horde, she had learned if they were calm and if whoever interacted with them was also calm, everything went smoothly. If anything got them stirred up, it would set off a chain reaction and suddenly the entire horde, save the chosen, would start attacking each other. Renee had fled more than once to get away when things turned violent, but she understood how Zane started a culling now.

If the horde member was calm, she could *almost* talk to them. They didn't have as many words as the chosen and they couldn't truly converse. It was more like when Renee would interact with intelligent animals, limited but still a form of communication.

Renee kept her movements slow and deliberate so they saw her coming. Although Brie had mocked her for being too friendly and smiling too much, Renee found it made the interactions much better with the horde.

She tiptoed toward one of the horde members who Daisy seemed to watch over. It was odd because there were thousands of them and it wasn't possible to remember all of them, but Renee found that more and more she not only recognized them, but she had some idea which of the chosen looked out for them.

Renee plastered a big smile on her face and crouched to seem less threatening because the large male was sitting on a rock. "Hi." She tugged her right hand out from under the coats she had in her other arm, using her knee to hold up the right side of the pile. She pointed to herself while speaking, "Renee."

He grunted and made a couple of noises that reminded her of words. Although his lips moved, it did nothing to give her a clue of what he'd said. She pointed to the coats.

"Warm," she said and slid the pile to the ground before pulling the one on top. Renee pretended to shiver and then wrapped the coat around her shoulders and then let out a sigh of relief. "Warm," she repeated. She tugged it off her shoulders and held it out. "Take. For you."

A horrible expression twisted his face but as Renee stared, she could see he was trying to smile. He reached for the coat. She held it forward and tried not to cringe when his fingers touched hers. Guilt ate at her for being repulsed, but she internally acknowledged, most of the horde was dirty and often covered in the remains of what they last ate.

He made a few clicks before he bowed his head down and said, "Queen."

Renee's eyes widened. She almost fell on her ass in surprise. He'd spoke an actual word, and he'd said... "queen."

"What?" she whispered.

He lifted his head and made the same sequence of sounds, but this time she didn't hear the word queen. Embarrassed by her stupidity, or perhaps it was her desperation for acceptance that she thought he'd said that specific word, she nodded and stood. With a quick glance at Garren she picked up the rest of her pile.

"Let's go up further, most of them don't have anything," Renee said and hurried away as if that somehow erased what happened.

"*Stupid*," a nasty voice said in her mind.

She tried to ignore it and stole another glance at Garren to assure herself that he hadn't heard anything because if he had, he would have reacted, right? Renee called herself queen if she was talking to Zane or in her mind sometimes but never in front of anyone else. She *wanted* to be their queen, their real queen but she wasn't arrogant enough to assume she had done anything to earn that title, yet.

They quickly gave out the other coats. Garren was efficient but not as friendly as Renee when he distributed things, but he was gentler than Brie was. She loved that Brie helped her with her secret project, but most of the time, Brie wasn't the best at being kind. It wasn't intentional because Renee understood how much Brie cared about the horde, she just didn't have great interpersonal skills.

The horde was in the thousands but Renee had been working hard to do what she could for the horde and more and more of them had some type of cover. In the last city, they handed out umbrellas, although that seemed to befuddle many of them. She and Garren had to show them how to open the umbrellas at least three times before most understood how to work one.

She never gave the chosen anything because she wasn't sure if they would tell Zane. Except for Garren, he'd never rat her out. But Brie was right, at Renee's current pace, it wouldn't be long until Zane realized what she was doing.

After the last of the coats were distributed, they headed toward the center of the city. Her steps slowed as they passed a cluster of the chosen. Mace and Hawk were there with others she didn't recognize but she grasped they were chosen because they were talking and *sparring*. Her mouth dropped open. She didn't know the chosen did that, but it made sense. And clarified part of the mystery why the chosen seemed to be natural combatants.

Renee continued walking but didn't speed up, mesmerized. Mace caught her stare and raised his palm to acknowledge her. Heat rose in her cheeks as she waved and turned her attention to the stores ahead.

"I didn't know you practiced," she said to Garren. Garren just shrugged and continued his graceful strides.

Renee yawned as they passed a woman's store, she peeked in the window but didn't see coats so she kept moving, not quite ready to return to Zane yet. Garren stopped. She turned to see what he was peering at. He pointed a claw at a pretty green dress in the window and gestured at her.

She strolled back, cocking her head to the side. "You think that would look good on me?"

Garren's narrow, reddish irises lit up as he nodded.

"I don't wear dresses much. They're not very practical. I know, I know, Brie does, but she's awesome and graceful." Not that Renee didn't want to wear dresses, it just didn't make sense for her life.

Garren crossed his toned arms and stared at her. His perfectly straight black hair danced with the slight breeze. It still reminded her of silk. Other than Brie and Zane he was the next cleanest of the chosen.

Renee threw her hands in the air. "Well, she is!"

His wide mouth smirked before he pointed at the dress and then at Renee.

"Okay. Okay. I'll get the dress," she grumbled as they entered the store. Renee rifled through the rack of dresses until she found the right size.

As they left the store, she turned to Garren and put her palm on his arm. He stiffened as he always did when she touched him, but she'd learned to ignore it, mostly. Unlike Zane he was only a few inches taller than she was so she didn't have to look up at him.

"Hey... um, so I know sign language. Do you? If not, would you want to learn it? I'm not trying to make you feel bad or anything, but I'd really like to hear your thoughts."

His response was to put his hand on hers as he nodded. It didn't even bother her — his long sharp nails grazing over the skin. Holy crap, he almost never touched her. He was her friend, too. Without thinking, she threw her arms around him and hugged him. He became as still as a statue before he returned her hug.

"I'm so glad we met," she said before she let him go. "Thanks for helping with the dress."

A huge smile made his broad mouth appear even wider, taking up the bottom half of his face. If she didn't know him, it would be terrifying because it showed his sharp teeth.

"You better not let our king see you doing that," Brie said loudly beside them.

Renee jumped. She hadn't heard Brie sneak up on them. Garren paled at her words.

"It's fine Garren. I'm fucking with you. I like you; I don't want you dead." Her ice-blue irises turned to Renee. "If you like him too, you better cut that shit out or he's dead. You finished getting the coats and whatnot or do you want help?"

"Don't sneak up like that!" Renee said. "I was done, but we could make one more run before I go back if you want."

Brie tilted her head up looking at the sky. "Yeah, we probably should. I think it's going to get a lot colder soon."

"Where do we stay in the winter?"

"We don't. We don't *stay* anywhere ever. Most of the time, we head south by now. It's gonna be a hell of a winter," sarcasm made her tone sharp.

"We aren't going south?" Renee asked as they continued their search for outerwear.

"I don't think so. Usually we're already headed that direction, but the scouts—" she stopped.

Garren and Brie exchanged looks. Garren seemed to shut down and tensed beside her. A crease formed between Brie's brows as the corners of her mouth turned down.

"What? Did the scouts find something?" Renee asked.

"Not my place to talk about. Ask your boyfriend." Brie said in a sour tone before she and Garren continued walking.

"Hey," — Renee hurried in front of them, turned, and stared straight at Brie — "I don't understand what that was about earlier, but I know you weren't afraid. At least not at first. He won't hurt you."

Brie laughed, but it sounded all wrong. "You don't really know him, Renee. I don't understand it, but with you... he's different. Trust me, what I did earlier was fucking stupid. I'm lucky to be standing here."

Garren nodded in agreement. Renee twisted her lips. Why did everyone see Zane as a monster? He technically was a monster, they all were. What made him so much worse?

"I'm not saying shit because he isn't lying. You follow orders. You submit or you die." Brie turned and entered the nearest store.

Chapter 5 - Zane

Zane paced in the living room making guttural noises that sounded similar to his less advanced creatures. He detested bickering with Renee. She wouldn't understand his perspective but after years apart, he didn't want to waste even minutes arguing with her, especially about the horde. They were... his burden. Even when he was sequestered far from them, he still sensed his creatures. He was *always* aware of them.

No escape.

He paused his steps and rubbed his forehead and then the rear of his head. *It* was irritated. Although he could not directly communicate with his parasite, there was a connection and a general sense of its inclinations and wants. Since Renee had become a part of his life, he was usually in control of most of his actions and words.

It was a tenuous existence. *It* wanted him to return to the way things had been. Where Zane had retreated in his mind because he didn't see a point of being present. Allow it to control his body. Continue to create more creatures. He wasn't sure but sensed its entire goal was to amass the largest army of creatures that ever existed. For what purpose he couldn't say, but he assumed because that was its nature. Conquer and destroy.

His jaw tightened. His father had been the same in his business practices and the military seemed to have the same goals, at least when Zane had been in active duty. It was strange he was thinking about his past, he rarely did. Or rather he *had* rarely thought of it until Renee appeared.

She couldn't understand his obsession with her, she never would, or the significance of her existence. What it had meant to him when he was still human. How it inspired him to be something different, better than what he had been. Part of him wondered if he wanted her to know the truth. Would she reject him if she truly understood how long he had desired her? If she knew how long he had watched and waited for her?

Now that he was in control of his body and mind, the memories from before he had turned into the monster he was, surfaced. Initially, it was like a gentle wave lapping at the shore. But the longer he remained in control the more memories returned. It often felt like a tidal wave threatening to consume him. Although many of the remembrances were painful, he accepted them because they also came with images and sensations of Renee before he'd damned her.

Zane brought his fist down on the counter as he entered the kitchen. A crack signaled that he'd broken at least part of the cabinet base. It didn't matter, they would leave in a matter of days. He grit his teeth. He didn't want to leave. He didn't want to lead the horde. Cursed with his crown because of *it*, resentment filled Zane as his knuckles turned white.

A sharp pain in his head made him double over and gasp for breath. Fuck. He'd irritated *it*. With odd jerky movements he shuffled back into the living room. Bastard parasite was trying to force his movements to leave the apartment, no doubt to commit some violent atrocity. It made his mouth water with anticipation of hurting something, tearing something to pieces.

No.

He wasn't that person anymore. He would not give in to the temptation. Zane endured the fire in his limbs as he stopped his movement and crouched, trying to catch his breath and clear his mind. Images of humans being ripped apart, blood spraying the air, and flesh being torn into pieces flashed in his mind. Superimposed over those images were memories of desert terrain. More violence and blood, only then, he delighted wounding humans in a different way.

∞

"Fucking monsters are real?" Zane's voice in the memory sounded odd. He struggled to understand the words, even though he'd been the one who spoke them at the time.

"Kid, this doesn't even begin to cover how real they are," Levitt responded as he dusted the bits of gore off his uniform. He fished a black cigarette from his pocket and frowned at its slightly crushed appearance before lighting it. *"Listen... I get this freaked you the fuck out, but I'm gonna need you to keep your trap shut."*

Zane swallowed and considered his options. No way would the sarge think he was telling the truth if he spoke about what he'd seen—what he'd been part of, but how in the hell would they explain the dead grunts that littered the ground? He lifted his blood covered palm and rubbed the almost hairless side of his head, trying to figure out a response that wouldn't make him just as dead as the bodies at his feet. He'd seen some shit in his life but nothing like this.

People who were snakes but also people? It was like shit from sci-fi movies or maybe horror movies. His eyes flicked to Levitt who was still smoking and staring at him with narrowed eyes. He'd always known that Levitt was unhinged, that crazy bastard charged in ahead of everyone and became the Colonel's pet after pulling off a mission where he should have died.

But what Zane had just seen... something was off with Levitt. Zane didn't know what Levitt was but there was no fucking way a regular person moved that fast, no way they could shake off the injuries he sustained. Zane's eyes drifted over Levitt's fatigues, they were soaked in blood, from the monsters they'd just killed and his own.

Somehow, because of Levitt, he hadn't been injured. He grimaced with the knowledge that Levitt had saved his ass more than once, especially today. He should have died at least twice. He owed this crazy bastard his life.

Zane cleared his throat. "Yeah okay. I didn't see shit but how are we going to explain... them?" He glanced at his fallen comrades.

"Don't worry about that. I'll talk to Stein. You just act like you were never here and you can stay... normal." Levitt inhaled his cigarette.

Zane was relieved Levitt decided to smoke because the cloves and standard smoke smell somewhat covered the rank odor coming from the snake people. He *found it bizarre that Levitt referred to Colonel Stein by his name only. That made Zane feel even more uneasy around Levitt.*

"Are... are there more of them?" Zane gestured to the tail of one of the snake people.

"Trust me, don't ask questions. You won't like the answers and then I have to get rid of you." Levitt flicked his ashes on the snake person Zane had pointed out. "Stay in your bubble. You don't want to be here and you're done with the military in a few months. You'll be free."

Zane's brow furrowed. Something in Levitt's tone sounded wistful when he talked of freedom. Zane thought Levitt enlisted on his own accord versus when Zane had been forced by his father. It was the military or jail. Of course, perhaps he deserved to be incarcerated.

"Yeah okay. Do you need me to do anything?"

Levitt dropped the butt of his cigarette and stomped on it. "Nah, I got this. Get lost before the others show up. I'll check on you later. Don't fuck this up. I don't mind you being in my platoon, you're better than the lot of them, but if you talk, I'll break your fucking neck." He raised his intense gaze to Zane's to make his point.

They weren't in the same squad but saw each other daily because they were in the same platoon, so most of their objectives were related. Zane wouldn't say they were friendly, but they were cordial. However, Levitt was known for his temper, enthusiasm for combat, restlessness and sometimes he was a complete bastard. When other soldiers would hesitate during a grueling battle, he would laugh and act as though he enjoyed the carnage. It was part of why Zane usually stayed far from him; they were too similar given how much they were each drawn to pain. Either receiving it or giving it, they both liked bloodshed.

The only reason Zane wasn't feeling the gleeful high he typically did after causing harm or taking lives was because he was freaked out from those snake people — monsters. They were fucking real. As much as he wanted to pretend that nothing had happened, he knew Levitt wasn't lying. Levitt was a wild card and often unpredictable. Just because he saved someone's life one day, didn't guarantee he wouldn't take it the next.

Zane didn't verbally reply but nodded as he backed away. He took one long last look at Levitt, standing in a godlike pose surrounded by fallen comrades and monsters staring at him, and turned away. He had no fear of Levitt attacking him from behind, that wasn't Levitt's style. He always wanted to confront people up close so he could be certain whoever he went after was dead.

Zane frowned. He wouldn't say anything but he couldn't go back to being normal or how did Levitt put it? Stay in his bubble? Unsure why Levitt chose that phrase but it was already too late. How could someone witness something like that — be a part of something like that, and just continue on as they had?

Zane fell to his knees and pulled on his hair as another sharp pain originating in his skull shot through him. He wasn't sure how long he'd been lost in his memory or how much time had passed, but he was worried Renee would find him on the floor. Then she would question him even more than had been.

He understood that she believed she had fully accepted this life, him, and what he'd done to her. But there were signs she hadn't, and he didn't want her to have another breakdown by overwhelming her. She didn't know about his parasite or the rival horde. She didn't need to, yet. It could wait until she fully accepted herself.

Zane didn't want to burden her with the weight of his crown. It was only when he was by Renee's side that the battle for control over his own form didn't exhaust him. He would deal with *it*, on his own as he always had. Although he hadn't genuinely fought over control of his body daily until recently.

He fell forward onto his elbows and knees, still cradling his skull as he gnashed his teeth. *It* was urging him to act, get up and leave the room, but Zane didn't trust *it*. He didn't know what the parasite wanted him to do, but it was bloodthirsty and he refused to be that person anymore, he finally had his chance to be different — better.

His life was now a twisted version of the dream he'd used to survive when he wanted to give up. Renee was his, and he wasn't a monster... except he was. Zane smacked his forehead against the floor. Even attaining his goals hadn't changed him from the heinous thing he was, the only difference was that now his outside matched his black soul.

He bit down to hold in a scream. His brain felt like it was on fire, and as far as he knew brains didn't have nerves to feel anything. Was his parasite trying to kill him and itself in the process? Zane laughed bitterly. All these years of not wanting to exist but unable to die... and all he had to do was fight back and it would have ended both of them. Fuck. But things were different now, he had Renee; he had to live.

Chapter 6 - Renee

Renee barely got the door open before Zane sealed his lips on hers. When he finally broke their kiss, she was lightheaded from lack of air. He studied her as his fingers caressed her neck.

"You ate."

"Yeah, Garren brought my lunch while I was out." She closed the door behind her.

"Garren." he repeated with an edge to his voice.

Shaken from her conversation with Brie, she took his hand and led him to the living room. "Do you want me to show you what I got?" she asked, keeping her tone playful.

"Yes. Of course."

"First" — she took out three new black t-shirts for him — "because this is all you wear." She giggled.

He frowned. "They're practical."

"Sure. You just want to be intimidating."

He scrunched up his face the same way he always did when she was right but he didn't want to admit it.

"I'll be right back. Close your eyes and don't peek."

Renee scampered into the bedroom and shed her clothes and threw on the dress. The dark-green material was made of something light and silky, and it fluttered around her legs when she moved. It was a simple, but elegant dress. Her mind wandered to her favorite romantasy series as she smoothed her palms over the material.

Unable to resist, she spun in a circle and grinned like a child. As silly as it was, she closed her eyes and slowed, imagining she was in a ballroom and that her dress was suddenly adorned with gems that sparkled when the candlelight hit them. It was hard for her to force her eyelids open because she wanted to imagine Zane in a king's regalia, meeting her on the dance floor.

No. Her life wasn't one of her books and she needed to stop trying to make it one. She bit her lip remembering how many times various people in her life told her to "grow up and give up her fantasies, be an adult." There wasn't magic and life wasn't a fairytale. Renee pulled her lips into her mouth, for some reason those words, even when she said them to herself, still hurt. Perhaps she really was a child.

She shook her head to clear it, not wanting to think about it anymore or the conversation with Garren and Brie — or Zane's temper. His moodiness hadn't escaped her; it'd been worse the past couple of days. Unsure why, but she didn't want him to take it out on Brie, Garren, or the horde.

Renee glided toward the door; the material swirled around her legs. She poked her head out, her chest tightening when she saw Zane. He sat on the couch with his eyes closed, just like she'd asked him to do. He almost always did what she asked him to do, and mostly without complaint. Unless it came to others, then he was an inflexible ass. She padded out in the flowy dress that clung to her in all the right places fanning out at the bottom. Garren picked a good style and color for her.

She leaned down and planted a soft kiss on Zane's lips and stepped back. He opened his eyelids and sucked in air.

"You're beautiful." His irises brightened as he tugged her on top of him so she straddled him and kissed her until she was breathless. His fingers traced over her lips. "There is nothing without you."

Her eyebrows drew together. Shit. He was in one of those lonely, morose moods.

His voice was rough when he spoke, "We need another culling soon."

Renee moved her hands to his shoulders. "Already? But it hasn't been... I don't know how long, but it seems like you just had one."

"Yes. But winter's coming early and we won't survive if I don't thin the horde." Although she appreciated the vibrations from his words against her, the topic ruined the pleasure of the sensation.

"Thin the horde?" she repeated his words in horror. Blood rushed in her ears from the memory of the last culling.

"I know you don't like it, but it's better for the overall horde. It isn't as easy to travel when it snows." This time the vibrations from his voice soothed her almost as much as the palm he slid up and down her back. Not enough to remove her discomfort, but it helped.

"Brie said we would go south. Can't we just try to make it and see if—"

"No!" he snapped, and then swallowed. "Going south isn't an option right now." He rested his palms on her hips.

Renee noticed the skin near the corners of his eyes was tight and there was an almost imperceptible twitch as his fingers pressed into her hips. Over the past few weeks, she'd noticed whenever they talked about the horde, she saw the same tells, but she didn't think Zane was aware of it.

She swallowed before she spoke to keep the tremble from her voice, "Okay."

His eyes widened. "You're not going to fight me?"

"No, if you say we can't go south, then there's a reason. I don't want to... thin the horde, but I understand why." She tried to disguise her sadness by keeping her voice level.

He cupped her face. "I'm trying. It's not in my nature. It's not in any of our natures to... care the way you do, but I'm trying."

For a second, Renee didn't respond because it was absolute bliss with the sensation of his fingers against her cheeks and his heartfelt words repeating in her mind. But the overwhelming sadness she felt, knowing many of the horde would die because it was needed, gutted her. The cruel reality of their existence was like a thousand paper cuts. Not enough to kill, but left one in torment all the time.

"I know you are. I don't mean to question you. I guess I still think too much like," she paused and couldn't say it.

"Like a human," he finished for her. "You are the only one who is…" His voice drifted as a crease formed between his eyebrows. "When I first turned into this, or as I witnessed the other transform… none of them were like you. You are…" he paused.

"Weak," she finished for him and dropped her gaze to their laps.

"No," his voice was firm. "Don't say that. You aren't weak, Renee. You never have been. You're a fighter. You don't give up," he said resolutely.

But she *had* given up, so many times, she couldn't face him. He moved his hands and tilted her chin until she looked at him.

"Every time you wanted to let go or give up; you always chose to stay. Even if it was hard. Even if you hate it here, you stay."

"I don't hate it here. I like being with you," she assured him.

A ghost of a smile crossed his face before he pulled her into a hug. "Stay with me."

Again, that pleading tone laced his voice. It eviscerated her and made her think that even after her declaration of love, her choosing him—he didn't believe she would stay. Renee couldn't fathom why he thought she would run, but his words meant he still believed that.

She squeezed him tighter. "If we don't have to leave until later. Why don't you see how easily my new dress comes off?"

He laughed his real laugh. All the tension gone. Renee tightened her legs around his waist as they went into the bedroom.

Chapter 7 - Eric

Near Syracuse, NY

Eric yawned as he finished taking a whiz. He wanted to sleep but couldn't because it was his watch. He'd been taking two watches at night because he was paranoid about what would happen if anyone else was around Ander for too long. They had a strained alliance, but so far, no one had been injured and Ander had kept his word. They'd run into a few rogue demons but with Ander's zombies, the huge werewolf, and Ander's powers, his group barely had to do anything. In fact, he sort of thought that Caleb, Seth and Zaila were disappointed.

Eric turned to head to camp when he heard Ander's hushed voice. He always seemed to speak just above a whisper unless he was angry.

"I do not know if I can continue like this. I understand I am a failure to you, to everyone. Each night is more painful than the last." Ander's voice broke, which made Eric freeze. Never had he heard Ander speak with so much emotion.

Eric's feet tiptoed close enough, that he found Ander just inside the tree line on his knees like he was praying.

"I will never abandon you, my love. I will not stop but I... please do not hate me." Ander's last words were a whisper. "But I do not wish for him to be in that form anymore. I need... I cannot do this alone. Please, forgive me."

Eric's eyes widened. He was talking to Maeve again. He'd heard Ander speaking the other night, but Eric was so exhausted he thought he might have imagined it. Ander leaned forward until his forehead touched the ground.

"We are more..." Ander whispered, and closed his eyes. "We are forever." He stopped speaking when his voice cracked. His body shook with sobs but no sound escaped his lips.

Eric's lips trembled from his own memories of learning how to cry silently. This horrible creature, that didn't seem to possess any humanity before, was now breaking in front of him and seemed very human. Ander seemed to understand pain just as well as Eric and others in his group. A shiver ran up Eric's spine as light sounds moved toward Ander.

It was the wolf that approached him cautiously. It ran its muzzle up Ander's side and dropped its head on his shoulders. Ander didn't move, he remained on his knees face pressed against the dirt for several minutes.

"I do not mean to be dramatic," he told the wolf.

The wolf grumbled at him.

"I have traded our souls for hers, but I do not think it is enough. We are not worthy of her. Perhaps we will never—"

The wolf growled at him, stopping his words.

"I assure you; we will never stop. It is only that if she were here, if we had not failed her, she would want us to help the humans. She would not be pleased with our choices."

The wolf huffed and lifted its head before it sat beside him.

Ander lifted his body but remained on his knees. "I know she would forgive us if we did nothing, but she would want us to try, she would want us to attempt to prevent the destruction of everything."

The wolf grumbled again and turned its snout away.

"I agree, but she did not want us to destroy monsters or anyone for that matter, unless they were our enemies. Not all are our enemies."

The wolf got up, padded over to Ander, showing its teeth, bumping its snout on the glowing marks on Ander's arms.

"I cannot agree to that. I must protect us or we cannot continue. I am unwilling to risk you each time we encounter a large mass of the undead."

The wolf snapped its jaws at him. Eric felt fear crawl up his legs, making his bladder once again feel full.

"We cannot trust others. Do you not recall the first years? We lost everything. We only recovered and became strong when I gave in, when I stopped fighting what I was meant to be. I understand you do not agree but I cannot lose you. We agreed until the end."

The wolf closed its mouth and whined, rubbing its face against Ander's shoulder. Ander reached for its head and petted it behind its ears.

"I will agree to a compromise. If we find trustworthy humans and an alliance is possible, I will consider it as a way to fulfill what she wanted and also, to stave off my corruption. Is that agreeable to you?"

The wolf made a pleased sound that reminded Eric of a cat purring. Eric didn't know what to do, but didn't want to leave his group unprotected. He saw the fire from where he stood but was afraid of Ander's reaction if he knew he'd eavesdropped on his private moment.

One thing was for sure, after witnessing Ander's despair, it changed how Eric was going to interact with the necromancer. He saw him during a moment that was raw and painful and... human. Under all that evil power was a man. A broken, possibly insane man, but still a human man. And Eric had just learned something that could not only help his own group, but maybe other humans too.

Chapter 8 - Renee

Things were tense the next few days between Zane and Brie, but they managed. Renee couldn't help but feel loved because she understood they were only civil because of her. When Zane revealed their travel plans, Brie scoffed but accepted them. Later, she told Renee they were going in circles, but Zane wouldn't tell her or anyone else why.

Today they were headed east, and it was even colder. Renee shivered. "Why do we usually travel during the day?"

Zane asked her multiple times to come up front with him and the chosen when they traveled, but she'd been stubborn and stayed in the horde's mass with Brie. It wasn't until recently that Brie admitted she used to be up front and not in the horde's mass.

Brie lifted a shoulder. "We didn't use to. When I was first changed, we always traveled at night. Can't remember when we switched, but now we always camp at night."

"Do you want to travel in the front instead of here?"

"I don't want to spend any more time with our king than I have to," Brie said with a huff.

"Does Zane talk to you less because of me?"

Brie's face tightened at her words before she tossed her long hair behind her shoulder. "He talks to everyone less. Well, kinda."

"What do you mean?"

"I told you before, he's always been a bastard. He's only different with *you*. He talked to me more before, but only to give orders not to chat."

Renee fiddled with the sleeve of her shirt. "Is that why you didn't like talking to me at first? Because you didn't have many conversations?"

Brie turned her face to Renee. "No, you silly bitch. I didn't want to talk to you because it pissed me off that I was on baby-sitting duty and—" she stopped and averted her eyes.

Renee's fingers froze on the cuff of her shirt. "And what?"

"I knew you were different. It freaked me out. Then when you started talking and wanted to be my friend, I knew I was screwed," she said with a laugh. "It's impossible *not* to like you, Renee. I tried, but you're so damn... nice? No, that's not the right word." Brie scratched her head and studied her. "It didn't matter that you were as dead as we were — you're everything we lost."

Her shirt forgotten; Renee pinched her brows together. "I don't understand."

"You wouldn't because even now you're still not like us," Brie said as she gestured around her to the horde.

Several stared at them with interest. Shit. Shit. They were listening to their conversation. A nudge, like intuition, told her she needed to be more careful.

"You're still so... human. It's not a bad thing. Makes me kinda jealous and sad, but I don't want you to change. It makes this shit more tolerable."

A couple of the zombies nodded or made clicks at Brie's words which meant they understood her words or at least some of their meaning.

Renee scanned the surrounding horde. "I don't want to make you sad, Brie. I don't want to upset anyone."

"Hey," — Brie's fingers brushed her arm — "you're not. Not like that. We like you being around. You're *so* much better than that prick." She laughed.

More of the horde exchanged glances and nodded. Renee felt fearful and flattered at the same time. Flattered because Brie honestly cared about her, and perhaps some of the horde did too. Fearful because she was certain if they didn't fear Zane, they would eventually stop tolerating his behavior.

"I'm trying to get him to be better," Renee said.

Brie flashed her a wistful smile. "We know."

Renee leaned toward her friend but raised the volume of her voice to speak to all of them. "Please give him a chance, there's more to him. He can be a good king."

"Yeah... he's a king alright. There have been lots of assholes who were successful kings in history. It might have sucked for the King's people, but *he* was strong." Brie paused, glancing at the sky above her before she leveled her view back to the horde. "It just depends on how someone looks at things." She shrugged. "Even if it sucks for the subjects, sometimes they *still* had better lives than they would have had with other prick kings who were worse. Am I right?" Brie glanced at the members of the horde.

To her surprise, Renee watched as almost every one of them nodded or made noises in agreement. It was all so confusing. They didn't like Zane, but it didn't seem like they hated him either. Other kings? Did she mean there were other hordes ruled by others like Zane? Renee wanted to ask but understood it wasn't a good idea with everyone tuned in to their conversation.

"We know you're trying to be a good queen." Brie's lips twitched with amusement when she said queen. "The point is, the horde notices and we dig it. Right?" She gestured around her again.

Guttural noises and clicks sounded around her. Renee's cheeks filled with blood as her eyes grew moist, touched by their comments. Strange that she could decipher the sounds of agreement and translate them into words, she figured it was because of all the time she'd spent with them as well as her ability to read body language.

She glanced at her statuesque friend. Brie was the horde's real hero, their Knight Commander, who always put them first. Renee wanted to be less selfish and put the horde first, but she couldn't, not before Zane. He was so awful to others, and he was still an ass where it concerned them.

Brie put her arm around Renee's shoulders. "It's so much better with you here, if for no other reason — you notice when I change my hairstyle." They both laughed and kept marching.

Chapter 9 - Brie

2007

"Angel, come and meet our guest." Her father's voice was louder than her heels that clicked on the marble.

Brie shuddered internally, understanding she had no choice but to obey her father. She plastered on a fake smile and pushed her shoulders back, moving gracefully, like a lady.

Both of her parents sat in their parlor with a middle-aged man with light hair and wire-framed glasses. Her mother insisted they call it a parlor because she loved all that old shit. Brie entered and waited to be introduced, keeping her posture proud but her eyes down to show submissiveness. She wasn't submissive, but she knew how to play the game with her parents.

"This is our daughter, Brie," her father said, but as always, that was her cue.

She slowly raised her eyes and morphed her smile into something more demure.

"This is Dr. Stevenson from Greystone Industries." Her father emphasized the company name which wasn't necessary because he'd talked about the deal he'd made with them for months. Her father owned several pharmaceutical companies spanning the globe, he was always writing up business contracts with the military, corporate assholes or someone in the medical field.

Dr. Stevenson reached for her hand as she extended it toward him and he raised it to his lips. She couldn't make herself blush but she blinked her lashes several times and averted her eyes. His paternal expression annoyed Brie, but she wasn't sure if it was because she just didn't like the look of it or that her own father never wore one.

"It's so good to meet you. I've heard wonderful things about your company." Brie kept her voice light and soft.

Dr. Stevenson chuckled, still holding onto her hand. For some reason it made Brie's stomach tighten. Not his laugh, but there was something about his touch that set off warning bells in her head. He was probably as sleezy as her bastard father.

"I wanted you to meet him because he will be staying for dinner tonight," her father clarified.

Fuck. She understood what that meant. She wanted to groan but held it in and instead, brightened her smile. Thankfully, Dr. Stevenson released her fingers.

"That sounds great. I should get ready." Brie realized it was two hours until dinner but she'd spent years training her parents, they understood it took her forever to get ready. In reality, it took about half of the time, but they didn't need to know that.

"Yes, of course. We'll see you soon." Her father turned away, done with showing her off to their guest.

Another fake grin and she slid out of the room, not breathing until she'd closed and locked her bedroom door. Brie inhaled several times to calm down. She hated being home when her father wasn't traveling. Her mother irritated her daily and was likely just as much of a bitch as Brie was, but at least she didn't raise a hand to Brie.

Her father was a different matter. Brie never knew when or why her father would hit her but it was a guarantee, he would. Hell, he was the reason she'd started wearing makeup in fifth grade, to cover up any marks that were left. She was a quick learner and had become a pro at applying cosmetics in no time.

Brie took out her phone to message her new boyfriend. They were supposed to go out tonight, but now she was stuck having to pretend that her family was the upstanding unit everyone believed they were. Damn it. Her boyfriend had promised to take her out on his motorcycle that he'd just got, but now she was stuck with these assholes.

She flopped on her queen size bed and grumbled. Maybe it was better to be poor like the plebeians who worked for them. Unless her asshole of a father was around, they were mostly happy working for her family. They also seemed to have simpler lives. Brie's maid told her that none of her family had arranged marriages. No one told them who they could or couldn't date.

They didn't force their kids on a strict diet so their weight wouldn't fluctuate. They didn't have mandatory hair, nail, and facial appointments. The house staff considered the requirements she'd become accustomed to, a luxury. But to Brie they were tiny forms of torture because although she didn't mind getting her hair done, the rest of the beauty treatments she could do without. Some of them were painful and all her mother had to say about it was "beauty is pain."

During her early teenage years, they sent her to a fat camp because she was "dumpy." Brie rolled her eyes. She was going through the awkward stage everyone went through at that age but of course, her parents didn't care. Recently her mother had commented that Brie hadn't "filled in" the way she'd hoped and that she might have to get a boob job if they didn't "come in" the way they were supposed to before she turned eighteen.

Both of her conniving parents wanted to marry her off and use her like a fucking trophy for her father's empire's gain, seeing which rich prick had the most money, influence, or power. They wanted her future husband to be useful to them and her father's success. Brie frowned. What if that guy, Dr. whatever his name was... was another candidate. She smacked her face and groaned.

Her phone beeped, with a sigh she opened the message app. Of course, her boyfriend was annoyed — she was annoyed. But her lips tilted up when he suggested sneaking out of her room to meet him after dinner. It was a school night... fuck it! If she had to suffer through a boring dinner with a creepy older person her dad seemingly wanted to marry her off to, she deserved a little fun.

After finishing up her message, confirming when they'd meet up, she forced herself upright and padded to her closet looking for something appropriate, but boring to wear.

"So, you won that ribbon too?" Renee's voice cut into Brie's memory.

Brie nodded as the ambient sounds crept into her ears. Shit, she couldn't zone out like that. The horde was counting on her and the other chosen to remain alert, to protect them. Renee wasn't aware of the constant danger yet and she didn't want to tell her. She liked her friend's upbeat and optimistic attitude, even when it plucked her last nerve.

"Yeah." Brie tried to make her voice sound normal.

"That's so cool. My mom wouldn't ever let me do anything like that." Renee frowned. "She was convinced I'd get hurt or embarrass her. Or both."

Brie's face twisted at Renee's words, trying to hold back her own frown. Renee's mother was a class-A bitch, more so than her own mother it seemed. It was odd because Brie hadn't thought about her life so in-depth in years.

She still couldn't quite remember her early days as a zombie, part of her was convinced that she couldn't recall details because her brain wasn't working then like it did now. Her first clear thoughts were more... animalistic? Simpler than they were now. Brie couldn't quite figure out why, other than Renee made her talk and interact all the time, but the longer Renee was around the more... human her thoughts seemed to be. The more she thought about her past.

The reason she and Zane were okay with each other now was because he helped her kill her prick parents at the beginning of the end. Sure, it wasn't intentional, but she remembered enough detail that they'd done it together. After that, they'd dealt with each other while they worked to make the horde stronger.

"Horses are big and if you're not careful, it's easy to get hurt, but that doesn't mean you can't learn to ride. You just need a good teacher." Brie wanted to make Renee feel better and stop thinking about her bitch mother but she wasn't great at comforting people.

Renee slowed her steps and looked up at her with a hopeful expression. "If we find a horse, just you and me — would you teach me?"

Brie peered at Renee's big, green eyes and sweet expression and wouldn't crush her spirits. There was almost no chance that would ever happen, but as much as Renee's childlike innocence got under her skin, it also stirred something in her chest that caused her to be more protective of her.

"Sure, you silly bitch, but if you fall off and bust your ass, no blaming me. I don't want to deal with your boyfriend." Brie chuckled.

Renee's face pinched as she grumbled, "We shouldn't tell him because he'd worry that I'd get hurt. He's as bad as my mom except that he's just worried I'll get hurt, not because it would embarrass him—he doesn't want me to be in pain."

Brie grimaced as her stomach twisted. That fucker was the worst. Over the years, thousands of them had died and Zane had scarcely noticed. Hell, they'd lost a good number taking the city and many of their scouts had died because of their enemy. Losing members taking the city couldn't be avoided and if she was honest, she only somewhat felt anything about it. Mentally she understood the impact, and it bothered her, but actual emotions about the deaths? That was still elusive to her.

However, the scouts, who could only be of chosen status, were not easily replaced. How many times had Zane told them they were the future? That they were called "chosen" for a reason. They *did* matter. He had told her once that one chosen was worth over a hundred of the non-chosen horde.

Brie had tried to convince Zane to stop being on the defensive and be offensive. Strike when their enemy didn't expect it because after the last few months of travel it looked like they were running. Their enemy wouldn't see it coming.

She took a deep breath. They hadn't been in an all-out battle for years. Sure, they fought against humans, random groups of monsters, and sometimes other zombies, but nothing substantial. Brie didn't crave the violence exactly, as she had in life, but things were shifting. She didn't quite understand how just yet, but she sensed it. A nagging, subtle urge wanted war. But if she thought about it too long... that *sensation* would make her head hurt, like a headache, but worse.

Brie and the other chosen had learned to stop their spiraling thoughts early on. They all witnessed what happened to Bramble. He kept asking questions, thinking about their origins all the time, for months. Even when Zane scared him so bad he would have pissed his pants if they did that, Bramble didn't stop. Even when his headaches were so painful he could barely move, even when his vision went, even when he no longer spoke anything but gibberish. His behavior got more and more erratic until one day, they lost him during a raid only to find him dead on the ground. No wounds from the fighting, but blood pooled around his head leaking from his mouth, nose, eyes, and ears.

It seemed like a random event until Cloud followed in his footsteps. After they found Cloud the same way, the rest of the chosen agreed they wouldn't poke into what they were anymore. Brie cleared her throat wondering when she'd gotten so damn introspective.

"Yeah, he's real... sweet that way." Brie did her best to keep the sarcasm out of her tone.

"He is, well, okay I know it's only to me." Renee's cheeks filled with color. Brie still wasn't sure how blushing happened; it was rare among the chosen. "But I keep talking to him. I know if I help him see the horde the way I do he won't be so... cold toward them."

"I know you want him to be a good king but I think you might need to consider that he's already as good as he's going to be," Brie said and flicked her hair back. "He takes care of us, but you, wanting him to be... nice? We're zombies. I don't think zombies can be nice like that anymore."

"That's not true! You can be really thoughtful, Garren is kind, Hatchet has a great sense of humor, Mace is really protective if you're with his hunting group–"

"Okay, but I was talking about being nice. The only "nice" one of us is Garren, unless he's hunting, and you said Hatchet was funny and Mace was protective — that's not nice," Brie cut her off.

"Fine!" Renee snapped. "Garren is kinder than the rest of you but you really are thoughtful, which is kind of like being nice in a way. And the others... I'm just saying you all have good qualities. Like..." Renee leaned closer and almost whispered, "human qualities." Her eyes darted around like she'd cussed at church and was worried someone heard her.

Brie burst into laughter. This was why she loved her silly friend. She'd been in a shit mood, thinking about her crappy past and then was stressing over their enemies, but Renee, as always, made her laugh. Sure, sometimes she was laughing at Renee's expense, but not in a nasty way. Brie didn't think Renee was ever going to be that different from humans and it made her so damn happy, even when it complicated things, because it also made this existence more like... living.

For Brie's entire existence she'd wanted nothing more than to have freedom and live, really live. Not walk about like a talking doll with nothing to look forward to other than being sold off in marriage to someone identical to her father. As odd as it was, in death she'd found life, but not until her friend showed up and reminded her of what that was.

"It must be your bad influence," Brie said with her genuine smile.

Immediately Renee's features lit up which only caused Brie to look like an idiot and widen her own smile.

Chapter 10 - Renee

"Tomorrow, we take the city," Zane said as he brushed her hair off her face.

Renee shivered, but not from the cold, even though they were both naked. She hated the death that surrounded them so much.

"You won't be near any of it. I'll have Garren take you to a safe place," he told her and tried to not sound shitty when he said Garren's name, but she caught it.

"Zane," she said in a warning tone.

"I don't like him being around you all the time," he snapped.

"He's protecting me for *you*. He's following *your* orders and you know you can trust him."

Zane adjusted them so they were on their sides, facing each other, but didn't reply. His hand slid down her side to her hip and caressed her stomach, over her scar. Renee touched his thin face.

"He's yours. We're all *yours*. They obey you because you're their king," she reminded him.

Disgust crossed his features. "They obey me because I own them, not because I'm their king. They would destroy me if they could." He rolled to his back and stared at the ceiling of the van.

"You don't know that."

"Yes, I do. I told you before, they obey me because they have no choice. *It* controls everything. They aren't loyal, they fear me."

Renee rolled until she was on his chest. "It doesn't have to be that way. If you would just show them a sliver of what I see then—"

"No!" Zane sat up, forcing Renee away, and she sat up too. "You don't understand."

"You're right, I don't, and you never fully explain. I'm really trying, but you make it almost impossible!" Renee crossed her arms over her chest.

"I can't. It's better if you don't know." He dropped his eyes to his lap.

"According to who? You? I don't agree. It's screwing things up between us."

His head snapped up. His fingers curled around her shoulders, worry furrowed his brow. "The horde has nothing to do with us."

"Of course it does. They're *yours* Zane. It's like I got married to a dad with thousands of children he more often than not, neglects. It makes me wonder how I can love someone who can be so cruel to their children."

"What?" The shock made his eyes large. "Married?" His fingers pressed into her shoulders as his pupils dilated. "Children? The horde is not... they aren't people." He shook his head. "Renee, I keep trying to get this through to you. They aren't human." He let her go and sat back.

"Maybe not, but they're not mindless either. I think you want them to be because it makes what you do okay. But they have feelings. They worry about things. They notice things." Renee uncrossed her arms and leaned toward him.

"What are you talking about?"

"You're always up ahead with your chosen, and leave the rest of the horde to fend for themselves. Just because the chosen are more functional doesn't mean the horde isn't just as important."

"I didn't say they weren't, but you don't under—"

"Don't you dare tell me I don't understand! I'm the one who has spent months with them. I'm the one who can see how worried they are about the winter approaching. Not just because they're getting cold, but because they're also worried about food. The families are already–"

He laughed. The bastard actually laughed in her face. "Families? Are you insane? The horde doesn't have families."

"You sonofabitch!" She shoved him, and he fell against the wall of the van. "How dare you! They *do* have families and if you knew anything about your own horde, you would know that!" Renee snatched the sleeping bag off the floor of the van and wrapped it around herself before she flung the door open and stormed out.

Five seconds later, she regretted her decision. Not only was it cold, but she was obviously naked, wrapped in a sleeping bag, several of the horde staring at her. Shit. Shit. Just as panic set in, Brie stormed in front of the still figures of the horde. When she saw Renee, her mouth dropped open in shock. Renee regretted it so much but couldn't take her actions back.

Behind her, she sensed Zane. Brie's eyes flicked to him, so much hurt reflected in them. Renee's feet were freezing, but she didn't move. Brie moved in front of her, glared at Zane, and put her arm around Renee. She heard Zane's heavy steps approaching, but Brie flashed her teeth and he stopped.

"You can stay with me tonight, alright?" Brie said in a tight voice.

"Thank you," Renee whispered.

"She'll be safe," Brie told Zane, as she led Renee to another van. This one wasn't the work kind she'd been in but more like a minivan. Two of the seats had been ripped out and placed by the rear doors. A couple of the horde occupied them and stood when they neared. Brie gestured for them to sit down.

"Keep watch," she told them in a guttural tone, and opened the back for Renee.

After they climbed in, Brie went to a backpack Renee had never seen and took out a dress and underwear. She gave them to Renee. "They might be too big but it's better than being naked."

"Yeah, thanks." Renee dressed as quickly as she could.

"Did he..." Brie paused and grimaced.

"No. It wasn't like that. It's not," Renee floundered. She didn't want to lie, but she couldn't tell her the truth either. "We had an argument."

"You had an argument naked," Brie said with sarcasm.

"Actually yeah, I guess we did."

"Why the fuck were you naked?"

"That's not important. He was being a jerk about the horde and I got mad–"

"He's always an asshole about the horde, Renee. Why were you naked?" Brie's icy irises locked on her.

"He said..." She swallowed. "It's complicated."

"No, it's not. Either you wanted to be naked with him or he made you."

"He didn't... he didn't make me," Renee whispered.

Brie ran her fingers through her hair. "Are you fucking?" Her words were like bullets. She leaned forward as her eyes widened. "*Can* you fuck? Is *that* what you do every night?"

Renee felt the tears as they slid down her cheeks but didn't bother to wipe them. She wasn't ashamed of her relationship with Zane, but she sensed it hurt Brie somehow and didn't want to tell her.

"It's not that. Fucking, I mean," Renee said in a quiet voice.

"What?" Brie's face scrunched up with confusion.

"We don't do that because we love each other and—"

"Are you fucking kidding me right now?" Brie's tone caught between disbelief and anger. "Were you about to say make love?"

Renee stared at her lap and nodded.

"I need air." Brie shuddered and hurried to the rear doors.

Renee's hand shot out and clasped her arm to stop her. "Please don't leave. Do you hate me now?"

Brie's face twisted. "I don't hate you, Renee. I just... fuck, you have no idea how screwed up this is and I can't..." She averted her eyes.

"I put you in a bad position with him again, didn't I?"

Brie laughed, but it was harsh and bitter. It traveled through her arm to Renee's fingertips. "I wish that was all it was. I can't talk to you right now. I need time." Her fingers reached for the handle. "It'll be okay. We're still friends." Brie pulled away and left the van.

Renee didn't fully understand Brie's reaction, but Zane had been right, she shouldn't have told Brie. It hurt Brie, made her furious and Renee swore a hint of fear had been in her eyes.

Life since the end of times had always been difficult. Some days were harder than others. Since she'd been with Zane, things were more complicated than she could have imagined. She was so grateful for his love, her best friend Brie and her chosen family, the horde, but all the unspoken words were corrupting everything.

He might not want to tell her things, but he *had* to. It didn't matter what the truth was, it wouldn't change her feelings for him or anyone else. They would deal with whatever it was. He kept insisting she was strong but wouldn't completely trust her. Renee decided she would call his bluff. Either he believed she was strong and told her the truth or that message was a lie and she'd force him to admit it.

"Tomorrow, Princess. Tonight, you need to rest," Liam said behind her.

"Okay, you're right. It will make things worse if I try to resolve anything tonight." She kept her eyes down as she settled in for the night. "You'll stay with me?"

"Of course. Big brothers don't leave. I'm always here for you Renny."

She closed her eyes and ignored the tears that escaped her closed lids. When Liam's hand touched her shoulder, she let out a breath. Her insides stopped shaking. She wanted to tell him how much she missed him but kept the sentiment locked inside because that was one of the quickest ways to accidentally cause Liam to leave.

"Tell me one of our adventures Liam, like you used to when we were little," she whispered.

"You've heard these a million times," he countered.

"I know, but I like when you tell me."

"Anything for you, Princess."

Renee smiled through her tears as she felt the press of him against her back. It wasn't real, but in the moment, it didn't matter because it felt real.

"Once upon a time there was a princess, trapped by an evil king and queen. They wouldn't see how special she was or that one day she would rule over the largest most powerful kingdom in all the lands."

"But her knight commander knew," Renee chimed in.

Liam chuckled. "Yes, he knew, and he vowed to protect her and stay by her side until she was the queen she was always meant to be..."

Chapter 11 - Zane

Zane held the rolled up sleeping bag out to Toad who accepted it eagerly. Zane glanced at Mace who stood a few feet away. Brie's idea of having certain members of the horde mentored by specific chosen members was paying off. Toad was almost at the level of a chosen and was being treated as such. He made a mental note to mention it to her once things were more amicable between them. It helped the slower horde members evolve faster which was less irritating to Zane.

He scarcely tolerated the chosen's presence, but the hordes' was fouler to him. Their obsession with eating and killing things made him nauseas. Renee wanted to see them as humans but they weren't, they were hardly more than animals.

"You were chosen to carry this for the Queen. Do not fail me."

Toad tried to smile, but it distorted his face in a grotesque way. He nodded enthusiastically and held it close to his chest. Zane was relieved that Mace had managed to get Toad to bathe daily.

"Has Flint acted on his words?" Zane asked Mace.

Mace shook his head. "Not yet, but we have been watching his group. Brie is still looking for the snake."

Zane grunted. Brie was relentless. He'd told her he didn't sense any other traitors in the horde since they'd caught the other two, months ago. Only Flint's group seemed discontent, but more than anything, it was Flint.

"She won't stop until she finds whoever it was," Mace continued.

"I know," Zane said, and felt an odd urge to touch the sleeping bag. When he delivered Renee's pillows to be carried, he'd had the same urge. He wanted to touch Renee or at the very least something she had touched. He cleared his throat. "Have the scouts returned?"

It still bothered him that they had fewer scouts now, many that were new. Both he and Steel had trained them on their assigned roles and he had used his will to be certain they were loyal before he sent them out, but they weren't as efficient as the previous ones. More than ever, they needed the scouts to bring back information so he could strategize their movements.

Each day that passed his growing concern for the next few months invaded his thoughts. The horde had survived through more than one harsh winter but they hadn't been forced so far north before and there were far fewer humans to consume than there had been in the beginning.

"Yeah, they got back a little while ago. They should have eaten. Do you want to talk to them now or on the way to the city? Mace asked.

Zane tried to stay focused on the upcoming city, while his worry over the approaching winter bludgeoned his mind, but he was still thinking about his argument with Renee. It didn't help that he didn't want to attack the city. Yes, it needed to be done. It always needed to be done but this life... violence, pride, and pain — it made him want to disappear. When he and Renee weren't fighting, it was tolerable.

He didn't like that she refused to travel with him. He assumed his company was so awful that she didn't want to be around him unless they were alone, which was only at night. The weaker part of him wanted to beg her to travel with him because he knew if she was at his side, the presence of the horde in his consciousness would be less, it wouldn't weigh on him so much. He imagined her walking beside him, viewing various landmarks, eager and talking his ear off about them. It would make the travel so much more enjoyable. Perhaps they would walk hand in hand.

"On the way," his voice was gruffer than expected. Zane turned and strode to the front of the horde, giving orders as he passed through. He knew what to say and how to say it to motivate his horde but it wore on him. By the time they were marching he'd fallen back into silence.

Another shot rang out and hit its mark. Him. He grit his teeth and circled around to draw more attention to himself and away from the horde. These humans had been more prepared and had more ammunition. It varied from city to city or from human group to human group.

Zane knew the horde would be successful, but he wanted to keep as many creatures alive as possible. The culling would take care of the weaker ones, but he'd rather keep them now so they would be consumed later to make the horde stronger.

Pain wracked his body. Damn it. He couldn't pause to figure out how many had died, but it had been a group because each one of their deaths spiraled through him. Not as strong or debilitating as it had been in the beginning but the losses still shook him up from time to time.

They were all connected to him. It made it easier to keep them obedient, but their pain was his pain. Zane pushed his aching legs faster and knocked over a chosen as a long blade cut into his own back. All logical thought stopped as he destroyed the sword-wielding human, leaving the pieces for his horde to consume.

The chosen he'd spared stared at him full of awe as he hauled them to their feet. He nodded and sprinted to where gunfire lit the sky. He healed faster than any of his horde, if possible, he tried to take their wounds as his own in a more literal way, instead of just sensing them as they happened.

Renee believed he didn't care for them at all but that wasn't the truth. It just wasn't in the way her human heart was used to. She might be a creature like himself, but her thoughts and behaviors were still very human. Renee, his sensitive heart, cursed by his selfishness, would always struggle in this life. He reminded himself it was his doing that caused her pain and as much as her arguments about the horde frustrated him, he had to be patient, to understand. Well, as much as he could.

More shots hit his chest and shoulders as he dodged one meant for his skull. He never needed to think or even use muscle memory to keep them from his head. The parasite saw to that. Regardless of how wounded he was or even if he was nothing more than a wild animal, he was confident that the parasite would ensure his survival.

The horde thought he didn't feel pain, that he was indestructible, but it was all an illusion built and controlled by the parasite. Even when he was so consumed by pain he couldn't think, let alone move, the parasite would move his body like a puppeteer. Pulling the strings to make him seem regal, proud — in control at all times. At least that's what his horde saw.

Before Renee, it was no wonder that he didn't believe he was alive. That he no longer existed except in vague memories. The parasite might seek to keep him distant from Renee, perhaps even try to drive a wedge between them, but he wouldn't let it happen. It could have whatever it wanted; he didn't care. He hadn't cared in years, at least not enough to stop it from its goal of world destruction, until Renee.

Zane refused to let her go. If he had to rip that fucker out of his skull, resulting in his own demise, he would accept it as long as she was the one holding him until his last breath.

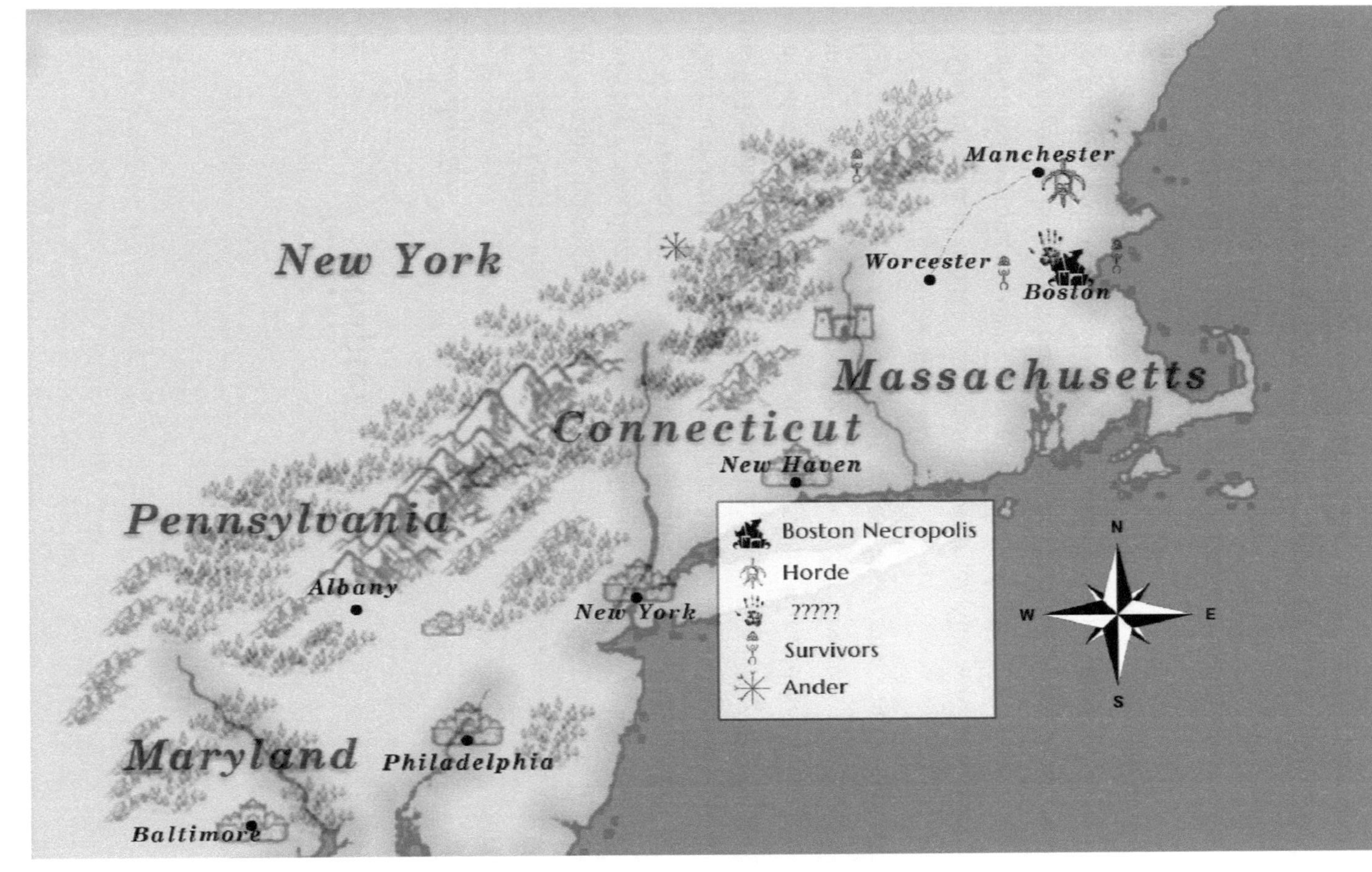
New York
Massachusetts
Manchester
Worcester
Boston
Connecticut
New Haven
Pennsylvania
Albany
New York
Maryland
Philadelphia
Baltimore
Boston Necropolis
Horde
?????
Survivors
Ander
N
W
E
S

Chapter 12 - Renee

Earlier that day...

Renee sighed and trudged along with the horde. She was concerned at the faint buzzing in her ears that had been present since she woke up. It was subtle, but it was there, and from what she could tell, no one else heard it. Yes, she'd wished for silence because she couldn't stand the sounds of violence and death, but she didn't mean it. She enjoyed being able to hear now. When she was younger, shortly after her implants, being able to hear sometimes seemed like a burden and other times it scared her. Her early months with implants she would go from wonder, to terror, to putting a pillow over her head in an effort to find the silence again. Maybe she had never been good with big changes.

Garren walked beside her instead of Brie. She was now more comfortable, wearing her own clothing, because when he arrived at the van in the morning, he had her backpack with her belongings. But Renee was upset that Brie didn't return. To distract herself from her sadness, she spent most of the day teaching Garren, and some of the other interested horde members, sign language.

She smiled at how quickly Garren picked it up and she also grew more depressed at the speed some of the horde members did not. They were much smarter than Zane wanted to admit. Her new family was a stinky, gross, dead bunch, but damn it, they had heart, even if Zane wouldn't see that. Zombies couldn't be that friendly and want to learn if they weren't like people. He was wrong.

Renee shook her head no. "Like this," she said to Flame. Renee had named her Flame because she liked to help make the fires at night and also preferred to sit near them. Although Flame couldn't say her own name, she smiled every time Renee said it and pointed to her.

Renee balled her hands into fists and crossed her arms in front of herself. *Guard.*

Flame repeated the motion correctly this time and looked to Renee for approval.

"Yes!" Renee bounced with delight. Then she pointed to Garren and positioned her right hand into a bent shape as she pulled her left arm up and put it into a horizontal position to resemble a horizon. She brought her right hand down to resemble the setting sun.

"Night," she said, and then repeated the motions for *guard.* It wasn't exactly correct for the word "sentinel" but Renee wasn't focused on that for the moment. She had tried to teach individual letters to some of the horde but many of them didn't have the coordination to manage it or even if they did, they could only retain a few letters.

Renee pointed to Garren again and repeated the motions, Flame imitated them. Renee clapped; she was so happy. Then Flame clapped too. She pointed to Flame and said, "Guard," as she signed again.

Flame nodded and did the motions. Then Renee pointed at Garren. Flame stared for a few seconds before she signed *night* and then *guard.* With slow movements so as not to startle Flame, she extended her fingers to Flame's arm and gave it a tiny squeeze.

Renee removed her hand, balling it into a fist with her thumb sticking out, using her thumb to trace a path up the middle of her chest and then pointed at Flame. *I'm proud of you.*

Flame's lips trembled as her eyes became watery. Renee was so stunned she stopped walking. Garren stilled beside her. Flame stared at Renee for a few heartbeats before she balled her fist in front of where her heart was and smacked it several times and then pointed at Renee.

Renee had to fight the urge not to bound forward and hug Flame. It didn't matter that Flame was filthy or had a nasty wound on the left side of her ribcage that would probably never heal. Renee had reached her, whatever was left of Flame as a person was still in there. Perhaps it wasn't who she'd been in life but there was something, and it was real. Never had she been so certain Zane was wrong about his horde.

She almost didn't notice how many other horde members had stopped and surrounded them. They were staring at her and Flame. Renee's heart raced uncertain of what it meant until they all made the identical gesture to Renee that Flame had.

Renee's fingers flew to her mouth as she teared up. Without thinking, she reached for Garren's hand. He slipped his into hers and held it tightly. She knew Zane would be furious with her for touching Garren but she needed something to steady her, something to keep her grounded, or she was going to sob like a baby.

Once she calmed her breathing, she tugged her fingers from Garren's and signed *thank you* while saying it at the same time. They all lowered their heads before they turned and started marching again. Flame was the last to move, still looking at her with overwhelming emotion.

Garren moved forward and gestured for Renee to walk. *We will be at the city soon*, he signed barely missing any hand movements.

As miserable as she had been, now even more upset with Zane than before, she couldn't help but feel hopeful as she began moving.

The horde slowed as the city came into view. As always, they split into smaller groups with different clusters headed in opposite directions.

"Be careful," she called out to them.

A couple signed back, others answered her, and a few just nodded. Where was Brie? Zane told her he'd have Garren get her to safety, and she had faith he would, but she always saw Brie before they attacked a city. Not concerned that Brie would die, Renee was convinced that she could handle almost any situation, but it made her feel better to see her friend off.

Garren gently nudged her away from the horde and held up a finger in front of his lips before he took her hand and hid them behind a pile of wrecked cars. Renee watched the horde close in on the city. Before they even reached the outskirts, guns fired. The sound traveled through her and made her tremble.

Garren squeezed her hand. He was alert but calm. He usually maintained a steady presence when he was with her. Renee had seen him in only a few violent encounters, but even then, he was more reserved than the others. He made targeted deadly strikes as though he'd been taught how to end lives before ever being a zombie.

They stayed among scraps of cars until the shamblers weren't visible anymore and the sun was low in the sky. He tugged on her hand and crept closer to the city's border. Like two thieves, they'd move a couple of feet to hide and then did it over and over until they reached the city. Every time they stopped; his eyes would dart around. Renee studied how his head tilted one way and then the other as he homed in on various sounds. She wasn't sure, but she thought he had acute hearing because he heard things she didn't think were possible, usually well before others saw what was causing the noise. Of course, her hearing had been impaired when she was alive, so perhaps even though she could hear now, it still wasn't as accurate as everyone else's.

They made their way to the heart of the city, avoiding everyone, both the horde and the fighting humans. Renee and Garren even used sign language a few times when they ran from place to place, ensuring silent communication between the two of them. Once inside an apartment building, they ascended several floors before trying to find an unlocked door. Unfortunately, everything they found was barf-worthy. Rotting corpses or worse. What's worse than a rotting corpse?

One that had been attacked by zombies before and then died. Looked like some had turned but didn't quite finish the job and perished where they were. Half-eaten loved ones decaying beside them. Garren got her far from anything that might cause her to wretch in record time.

They went up another floor, but none of the doors were open. To her surprise, he took out tools from his pocket and picked a door. Score! The abandoned apartment was clean. He closed the door and wouldn't let her explore until he checked every room for threats.

The noise of the violence outside wasn't as bad given their height above the city. Perhaps that was why he insisted they went up so many floors. Once Garren was satisfied, he waited for her to check out the apartment and get comfortable.

"I didn't know you could pick locks." She peeked in the bedroom, ecstatic to find the bed was in good condition.

Garren shrugged and moved to the door. She grinned as he tried to sign to her, but forgot some of the new words. His lips flattened with frustration. Renee put her fingers on top of his.

"It's okay. You have a lot to manage. I'm kind of a pain in the butt. Don't worry about me, I'll lock the door. I want to know your thoughts, but I know you need to go. We'll talk later. Thank you." She let go of him and pulled him into a hug. "Please don't die," she whispered.

Garren squeezed her tighter before he let go and swept into a low bow. She locked and bolted the door so he'd hear it and shuffled into the living room to wait. After what felt like an eternity, she heard his knock. The one he'd made so she would always know it was him. She jumped up and raced to the door, still angry but more relieved he was there, that he was okay.

She opened the door and stumbled when he cupped her face and kissed her. The door thudded behind him as he devoured her. Trace blood was still on his lips, but she ignored it and ran her fingers over his chest and torso. It was wet with blood like it always was, but that bothered her less and less as time passed. As horrible as it was, she was always grateful it was someone else's blood and not his.

He winced, but didn't break their kiss. Renee tried to pull away, but he refused to let go. He pressed her against a door in the apartment's hallway as his palms ran over her waist and hips. When she was lightheaded from lack of oxygen, he broke their kiss. Zane buried his face in her neck and hair.

"I missed you," he rasped.

"Zane?" She picked his head up and inhaled sharply. Something was wrong. "Are you okay?"

"I'm fine... now." He collapsed against her and then passed out.

Renee tried to hold him up, but he was too big. They slipped and collapsed on the floor. She struggled to breathe with his full weight on her. Her back and butt hurt from when they slid down, somewhat falling to the tile. His weight pinned her down, but after a while, she wiggled out from under him and checked him for wounds.

Oh god, the blood on his shirt wasn't someone else's. It was his. She yanked his black t-shirt up his torso and bit her lip. How many times had they shot him? Not only that, there were multiple slashes, like he'd been cut by something too. So many deep, angry-looking wounds that were still oozing blood — his dark, red blood.

Tears made her vision blur. She wiped her face with her sleeve. He said he couldn't die and promised he wouldn't leave her. But how would he be okay after this? She sobbed as his words came back to her.

"I promise, I won't leave you. It won't let me die."

What was *it*? He kept bringing *it* up but never explained. Right now, with his torn-up body, she needed reassurance that he wasn't just crazy. There really was an *it* and it would keep its end of the bargain and not let him die.

"Please, please don't leave me," she begged. "I can't do this without you, please." Her own words haunted her as her brother's face superimposed on top of Zane's and almost made her jump out of her own skin.

Liam's deep brown eyes pleaded with her as he choked out his last words, "It's okay Renny, let me go…"

No. No. No. She couldn't relive his death. Her entire frame shook as she pushed the awful memory away.

Pressure on Renee's shoulder made her glance up. Liam was crouched beside her, clasping her. His brown eyes flicked to Zane and then to her. The memory of Liam's last moments vanished. The rational part of her brain knew Liam wasn't there, but it still comforted her to have him supporting her, even from the grave. His eyes twinkled before he winked and tilted his head back at Zane. She looked down at Zane.

Her mouth fell open as his wounds closed slowly. Disappearing like they'd never been there. It reminded her of healing magic from her books.

She turned to her brother. "Liam, look!" But he was gone.

Zane made a soft sound of pain from the floor.

"Zane." She bent and kissed his forehead and smoothed his hair back. "I'm here. I'm right here with you. Come back to me."

He gurgled, then coughed, rolling to his side. Pain made his body shake as blood trickled out of his mouth. Renee put his head in her lap and held him as he trembled. He turned his bright, amber irises to her.

"I'll always come back to you," he croaked out.

Chapter 13 - Renee

They'd moved to the couch when Zane assured her, he was safe to move. He had removed his shirt to show her how well he was healing, but she still was wary. Most of the wounds were gone, leaving no trace. A few of his scars remained, but she guessed they had been there when he was still alive. The only one she didn't remember was some uneven skin on his chest, near his heart.

"The city is safe," Zane said. His voice resigned.

"If it's really safe and you're really okay, then take off your pants."

A crease formed between his brows. "You want me to take off my pants?"

"Yeah, you may have more injuries and are hiding them."

He laughed at her words and then winced. She crossed her arms and narrowed her eyes. With a sigh, he stood and pulled off his pants, leaving only his boxer briefs before he sat.

"You *do* have more injuries!" she called out and pointed at his leg that was slowly beginning to heal. "How many times were you shot?"

Zane leaned his head back on the couch, staring at the ceiling. "I didn't keep track. I get shot a lot," he said with a grin.

"This isn't funny! You haven't been this hurt before."

"Of course I have. I've had better luck since you've been in my life. Until tonight, but that's because I was distracted." He turned his gaze to her. "But this time I got to come home to you." He placed his palm on her leg.

"As opposed to what? Passing out in the street somewhere?"

"No. I can't do that." He turned his head from her. "*It* makes sure I don't show weakness in front of others. I find somewhere private to heal."

"You mean you find somewhere to hide so they believe you're unstoppable?"

A sour expression covered his sharp features. "Something like that."

"But it let you get here, to me, *and let you* pass out?" Renee wanted to understand what *it* was. She was starting to believe that "it" was Zane's coping mechanism with what he was. He'd never used the word zombie and didn't seem to like it when she did.

He turned back to her and studied her. "Yes, and that terrifies me."

Confused, Renee leaned forward. "Why?"

He adjusted, so he sat up. "You are everything to me, always the exception. But *it* doesn't see anything, anyone, that way. I don't understand why."

Renee listened to his words, but stared in amazement at his legs, as every single wound healed in front of her. Nothing was left but dried blood. She scooted closer to him. "Could be *it* knows you love me."

"Yes, but that didn't matter before. It wanted me... it doesn't matter. Something has changed." His face tightened.

"Maybe because it can sense how you're the same, but different, too. You're not evil, Zane. You're good." She climbed into his lap and straddled him.

"I'm not what you think. There's nothing *good* about me. You... you are the only thing that makes me what I am now." He brushed his lips on hers. "There is nothing without you," he whispered and kissed her neck.

"Stop saying that."

He buried his face in her hair. "You wanted me to be honest."

As much as Renee enjoyed the sensation of him speaking directly against her skin, the tiny vibrations tickling her, she had to get him to open up. "Zane, look at me."

He pulled back and gazed at her. The pain in his expression twisted her stomach into a knot. She'd already decided. No turning back. He had to tell her, had to trust her.

"You have to tell me about *it*. You can trust me. You're not alone anymore." She brushed his hair back. "It's us now."

He looked away, but not before she saw his wet lashes. "It's not just us."

"What?"

He turned his teary eyes to her. "There's a reason the horde is mine, why I'm their... king." He cleared his throat. "It's because of the parasite."

"The parasite?" Renee wasn't sure what she thought he was going to tell her, but the word parasite never entered her mind. She racked her brain thinking of what she knew about parasites. What kind she was familiar with? Ticks? Tapeworms? Weren't those parasites too?

"Yes. It's part of me. It's what made me like this. I guess what made all of us like this?"

Renee straightened. "Are you saying the reason zombies exist is because you're infected with a parasite?"

"Yes...not entirely. It's why *my* horde exists. There were others..." He averted his eyes. "The point is, when someone is infected by me or my horde, they have no choice but to bend to my will. It seems, with the others, it acts like a disease, but with me... it's different."

Her pulse raced, making the blood rush in her ears. "Different how?"

His eyes locked on hers. "I'm its host."

The realization of his words made her chest tighten. His erratic mood swings made so much more sense now. "Which is why it won't let you die and why it keeps making you consume even when you don't want to."

Zane didn't reply, but he didn't need to. It was why he always sounded like that when he talked about himself, because he wasn't talking about himself. He was talking about the parasite.

"But how does it make you do things?"

The skin near the corners of his eyes tightened as his hands trembled ever so slightly on her waist. "It's hard to explain, but it takes over my actions, my mind. I can see what's happening, but can't do anything to change it. It has its own agenda."

Was it the reason he was such a jerk about the horde? Or was that just Zane? It didn't make sense because he told her *he* decided to save her, but from what he said tonight, it didn't sound like the parasite wanted him to do that.

Her fingers threaded into his long locks. "But you said you were selfish and wanted me."

He touched her face. "Because you're the one thing that gave me the strength to force *my* will, what *I* wanted. I told you without you, there's nothing."

A million thoughts collided in her mind, but the foremost being that she'd never been so important to another person. It was like she was the only thing keeping him alive, and in a way, she was. The responsibility was overwhelming, but at the same time made her fucking swoon. Selfish to want someone to love her so much they would feel like they'd die without her, but she wanted it. Perhaps she was just as terrible as he was.

She slanted her mouth over his. Tomorrow, they would talk more about it, but tonight she wanted him to know how much she loved him and that even with his admission, her feelings hadn't changed. If anything, they were stronger. She hadn't been wrong. The truth had broken nothing. Renee never felt closer to him because he'd trusted her with something no one else knew. He picked her up and started toward the bedroom.

"We shouldn't. You were hurt," she said in alarm.

"All the more reason we should." He kissed her as he laid her on the bed. "Remind me what it's like to be human."

Chapter 14 - Renee

For once, Zane slept longer than she did, probably because he'd been so hurt and then insisted on them having sex twice. As amazing as it was, she worried because he had never passed out from being wounded before. When she realized the more, she protested, the harder he worked to please her, she stopped and enjoyed their connection.

She peered at him for a long time, her eyes tracing the blue and purple lines that crisscrossed all over his skin. Even with his pale, dead-skin coloring, he was gorgeous. He was the most beautiful man she'd ever seen. He was a man, wasn't he? At least in part. Sometimes he acted more like a monster, but when he was alone with her — vulnerable — he was only her Zane.

Her Zane wasn't a monster. He was her twin flame, the other piece of her soul. Perhaps darker, but that didn't mean evil. What was light without darkness? As much as she might not like how cold he was where it concerned the horde, a small part of her understood as the King of the Dead, he could only show so much warmth. Perhaps it was her job to show the horde the caring he couldn't.

The idea of the parasite bounced around in her mind and what it might mean, not only for him, but for the future. Renee was positive Brie didn't know about it, and she wouldn't ever tell her. This secret was more important than her and Zane's sexual relationship. She breathed out, still had to fix that or figure out how to make Brie feel better. Of course, she wasn't sure what offended Brie the most about that. It could be that the relationship existed at all because Brie thought it endangered the horde. Might be because of the unnaturalness of them being able to have sex at all.

Zane stirred and reached for her breast without opening his eyes. He made a satisfied sound once he cupped it and slid his palm down to rest on the scar on her stomach before cracking his eyelids open. Zane might've been hurt last night, but he'd eaten too, his goldish irises striking. He tugged her closer and hugged her before he brushed his lips against hers.

"This is all I want. You hate the violence and death and I hate all of it, except you."

"Don't say that."

"I don't want to be king," he said, clenching his jaw. "I understand nothing can change. That this, with you, is more than I ever hoped to have, but if I could, I would take you away. Let you live in peace. Be happy." His fingers traced her lips.

"I told you, I'm happy with you. Even with the violence and death. Whether I was with you or alone, I wouldn't be able to escape it, not in this world. Things before... that world is nothing but ashes now. Being with you makes all the difference."

"But it," — he paused — "it will keep making me consume. Continue to create an army." His jaw worked.

"Because it wants to spread? It wants to control everyone?"

"I don't know." He turned his head. "I didn't care before."

Renee's stomach knotted. "Before me."

"Yes."

"But you did." Renee turned his face back to hers. "You cared. You told me your plan. It was the only way you could think to stop it. To stop yourself."

Doubtless the slowest, most painful suicide plan she'd ever heard of, but if you weren't in charge of your own body, it didn't leave someone with a lot of choices. Zane said nothing and moved his head, so he stared at the ceiling.

"Once I was here, it complicated everything because you had to change your plans. If you don't want to do what the parasite wants, what can you do to stop it?"

"I don't think I can. Every time I try, my control only lasts days." Tears slid down the corners of his eyes to the pillow.

Renee swallowed before she spoke to give her a second to muster her courage. "Maybe you shouldn't try to stop it. I mean, stop fighting it."

His head whipped to her in shock.

She repositioned herself to see him better. "Just hear me out. If you can't stop it, but it can't stop you when it comes to me," — she scooted until she draped over him — "perhaps there's a compromise where you don't have to be so miserable all the time. You said you didn't understand why it let you come back to me last night. It never lets you show weakness, right?"

"Right," he said with caution.

"Okay, but it let you come to me. Let *me* see weakness. Maybe it trusts me or is at least trying to compromise with you about me. It's better if it lets you have me because then you won't fight it so much about what it wants?"

"Are you suggesting I keep infecting others and building the horde like I have been all these years?"

"I mean, isn't that what we've been doing?" Renee was confused because she thought that was why they went from place to place.

"No! I was taking care of the horde," his tone offended. Zane slid her off of him and sat up in the bed.

Shit. Shit. She sat next to him, unsure of what to say now.

"You keep yelling at me about them all the time. We have to consume, and the horde is large." He paused and shook his head.

"I know we have to eat or we turn into shamblers."

"Something like that," he snapped and took a breath. "There isn't enough food available unless we keep moving. We haven't... recruited for months. There were some mistakes, but I made sure no more creatures were added."

"But what about me?"

"I told you I was selfish. I couldn't let you go." He dropped his eyes to the sheets.

Renee threaded her fingers together. "I didn't know any of that."

"I'm surprised Brie didn't run her mouth about that too."

"If she had, it would only be because until last night you wouldn't tell me anything."

He twisted toward her. "I did that for you. Your transition to what we are was hard, and I didn't want to upset you more."

"Okay, but you keep telling me I'm strong, that I'm a fighter, but you keep shielding me. I need you to be honest with me. I'm supposed to be your queen and help you. I can't do that if you don't talk to me."

"You are." He swallowed. "I'm not used to having anyone who I can trust."

"That doesn't make sense. Brie is awesome and Garren—"

"Don't!" He took a breath. "It's not the same. I own them. They follow orders as you've pointed out. They aren't equals."

Renee was caught between wanting to strangle him for his arrogance and hug him for the compliment that she was his equal. She took several deep breaths and separated her hands from his before she answered.

"Okay, well, now you do. Don't just be my boyfriend." She picked up his hand. "Trust me. Be *with* me Zane."

"I only want to be with you. It's all I have ever wanted."

The sincerity in his voice made her stomach flip-flop.

"Will you consider what I said about the parasite? We can have a future you don't hate but not like this." Renee tried not to ponder about what she suggested. Rationalizing that she'd already believed that's what he'd been doing and been okay with things. Yep, every bit the monster he was. Crap.

"Do you think about a future with me?" he asked.

"I know, crazy, right? We're monsters and the world is a mess, but it's probably the only place where monsters could have a future."

Zane yanked her to him and slammed his mouth on hers. Unlike most of their kisses, this one hurt, but it wasn't as desperate as others had been in the past. This kiss was filled with fierce devotion and hope. When they broke apart, they gasped for air but held each other.

"I'll do whatever it takes to have a future with you," he vowed.

Chapter 15 - Eric

Near White Creek, NY

Eric peeked at Ander, who perched on a log near the fire, his giant wolf beside him. Over the past week, Eric had somehow kept his crew under control, although there had been a few intense interactions with the necromancer. Eric had spoken with his group and told them unless he gave the okay, he needed to be the only one to talk to Ander. Valen, Caleb, and Zaila were too hot tempered. Seth wouldn't leave Lucy's side because he didn't want the necromancer anywhere near Lucy. They had all begrudgingly agreed, but it was hard for Eric to get any rest because he wasn't one-hundred percent certain that someone from his group wouldn't try something when Ander rested. As irrational as it was for them to try since the wolf always watched over Ander when he slept, and showed its teeth to anyone who came within ten feet of them, they might risk everything if they believed they could defeat him.

Eric understood they could probably kill him, but not without one or more of them dying, and he wouldn't accept that. They'd been through so much, not only surviving this hellscape but still putting the pieces together from what happened at home. His eyes traced over Ander's glowing marks and noticed a multitude of scars on his arms since his sleeves were pushed up. Perhaps the only difference between his and Eric's group, was that he wore his damage on the outside instead of hiding it like they did.

Ander seemed most at peace late at night as he stared into the fire. He ate and slept, which meant he was probably human. Ander didn't talk to them much and when he did, it was always about their abilities, figuring out how they worked or their origins. They had all been dodgy about telling him where they came from, except for Valen. She was proud that her grandmother had been a witch.

Eric noticed that if Ander wasn't in a mood, and no one interrupted him as he stared at the fire for a while, sometimes he'd talk to Eric, even answer questions, provided the others clustered near them, but not with them.

"Do your tattoos always glow?" Eric dared to ask.

"No. Only when I use magic." As usual, Ander's expression didn't change when he spoke.

"But... they haven't stopped glowing since we started traveling with you."

"That is because I have used magic every day."

The wolf grunted and changed position, knocking into Ander's side. Ander turned his head to the giant beast and rubbed it behind its ears.

"I am aware of how much this upsets you, but you understand it is necessary." The wolf let out a rumble and snapped its teeth. Ander sighed. "I will not allow that to happen. We must find her. I will not rest until our work is done. Bloody and broken... but together." Ander tugged the wolf closer with his final words and the wolf let out a little moan of agreement.

Eric's eyebrows shot up. The only time Ander showed kindness or compassion was for his wolf. Unless he spoke of the woman they were supposed to find, he was like an animated corpse. His wolf was the only thing he cared about. Valen had figured that out immediately, god she was amazing.

"Stop with the death pact shit, Ander. You need to help him find himself — not remind him of this pointless search," the ghost of the older woman that was constantly around said.

Eric used his abilities sparingly most of the time. There were too many restless spirits since the apocalypse began. If they were in the wrong location, it would incapacitate him because his power would overwhelm him. But at night, when it was calm, by the fire, he let them surface. Mainly to hear what the woman said. Ander would get angry and sometimes hurt her, but he never destroyed her like he threatened to. As nuts as it sounded, it made Eric feel better to see the strange exchange. It meant that somewhere deep inside, the malevolent necromancer was something that wasn't inherently evil. What he'd witnessed days ago, gave him hope that he would figure out how to gain Ander's trust so he could protect his group and help their settlement of people.

Both the wolf and Ander growled at the ghost. She put her hands up, palms out, to show she would stop.

"Don't be a shit. I'm only saying it because I hate watching you two hurt like this," she explained.

"While I appreciate your words, we have discussed this; neither of us will stop until she is whole," Ander replied through gritted teeth.

"Okay. Okay. But wouldn't it be easier if he was himself?" she questioned.

Eric forced his posture not to change as he listened. He understood the wolf was actually a werewolf, but had no clue why it couldn't turn back into human form. He'd assumed it was like Zaila had explained—sometimes, if they shifted too much or were in general, more bestial, they couldn't return to their human form.

Ander gazed at the wolf; his sharp features softened. "You understand why he cannot. He must remain in this form until we return her to this plane. It was his choice."

"You surly prick!" the ghost snapped. "I need to know if you're okay." She floated closer, right next to the wolf's head. "I know you're in there. You fucked up. We both did. And we're paying for it, but you can't hide forever."

The wolf showed its teeth and started a low growl.

"I know you too, asshole. We're supposed to have moved past all this bullshit. I'm dead! I paid for the mistakes I made with both of you, and her. I can't fix what happened, but you understand I wouldn't keep you from her. Let him out, damn it!"

Ander winced from her raised voice as his markings increased in brightness. The woman noticed and hurried away.

"You have said enough and upset him. Stop or I will make you." Ander's voice was level, but there was a hint of a threat lacing it.

"Fucking fine. I'm done." The ghost pouted on the other side of the fire.

Ander turned his glowing, mismatched eyes to Eric. "I suppose you heard all of that, since you appear riveted by our family interactions." Although his face hadn't changed, Eric got the sense he was trying to make a joke.

"Everyone has family drama. It's no big deal." Eric lifted a shoulder.

"Perhaps, but I assume it is less... aggressive?"

"It depends on the family. My dad had a temper, but he never smacked me around the way Lucy and Caleb's father did."

Ander and the wolf studied Eric. What he'd said meant something to both of them, but he wasn't sure what. After a moment, they both returned their attention to the fire.

"Do you find my presence disturbing?"

Eric stiffened from Ander's question and debated on how to respond. He hadn't forgotten that Ander had told them at their initial meeting that he could sus out a lie. Eric didn't know if that was by magical means or just because he was good at it.

"Sometimes," he responded, choosing an honest answer. He didn't mention that sometimes was actually, most of the time.

"I have... never been able to interact with humans well. There was a time when my mask hid what I am, but since she..." He paused as his features tightened and made his cheekbones look like razors. "I am not capable of it anymore."

Ander cleared his throat and adjusted how he sat on the log, pausing for a moment to stare at the enormous trunk of the tree. "I recall sitting with her on a fallen tree." His fingers traced over the rough bark. "Do you remember? It was when we discovered the gorgon and that she spoke Greek." He glanced at the wolf, who huffed in response.

"Did... did you say gorgon? Isn't that a monster from ancient times?" Eric vaguely recalled reading about myths and legends in school. He'd read about them because it irritated his father, who believed they were nonsense.

The corner of Ander's mouth tilted up, almost resembling a grin. "Yes. We had not realized at the time it was a gorgon and were not prepared. However, the angel that arrived aided us in weakening the creature so we were able to destroy it."

Eric's mind buzzed with a million questions. He wasn't sure which one to start with or how long Ander would talk. Over the years, they had seen many creatures that, until all hell broke loose, everyone assumed were made up.

In the early years, there were what seemed like thousands of werewolves. For the most part, they died protecting humans and killing the zombies. Zaila had explained that most werewolves, unless they were corrupted, didn't want to hurt people, and they loved the earth and wanted to make it better.

Of course, from the beginning, there were demons. There would always be demons. As long as Hell existed and people's souls went there... there would always be an endless population. Although over the years, many retreated to Hell, preferring to wait out the apocalypse. All except the ones that declared they were from House Executioners. Most humans just called them savages or butchers because that was all they were. They were wrath unregulated and their only goal seemed to be to end whatever was left of humanity.

At one point, it seemed like the vampires were going to help people, but they only wanted to help to secure their food supply, so things disintegrated into yet another battle humans had to fight. It was exhausting. Ever since the zombies rose up, it was like a switch got flipped and every monster in hiding came out — ready to fight.

Eric and Valen had talked about the monsters more than once. Back home, everyone looked down on Valen for being different, and they didn't even know she was a witch. If their hometown had known, they'd likely have screamed to have her burned at the stake. He pressed his lips together in irritation at the memory.

Eric wasn't sure how much time humanity had left. Both Lucy and Valen were convinced the remaining human population could be saved and urged them all to keep trying, but it got harder with each passing day. He wouldn't debate with either of them, but the longer things went on there were less and fewer humans and more and more monsters. His eyes flicked to Ander. He believed at some point, Ander was human, perhaps part of him still was, but it seemed like any humans that had survived turned into monsters just to keep breathing.

The one creature none of them had witnessed was an angel. "An angel? A real angel?" Eric said cautiously.

The wolf grunted and turned its head away. In response, Ander petted its back. "Yes, it was only an emissary, thankfully. We would not have been able to best a sentinel. Have you not witnessed an angel? I have seen several in the last few years."

Eric shook his head. "I'm sure we would have remembered that. I didn't think Heaven cared about anything going on down here." He tried to keep the bitterness from his tone.

"It is not invested in what is happening."

Eric sat straighter as anger made his face hot. Typical. All those years spent praying, doing all the right things, even when it hurt, even when the people in the church they should've been able to trust betrayed them—and now this. To know that Heaven had abandoned them.

"Doesn't it *have* to be invested? Don't they need us—our souls?" Eric snapped.

Ander sighed. "Given the rate of daily deaths... no. Both Heaven and Hell are being supplied with souls. If there was an imbalance, then one or both sides would intervene."

"How many people have to die before they care? Millions of people are dead. Hell, at this point probably billions—that's not enough?" Eric tried to keep his voice down so as not to wake the others, but knowing that humanity had been forsaken was killing him in ways he wasn't sure how to process.

"I see. How unfortunate. You had some amount of faith left." Ander faced him again. "I had many years to work through my disappointment."

Eric scrunched up his face. Was that Ander trying to comfort him? If so, it was terrible. "Disappointment?"

"Yes, you are disappointed in Heaven, and by extension, God. He does not care in the way you perceive. However, anger is a more accessible emotion. For many young people, it is more comfortable."

Eric grit his teeth. He was used to older people talking down to him, but Ander wasn't *that* much older. "How old are you?"

Ander's eyebrows raised. He tilted his head in calculation before he answered. "I believe I am thirty-two."

"I'm almost twenty-five. You're not much older than me."

"Twenty-five..." Ander's eyes glazed over and he became still. He did that periodically. He'd say something and then zone out for chunks of time, still as a statue, unaware of what was going on around him. But like every other time he did that, the wolf became hyper alert and watched for any threats.

Eric's gaze latched onto the werewolf. "I wish I could talk to you. I know you know a lot about what's going on. You understand him, but can you understand me?"

The wolf raised its head and then tilted it down twice, showing it understood him. That made sense to Eric because even when Zaila and Caleb were in their wolf forms, they still understood him. They didn't quite think the same way, but it was close. It was like a simpler version of themselves, more instinct and less finesse.

"Are you his only friend?" Eric asked the wolf.

The werewolf's irises shifted from amber to a steel-grey color for a couple of seconds before they returned to yellow.

"I'll take that as a yes." He felt kind of dumb talking to the werewolf since it was pretty one-sided, but it surprised him at how well he could see what the wolf intended to say. Perhaps that's how Ander communicated with it? But their communication seemed more nuanced.

Eric glanced at Ander, making sure he was still tuned out before focusing on the wolf. "I'm going to level with you. He... makes us uncomfortable. The only time he seems 'okay' is when it's just us sitting here like this. I don't know what your story, or his is, but we aren't going to try to kill you." Eric twisted his head and peeked at his group, all asleep, since he'd opted to take watch. "The only reason you pick up on aggression is because Caleb and

Zaila are like you and have trouble controlling their tempers." He faced the giant wolf. "But it's mostly because you both keep threatening us. We just want to survive. I... want to keep my family safe and alive. You get that right? Isn't that what you're worried about too?" Eric was going out on a limb, basing his words on the interactions he'd witnessed with Ander's group.

The wolf huffed and readjusted to a more relaxed posture, putting its paws in front as it stretched out. It stared at the sleeping group for a moment and then locked its gaze on Eric. Again, it nodded.

Eric took quick breaths and tried to not let his elation show. He'd felt pretty silly talking to an animal, but it had worked! He hoped the wolf would somehow communicate Eric's group's intentions to Ander.

"Kid, he won't kill any of you as long as you don't push him," the female ghost piped up at Eric's side. "And neither will he." She gestured to the wolf. "Before all this... they both risked their lives daily to protect humanity. They gave up everything for the code and in the end, it didn't matter." Her tone was miserable.

"Will you tell me more about what they used to do?" Eric asked the spirit.

"As long as those pricks will let me." The woman shot a glare at the wolf. The wolf huffed but didn't growl or show its teeth as it had in the past. "We were all soldiers in a secret army sworn to protect humanity from monsters. Didn't work out." She chuckled.

"Do you mean Greystone Industries?" Eric asked, wondering if they were part of the organization Zaila was affiliated with.

The ghost floated in front of him before he finished the sentence. "What do you know about GI?"

Eric drew a quick breath at the speed of her movement. "Zaila used to work for them... well, she was more like a slave. They had her on the team that came to our hometown just after the gate to Hell was opened, to close it before things got worse."

"Fuck. You were in one of the places that a gate opened. It's part of why this happened. Even with all hands-on deck and working with those fucks at GI, with all the damn undead running around spreading that sickness and Hell's gates opening all over the world—we couldn't keep up."

Eric scratched his head. "So, you worked with Greystone Industries but weren't part of them?"

"No, they were too corporate for my taste. We were all Soldiers of Night. We were the dollar store version of them. At least that's what we wanted them to think. They didn't see us as a threat, which was our intent. Never had time..." her voice trailed off as her ghostly form searched the starlit sky above them. "None of that matters now. Listen, kid, I need your help."

Eric's eyes darted to the wolf that seemed to be listening to everything before glancing at the ghost, concerned she would say something that might upset Ander. Ander was still frozen, staring at nothing. "I already agreed to look for Maeve."

"It's not about that. I've already..." She paused and took a metaphorical breath. "There's no changing their minds about that. I don't know how much longer I have, and I need to know that someone who isn't a complete asshole will keep an eye on them. And before you tell me they're older than you or they scare the shit out of you—don't."

"I don't... I don't understand," Eric managed.

"You know how this works. Shades can only maintain themselves for so long. Every day, I can feel it, feel *myself* slipping a little more. It's a fucking curse to exist as a shade. It's why they all turn into monsters. I'm only like this because of him." She gestured to Ander.

"Okay, but that doesn't explain why you're asking me to... watch over them?"

Her face softened at his words, and a motherly expression changed her appearance. Eric finally understood why the ghost put up with Ander's behavior. He had to be her son. Although Ander looked nothing like her. She appeared to be an older woman in her sixties, with deep lines on her face showing how hard her life had been. Eric was unsure, but since he'd first seen her, he thought the ghost was multiracial — like his girl — even though he couldn't see the rich bronze color of her skin, she was still more vibrant than a lot of other spirits he'd seen.

"I thought I could do it. That I wouldn't be such a bitch, but I guess this old soul is more worn out than I thought. You already know this, but if a shade's soul is worn out, it doesn't last long as a spirit on this plane."

Eric hadn't realized how tiny the ghost was until she was in front of him. She was only as tall as Lucy. Most of the time spirits appeared the same as they did when they were alive, unless their death had been traumatic, then sometimes they appeared stuck in that last horrible moment, and it was terrifying.

"I wouldn't have any idea how to do that. We don't trust each other and—"

"I know that. But we still have weeks till we get to your encampment. You've lasted longer than any others they've been around and he," — she pointed at the werewolf — "doesn't hate you, that's important."

"But we only agreed to have an alliance until we got to the encampment."

"Yeah, yeah, I know. But you gotta understand I've been saddled with these shits since I died and this is the first time in a long time, they have tried to act like anything more than monsters."

The wolf grumbled and shifted, giving her side-eye.

"You're a dick—stay out of this. Besides, you understand I'm right. You didn't listen to me in life. You can try now that I'm just a fucking shade. Ungrateful prick."

The wolf growled, but the tone was different, almost playful. Eric realized he'd spent entirely too much time trying to figure out the werewolf and Ander because he was starting to understand the wolf and sometimes picked up on the subtext in Ander's words.

"I get it's too much to ask. I get your young and still hopeful, at least I think so. You didn't take the news that Heaven doesn't give a crap about any of us well, but I need you to think about it. I get this isn't your problem, but it could be if you ignore me."

"What does that mean?" Eric leaned forward, unsure if she'd threatened him or not.

"Neither one of them, despite what they say, is a lost cause. I've seen a lot of lost causes. Hell, I've been a lost cause for a while." She shook her ghostly head. "But if someone other than me doesn't see them for what they really are... it doesn't matter. When they finally accept, she's gone..." She turned her body to face the werewolf. "They'll end everything. You won't have to worry about the zombies or demons because trust me when I tell you, they'll destroy the world."

Fear raced down Eric's spine because, although he wasn't sure if it was possible for two individuals to end the world, she spoke with conviction. He understood that while they may not be able to destroy the entire world, they could devastate a large area, and humanity wouldn't take another large blow to the population; they were barely hanging on as it was.

The wolf growled and snapped its teeth at her. She crossed her arms over her chest. "What are you going to do to me, asshole? I can still hurt you, but I'm immune to your bullshit." The wolf got up from its relaxed position, the hackles on its back raised. "But you know what? I'm not going to hurt you. I'm still trying to save your sorry ass. You have a chance to do something you never could before. You can actually create something as you preserve humanity — you've destroyed enough. I know you're in there and if you want to preserve Ander, if you don't want him to destroy himself, then fucking listen to me!"

Eric startled from her raised voice, his eyes darting around. His group was still asleep, and Ander remained frozen in thought. The wolf stalked toward her, which made Eric nervous because she was right beside him. He didn't want to be involved in whatever was happening. The wolf bared its teeth as it crept closer. Eric had to fight the urge to bolt up and run or grab his pistol. He understood part of his flight response was due to a rational fear of a large monster, but part of Eric's desire to flee was the wolf's ability to strike fear into people.

The wolf stopped in front of him and put its muzzle in his face. Eric wondered if he'd piss his pants as it peered at him. It leveled its gaze at him, studying him. The dampness from the sweat on Eric's back made him cold from the cool night air surrounding him. The werewolf twisted its neck and looked at the ghost before it retreated and padded near Ander.

Eric didn't move a muscle, still filled with fear, and unable to predict what was going to happen. His priority was his family and making sure they were safe, so if he had to sit there trembling as he tried not to piss himself to keep things calm, then that's what he'd do.

The wolf left out a huge breath and made grumbling noises. The spirit drifted closer to Eric with an almost unperceivable grin. Ander twitched and then blinked. His eyes flicked around before he reached out to the wolf and petted its head.

"I was recalling my twenty-fifth birthday…" His voice trailed off, but sounded different. It was quiet because he always spoke softly, but there was a hint of emotion, like he was nervous and needed to explain why he'd zoned out. The wolf huffed and rubbed its head against him before it moved and sat… directly in front of Eric.

Eric's stomach dropped to his toes. Crap. He couldn't read minds, but he understood what the gesture meant.

Ander tilted his head, his brows furrowed. "Did something occur?"

"Nothing exciting. He decided he likes the kid and, as it turns out, the kid likes him." The spirit faced him, her expression hopeful but firm.

Eric cleared his throat, racking his brain to find a way to get out of this. The woman raised one of her incorporeal eyebrows and slid her gaze to the giant beast.

"Yeah, he's not so bad," Eric said and tried his darndest to keep the tremor out of his voice. Sensing it was the right thing to do, he raised his hand. It shook, but he didn't bother to hide that, and he lowered the tips of his fingers to the wolf's fur, near its shoulders. The wolf stiffened, but allowed him to pet him lightly three times before he pulled his hand back.

"What is the meaning of this?" Ander was in front of them before Eric opened his mouth.

"Calm the fuck down Ander. All that happened is your cousin decided he's okay with the kid and the kid decided he was okay, too," the ghost blurted out quickly.

Eric cleared his throat as Ander's markings brightened. "I was… I was thinking, since we've been getting along, maybe" — he swallowed down his terror — "we could still be allies after we reach our destination? I understand you don't care about humans, but we need help against the zombies. We can't do enough because there are too many of them, but you could control them."

"I explained this. I do not control the undead. I control shades," Ander said in a sharp tone.

"Okay, but the ones you have will rot and will need new bodies, right?" Eric detested his words. He understood what he was saying, but didn't know any other way to appeal to Ander. He couldn't give him false hope of finding his lost love. He would *never* suggest such a feat unless he thought he could find her. Eric was pretty sure if he did, Ander would kill him and his family.

"Yes. That is true, but as a human, does this not bother you?"

"Of course it does. I'm not suggesting using people. I'm suggesting using the zombies we're fighting that are fresher than the shells your spirits currently occupy. Can't you transfer the souls to a new corpse?" Eric's stomach twisted with his words.

Ander's marks dimmed as he changed to a more relaxed posture. "I see. So, you want to enter an extended agreement? Once we travel to your encampment, I will aid your humans with the undead you are battling and in return, I will keep the corpses I choose?"

The breeze picked up and chilled Eric again. Or perhaps it was because he was entertaining the idea of agreeing to this. He wanted to glance at the ghost, as stupid as it was, because technically, she'd forced him into this and he'd never actually agreed. Looking at her would still have made him feel better about aligning all of them with Ander for the foreseeable future. Was the ghost, right? Could Ander and his wolf be redeemed in some way?

"Yeah," Eric croaked out.

Ander narrowed his eyes on him. "Your humans are so desperate for a solution that you will align yourself with someone like me?" There was a slight shift in Ander's tone, he sounded young, almost vulnerable.

The truth was, Eric understood how screwed up the idea was, but the leader of the encampment wouldn't hesitate to align with whomever to save the remaining humans. The leader couldn't see or talk to ghosts and wouldn't understand or realize what Ander was. However, Eric believed, even if the leader did, she'd still agree. Every human hated zombies so much so that they would partner with anyone who offered help, no matter what the price was.

"Yeah, they are, but I'm the one making the call here. I could never tell them about you and they wouldn't know the difference. I want to do this because... because even though I don't like what you're doing, I understand it. I'm scared of you." Eric glanced at the massive wolf in front of him before turning to Ander. "Both of you, but I still think there's more to you. I get you want us to be scared, to believe you're evil and maybe you are, but I don't think that's all you are," Eric finished with a shrug.

"I have done nothing to indicate otherwise," Ander stated in a flat tone.

"Yeah, you have. You care about him." Eric gestured to the wolf. "You don't destroy her, even when she pisses you off." He pointed to the ghost. "And when you talk about Maeve, I can see something in you — something better. I might be young and stupid, but even if I'm scared, I still think I can trust you."

"That is a foolish and unsupported train of thought. You will regret your words."

"Maybe." Eric peeked at his sleeping group. "They don't know what we're saying — this is just between us. If I'm wrong, if I regret my words, just make sure it's *me* that pays the price and not them. If you can swear to that, then it's all good."

Ander frowned and looked at Eric's family. "You are willing to die a horrible death for your foolishness? Trust those you've been warned that you shouldn't? You expect evil beings to spare your family?"

Ander's words from when they first met echoed in Eric's mind. *Your consent is not necessary, but I would prefer not to force you. I would like it if we could travel as companions instead of enslaving you.*

Eric locked eyes with him knowing exactly what Ander wanted. "I'll give you my soul if you pardon my family from any future devastation."

Surprise covered Ander's face. It was the first time Eric had ever seen any expression morph his face so much. "You wager your soul on us? On me?"

"Yeah, I guess I do. You think you're a void and maybe you are, but if you're not... it might change everything for us. I have to try."

"Stand." Ander moved in front of him and reached for his hand.

Fear made Eric's throat tight, but he clasped Ander's arm as he had the last time.

"You are far more senseless than I anticipated. You should not put your faith in us." His eyes drifted to the ghost and to the wolf. "But this benefits me and our plan, so I will allow it."

Eric wanted to reply but still couldn't make his throat work, so he nodded.

"I can almost taste your fear. You must cease and learn to better control your emotions, it is distracting."

"Distracting?" Eric managed, although his voice was rough.

"Yes, it makes me crave things I should not. We are all monsters in one way or another. Now, this agreement is made by you but extends to your group. Once we reach your settlement, we will collect the needed information to create a plan that is suitable for my needs as well as give your humans a measure of success. I will keep all the undead I choose and we will remain... allies until the matter is done with."

"Yeah," Eric said and stared at Ander's neck, which started to glow.

"If and when I choose, I will collect your soul should you betray me or my group. Or perhaps if I decide to destroy the encampment and the undead as well. However, I will not harm your current traveling companions. If they attack me, or my party, I can, and will, incapacitate them but not harm them until the matter is resolved."

"That's a shitty deal," Eric mumbled.

"It is what you desire, is it not?"

Eric breathed out. "Yeah, okay, it's what I said."

"Excellent," Ander said with an evil grin, before he spoke gibberish that made his entire form light up. Eric squinted.

Seconds later, Ander released Eric's arm and returned to the log he'd been sitting on. "Now tell me of the conditions of your settlement, as well as the undead that you are battling with."

Eric plopped down in his spot. Noting the wolf hadn't moved. He hated that the wolf remaining near him brought him comfort, but it did. Part of him wanted to pet the wolf, which was even more screwed up because he never thought about that when Caleb or Zaila were in their wolf forms. Then again, they didn't *stay* in those forms all day, every day.

"Our encampment is outside of Boston. We've been trying to take back the areas of Boston we lost over a year ago, but we have lost so many people. At one point, people were flocking to us because we had a better setup. We'd even made a deal with the other people who own the islands in the bay, we had running water again."

"I see, so your settlement meant to control the city."

Eric ran his fingers through his hair. It was getting too long, he needed to ask Lucy to trim it. "Yeah, humans had control over most of Boston for a few years and got a bunch of stuff up and running. We had power, crops growing... We thought it would work, but then everyone started fighting over what we had. After a while, we all split into smaller communities and kept fighting among ourselves. It wasn't hard for the zombies to run us out."

"All living creatures are inherently greedy. Always pursuing more. While it drives innovation and various achievements, our basal ganglia will eventually overpower our frontal cortex, returning us to the beasts we are."

Eric wasn't sure how to respond. He tried to recall what a basal ganglia was. He understood Ander was referring to the brain when he mentioned the frontal cortex, so he assumed the basal ganglia was what most would have called the "lizard brain," all instinct and survival. If that was the case, he wanted to debate it but wouldn't, because that was literally what happened in Boston.

"So, you seek to regain the territory from the undead?" Ander asked.

"Yeah, but the thing is... we don't know what's happening in their territory. Every group that has entered the zombies' land, they either die immediately or disappear and never return."

"They are presumably consumed by the undead, since they do not seem to be traveling for sustenance." Ander replied with a shrug.

"Yeah, that's what we thought too but after a few months, we stopped sending people in and came up with a different plan. The thing is" — Eric leaned forward — "the zombies never came out. They've been holed up there for months. They fight us if we get too close but haven't been expanding their territory, and we don't know how they've been eating."

That got Ander's attention, Eric had known it would. He understood after traveling with Ander and his group for the past few weeks that Ander liked to thoroughly understand things. He liked mysteries to solve, it's how the ghost got him to buy into things.

"That, along with zombies acting differently, is part of why we left. We went looking for medicines, weapons, and magical items that would help us figure out what to do," Eric continued.

"Did you find anything of note?" Ander's irises brightened for a second.

"No. We found medicine, although we had to go to Canada to get it. The weapons that were supposed to be hidden weren't there, already taken by other survivors and the magic items... no doubt they weren't real to begin with."

"There are thousands, perhaps millions of magical items in the United States. However, most are not helpful for what you desire and others are ineffective."

"I'm guessing you're not going to be more specific?" Eric said.

"No. It is not wise to use magical items without proper training. If someone tries, more often than not they injure themselves or those they are attempting to help. I am intrigued by this situation. It will help pass the time as we search for her. I appreciate your effort to make it tantalizing. I may have more questions but need to ponder the unique circumstances for a bit." Ander stood. "We will set off at dawn." He moved to an empty spot near the fire to lie down. The wolf got up and sat beside Ander as he closed his eyes.

Eric stared into the fire and wondered if he'd made the biggest mistake of his life.

Chapter 16 - Zane

The more time that passed the more his mind filled with memories he'd forgotten or perhaps he'd let slip away. It was hard to reconcile who he was, with what he had become. The long hours spent separate from Renee wore on him because of the deafening presence of the horde. He had started walking alone again, ahead of the entire horde, as he had in the beginning just to dull the noise in his mind. When Renee was near him, her presence was the loudest, muting out most of the others, giving him a peace he hadn't experienced before.

Renee, his queen. She'd assume he was fond of referring to her that way because she loved her court titles but it had nothing to do with that. He had spoken little to her about his human past, for the most part he was ashamed of who he was. The only honorable act he'd ever done was tied to her, of course she didn't remember that, which didn't bother him. She was his now, nothing else mattered.

His mind wandered over the miles he walked, back to Springfield when she'd attacked and killed that human woman who threatened him. The moment proved to him he had indeed damned her with his selfishness. He'd hidden her transformation from Brie and Renee, fearing if she found herself in a similar situation it would happen again, and he wasn't sure what he would do.

He'd casually poked around in the horde to see if any of the more cognitive ones had been scientists or doctors in their former lives but so far, he hadn't come across any. Zane understood when he created a creature, that although they were all similar, there were small, distinctive differences in each one, the same as humans. He assumed it had something to do with genetics. During the clinical trials, Dr. Landry had spoken about the treatments reacting differently with each person based on several factors, one of them being DNA.

The image of Renee — his heart — looking like one of his crazed, feral creatures, tore into him. It wasn't uncommon for the ones who had more animalistic tendencies to appear that way. But Renee didn't have permanent sharp teeth or claws, pointed ears, or odd bone protrusions. However, when she ripped the woman apart, she *had* claws, and her teeth were sharklike. His fingers grazed over the subtle scar on his chest where she'd torn a piece of him off when he'd calmed her down in Springfield.

Zane didn't know why Renee, and only Renee, seemed almost human one moment and a monster the next. It didn't matter; it was his fault for making her like him. If her transformation was different, if somehow, she'd evolved into something apart from the others, he would still love her, protect her.

A faint tingling sensation around his skull slowed his steps. *It* had responded to his thoughts—it liked these thoughts. His chest squeezed as his pulse raced. Was Renee, right? Did *it* want them together? He almost couldn't breathe as every internal alarm went off inside of him. *Why?* Why after all these years would it allow him any shred of happiness? Perhaps he was paranoid, but he'd always been at odds with the parasite, so he couldn't suddenly believe that they wanted the same things.

When the sensation of his horde pressed on his consciousness, he quickened his steps to put distance between them. It wouldn't remove the static in his mind, but over the years he'd learned tricks on how to lessen the intrusion. It was stupid to be so far ahead of his horde, leaving him open for assassination from his rival. At the moment they were headed north, away from the coast, so he didn't think the other horde would bother his, as it seemed they were retreating. Were they retreating?

"There's a dark veil over this world. It obscures the hidden truths of monsters living alongside humanity." A deep, guttural voice filled his mind.

Zane sighed at the memory, he learned the truth of that, but in the end, he was a coward and chose the safe path. He'd listened to his friend Levitt and abandoned him just as he'd promised Levitt he would do. But the guilt of his actions had never left Zane. Levitt had been dishonorably discharged because of the choices he made. But Zane had known Levitt's choices had been justified, and that Levitt was trying to protect the rest of the platoon.

Because of his remorse for being a coward, he'd kept his word to Levitt and hadn't spoken a word of what he'd witnessed during his time in the service or any knowledge Levitt had trusted him with. If he'd been in his right mind when everything went to shit, he might have tried to find Levitt. He imagined Levitt had the time of his life until he perished with so many others.

A grin made the corners of his lips tilt up. If anyone would enjoy the end of the world, it would have been Levitt. He and the others he called the Soldiers of Night were supposed to protect humans. Zane assumed that they'd all died in the first couple of years when everything was unstable.

In the beginning, although Zane was somewhat aware of his actions, everything felt more instinctual than anything else. If he had thoughts, he couldn't remember them — except when he discovered Renee wasn't dead. He'd assumed, when he found her brother's body, she was gone too.

He was unsure how much time had passed when he found her, but his horde was small then, only a few hundred when they found her group. His scared queen had run, unaware that her retreating form would set off the hunting instincts in his creatures. They followed her, just as he did. Even in his confused state he wouldn't have allowed harm to come to her.

He quickened his pace, his intent clear.

Take her.

Force her to stay with him. Zane leapt over a fallen tree trunk closing the distance between them. His strides were longer and faster than hers. She was smart to enter the wooded area, but he navigated the uneven terrain easily.

When he'd caught sight of her, he didn't think she was real and barreled toward her. The surrounding humans scattered in all directions, sensing their doom.

Consume. Devour. The urges pushed him closer to his prey, but he shoved back. It was her. *To his right, one of his creatures fell to the ground and screamed. Searing pain tore through Zane's shoulder from where the undead had been shot. He stumbled but continued moving so he wouldn't lose sight of her.*

A burning sensation blossomed in his leg as another creature dropped to its knees on his left. Black blood flowed from an injury in its leg. Zane grit his teeth and took another step. It was hard to concentrate with the pain that continued to assault him as more of his undead were injured or died. The buzzing in his mind got louder, and he struggled to recall what he was chasing until he caught another glimpse of her sprinting away.

Her. She was his.

Now refocused, he ignored the pain, he ignored the subtle urges to stop and consume, and shoved away the irritating mental presence of his horde. He frowned. What was her name? It was sweet and reminded him of a bird. A bird from her books. A bright bird made of flames. A gentle whisper caressed his mind.

Renee.

His jumbled thoughts snapped into ones that made sense, logical thoughts, closer to a human's thoughts, except the word mine *kept repeating in his head. It was like waking from a long sleep.*

She stumbled and then fell. He and his undead found her curled up on the ground shaking. With his will he forced his creatures to stop. One creature, only inches from tearing into her, resisted his will. Zane forced the creature upright, snapping its spine in the process.

His terrified queen's body jumped at the action as she peeked out. Realizing the creature was frozen, she couldn't see him or any of his other more obedient undead that had exited the area at his command, she started muttering to herself. Zane couldn't understand the words, but it sounded like a one-sided conversation as she tried to encourage herself to be brave.

Her courage impressed him; she scuttled away and reached into her pocket, never taking her gaze from the undead who remained frozen in place. Renee flicked out a tiny knife and waved her other hand around to see if the undead would move or respond. Zane allowed no movement. She scrambled to her feet darting her eyes around. He thought she'd run. If she did, no one *would pursue her except him.*

Mine.

She surprised him by clenching her jaw, gripping the knife harder and charged into the creature knocking it on its back before she stabbed it repeatedly in its chest and neck. Each stab made him wince, the sensation of being stabbed over and over made his muscles contract. Not the identical pain of when he was run through, but an echo of his creature's torment.

His queen screamed and cried in rage as she pierced it for as long as her body allowed. Spent, her body sagged, and she spoke again to an unseen presence. Her lips moved. Zane concentrated on her mouth but couldn't understand the sounds coming from her lips. Was she angry? She wiped the back of her hand across her cheeks to dry them. Her last words seemed fierce, determined. Although he was confused, he believed she'd made a vow of some sort.

His chest tightened. He wanted her — she was his. *She'd been his since the day he decided to live but... an unknown force stayed his actions. It was as if he no longer controlled his own body. Zane tried to force his legs forward. She was calming down; he needed to grab her before she left. Why couldn't he move?*

He didn't care if she hated him as long as she was with him. No. That wasn't true, he didn't want her hate; he wanted her love. He wanted her to smile and laugh as he'd seen her do for the smallest things, like a sunset or a flower. Would she see him as a monster?

No.

He'd seen her heart, how kind she could be. How she never judged animals or people based on appearance. It made her somewhat naïve to the evils of the world and she had the scars to prove it. She would accept him. If anyone could look past the monster he'd become, both inside and out, it was her. He lifted his foot and took a step before he couldn't move again.

Her head snapped up as she raced to get on her feet and hurried to her fallen backpack. Seconds later she bolted from him, tearing through the clearing and onto the paved road. Distracted by his own battle with his body and her fleeing, the injured undead groaned as it rolled to its side, pushing up, probably to give chase.

Mine.

A sharp pain behind his eyes made him squint as murderous thoughts filled his mind. He stalked to the undead and kicked it into a tree. He bellowed as he tore it limb from limb relishing as the blood splattered on him. No one would hunt Renee but him. None would touch her except him.

He dropped the pieces of the undead to the ground and turned to the direction Renee went. As he lifted his foot, another piercing pain stabbed his head. Unlike any other pain he'd experienced, even when he was human, it dropped him to his knees. Zane tried to move, but it was unbearable.

The pressure of the approaching horde buzzed in his mind and almost made him vomit. His hands let go of his head as he bolted upright and got to his feet. His stance shifted to one of authority and pride as the thunderous approach of his horde got closer. Growls, grunts, and clicks announced their arrival before many ran past him, headed in Renee's direction.

Zane finally got over the shock that he wasn't the one calling the shots in his own body. It was excruciating, like his brain was melting, but he bellowed, calling his horde back and directed them north, away from his heart. He had no idea what was wrong with him but he refused to let them have her. For now, he had to let her go. She was still strong, still a fighter, she would survive. The next time he saw her, he would do whatever it took to make her his.

Only now could Zane truly understand how fortunate he was that he hadn't taken her that day. The parasite had too much control over him at the time and he wasn't himself. If he hadn't recognized her, he wouldn't have had any thoughts other than to consume. Even then, when he was little more than an animal, she'd brought him back to himself.

She hadn't noticed him when he was still human. He was only in the background or a nuisance because he took the attention of the only person she loved at the time, her brother. The few times she acknowledged his existence was because she was irritated by his presence. It made sense, any time he was at their house it was unintentionally preoccupying Liam from her.

But through Liam, the precious times he'd seen her in person, and the inappropriate moments he'd watched her without her realizing, he grew to know her. He learned what a beautiful person she was, what a person *could* be if they tried. It made him think perhaps he could be different, more like her and less like himself. Perhaps he didn't have to be a monster like his father, he could learn compassion, patience, and kindness from her.

"Maybe not, but they're not mindless either. I think you want them to be because it makes what you do okay. But they have feelings. They worry about things. They notice things."

Zane frowned thinking over Renee's words. Perhaps Renee always pulled him back from turning into the monster he was, but he still wasn't what he wanted to be. He rubbed his forehead. It wasn't possible to be what he wanted to be.

He'd never known freedom. First his father dictated his life, then the military, then the scientists by choice, and now the parasite. He'd gladly serve Renee, but only Renee. His lips quirked up, maybe in a twisted way, he was serving her. Thinking of things that way made it easier to bear, existing felt like less of a burden.

Still, he hated that his behavior upset her. Even when her argument made no sense. How he ruled the horde had nothing to do with their relationship. But for the very reasons he loved her it drove him crazy. His sweet Renee would be the only one who would empathize with the undead that destroyed her world. The only one who fought for better treatment of them.

He understood what his species had done to humans, what it continued to do, but a part of him believed it was necessary. Zane was positive that Renee would not believe him if he told her, these were his thoughts and not the parasite's. But she didn't know about Levitt or what Zane had been a part of during deployment.

The fact that a world-ending event full of monsters hadn't happened before his species rose, was a surprise to him. People had no idea how long they had existed at the tipping point, and that anything could have set off a chain of events that would have resulted in the same outcome. An apocalypse that would end or change humanity forever.

Of course, his queen found the positive in any situation, even in the middle of the end, she wanted a future with him — saw the possibility of a future — and foolish as it was, he wanted to see one too.

Chapter 17 - Brie

"Are you going to tell us where we're going now that we're headed west?" Brie asked Zane.

She wasn't sure why Zane was so far ahead of the horde, but he'd done this off and on over the years. In the early days, they all traveled as one unit, but that was when there were far fewer of them, and the distinctions between the different types of zombies wasn't as obvious.

Brie glanced behind her at the chosen, and then further back, to the remaining horde. She didn't want to be far from Renee for too long. It was unlikely their rival would attack during the day, he almost never had, but still she was on edge. Both the opposing horde and Zane, seemed to prefer to strike at night. Probably because it seemed more menacing or fitting for what they were. Her lips twitched at the idea.

"No," Zane replied and then went silent. He never was a talker.

She hadn't come face to face with their rival yet, Zane wouldn't let any of them near him, refusing to allow his horde "to be tainted by his presence." But she'd seen that fucker from a distance ordering his horde around and he was big, as big as Zane, maybe bigger. Didn't matter, if she got within ten feet of that prick she'd die trying, as she attempted to tear his head off.

Although she hadn't lied to Renee, the horde didn't really care about individual deaths. She'd been around long enough to understand he wasn't just their rival for food and territory, he was an evil fucker that needed to be put down. He'd done things that were diabolical, things Zane didn't allow.

At least not since she was more cognitive. Her early memories were vague at best and she couldn't say what did or didn't occur; but as much of an asshole as Zane could be, she was pretty sure, as long as he was capable of independent thought, he wouldn't cross certain lines.

They had several battles with their rival's horde over the years, eventually it would lead to a real war and Brie couldn't wait. All of Zane's efforts to ensure his horde was strong and able-bodied were almost complete. Renee still didn't understand what it meant to be a zombie or what their problems were, and if Brie was being honest, she didn't really want her to.

"Is that all you want?" Zane asked, breaking her thoughts.

"Don't be a dick. I'm trying to do my job."

He slid his eyes to her. "Awfully belligerent for a Knight Commander."

She frowned, she didn't like when he called her that, only Renee. "The horde is nervous because it seems like we're circling, they're worried about food."

He sighed and shook his head. "I know. They're always worried about food."

"So, we're headed west for now?"

"Yes, they will have food." His voice was despondent.

"Is this because of *him*?" Brie dared to ask.

Zane sped up his steps. "No, but his power grows. He'll need to be dealt with soon."

Brie's stomach fluttered at his words, she hadn't forgotten the things she learned about their rival, Zane's promise of justice. "I'm ready."

He turned and relaxed his jaw before the corner of his lips tilted up. "You're always ready, but" — the grin disappeared — "the horde isn't, yet."

"The chosen have been training every day," Brie reminded him. "And the day guards are good enough to watch our borders at night."

"And the night guards?"

"Night Sentinels," Brie corrected, using Renee's words. "They're ready."

"The night guards aren't as advanced as the *Night Sentinels*. I'm asking what our most useful numbers are. How many in each division?" he asked.

Brie flattened her lips in response to his sarcastic tone when he called them Night Sentinels. She understood the difference between the guards at night and the Night Sentinels. Although the guards that patrolled at night were more advanced than those who kept them safe during the day and could handle more complex orders, their ability to judge and plan paled in comparison to the Night Sentinels. Only the best of the chosen could become Night Sentinels.

"There are over a hundred scouts, although they're still learning, after our loss of the others. Two hundred Night Sentinels, with over twenty of them training and monitoring new recruits for upcoming night guards. And our special... Apex, they are around seventy-five now," she spoke with pride.

"Apex? Is that what they're being called now?"

Brie nodded. "Yeah, we needed a name, and I figured Renee wouldn't know what that meant and it kinda sounds like something a chosen would name themselves." Brie chuckled.

Brie, along with Zane and the others he appointed, had been working with their vicious enforcers, similar to assassins, for years, training them how to be more silent and deadly. Making sure they were focused, could control their hunger and instincts. It wasn't easy to be a zombie; the hunger gnawed at your brain all day, every day, and no matter how much you consumed, the ache never left. The chosen were better at dealing with the constant hunger, but the horde, not so much, especially the feral ones.

But Zane found uses for them too, he kept them under control by making sure they got livers regularly, which seemed to sate their hunger more than other organs, and strategically used them for things where control mattered less. Sometimes he would get them worked up and release them like berserkers, their ferocious nature made them almost unbeatable in attacks.

"Good," Zane replied.

Brie waited for him to say something else, but he remained silent. She'd asked who the rival was before but he wouldn't talk about him except to say, they wouldn't go in without a plan. Ever since that night, when Zane recognized his rival and witnessed what he'd done, they had begun to plan.

Brie was half out of her mind with being forced to stay the attack, but Zane refused to listen to her.

"We're close. He's probably still stealing children," Brie said through gritted teeth.

"Yes. Possibly worse," Zane said as the corners around his eyes tightened.

"It's been... I don't know how long but we need to do something!" Brie snapped.

The memory of those kids being stolen, but not eaten, would never leave her mind. If she hadn't been so confused that night she might have done more, but at the time, she couldn't think as clearly and nothing made sense. She'd followed because zombies didn't *steal* people, they killed them and ate them.

They fought the rival horde for the city and the humans in it, while they simultaneously battled the humans. She and a few others discovered the rival's zombies were taking children. It wasn't until later they discovered why.

"He is taking humans, not horde members." His tone was flat, emotionless.

"You cold bastard," she said through gritted teeth.

Zane turned his glowing, amber irises to her. "Human children are not our concern. If they survive, they will become the adults who will hunt us, and unlike their parents or other adult humans, they will have known nothing but this world. Nothing but us as their enemies and by that time, more effective ways to destroy us."

Brie narrowed her eyes. "I know that."

He cocked his head to the side. "You do?"

She balled her hands into fists. "They're fucking kids, Zane! You don't let us consume them! I know you hate it as much as I do."

"The human children aren't innocent, no one who exists now is, as you learned, but their survival is key to ours. They need to age and breed so we don't run out of food."

Brie stopped and put her hands on her hips. "Bullshit."

Zane stopped and faced her. "I don't have the same viewpoint you do, but our goals are the same."

"Bullshit," Brie snapped again. "I know you think it's wrong to hurt kids, that you want to protect whatever innocence they have left, and I know why."

Zane was in front of her before she blinked, showing his teeth. She squared her shoulders. She didn't want to fight him because she knew she'd lose and fear rippled down her spine, but she wouldn't back down.

"What do you think Renee would think if she knew you only saw them as guaranteed food for the future?" Brie asked. It was risky to poke him like that but she needed him to understand the urgency.

A low growl rumbled from his chest and made her tremble. Fuck she didn't want to lose her limbs. But it wasn't about her, this was about something more important, she had to be brave.

"I already told you, our goals align, leave it at that. Do not speak her name to me like that again." His voice shook with fury but to her surprise, he didn't touch her.

She decided it was time to change tactics. "He took from the horde too, not just our food but us. He took some of *us* too."

"He will pay for that," Zane said as his jaw worked. "And yes, for taking the human children as well. I promised you justice and we will have it. Don't press me about this."

"I know you have a plan. I'm just..." Brie lowered her gaze.

"Impatient. You've always been impatient." He let out a breath. "But you are loyal, the horde needs that. Renee needs that."

Brie's eyes snapped to his face. Her nails dug into the skin of her palms. It wasn't his words that upset her, it was the tone shift when he mentioned Renee. He sure as fuck didn't care if the horde needed anything other than basic things. Thankfully—and fuck him—Renee did care, and she was trying to do something about it, even if it seemed silly to Brie.

"When?" she asked, because it was a safe question.

"Soon." He turned and started moving.

To hell with his vague answers. She didn't respond and made her way through the chosen, giving them a few orders as she passed into the horde.

Chapter 18 - Renee

Brie walked beside her as they headed west. Renee felt like they were backtracking, but Brie had explained it was because they needed more food because there hadn't been enough where they'd been. The knowledge made Renee uncomfortable for several reasons. She'd eaten when others had starved, several of the horde had died for others to consume. What distressed her most was her constant wondering if they'd already eaten too many humans and were running out of cities to take?

An odd buzzing sound made her scan the area. It reminded her of how things sounded when she first got her implants. Only it was so low she almost didn't catch it, and none of the horde members were reacting. Even Brie didn't seem to notice, which probably meant it was something in her head, or perhaps it was the one remaining electrode array on her right side. The transmitter, receiver, and antenna had been gone for a long time. Zane had pulled out her left one when it had been damaged from her head injury the day she died. As far as she knew, the electrode array was still in her right ear. It was still a mystery how she could hear at all. The buzzing faded.

Her eyes flicked to her friend and then to the surrounding horde. None were affected in the slightest about the deaths. Not of the humans or their own comrades who had fallen. Perhaps Zane was right; she was the only one who thought about things the way she did. It was unfathomable to her that not one of them didn't have lingering guilt over killing and eating people.

Zane made sure that anything she consumed didn't look like people or animal remains. Her lips pinched when it occurred to her that the last few times she ate, she couldn't tell what it was. More and more, everything tasted the same. Meat was meat. She blanched. Was this her becoming more like them?

"Did you hear anything I said?" Brie's voice interrupted her internal musings.

"No, I got lost in my thoughts."

"You always do that when you're trying to figure things out or you're upset. Otherwise, you talk my ear off." Brie stretched her arms above her head. "Which is it?"

Renee shrugged. It was a bit of both.

"I thought you... made up. We're not walking into a death trap, so that's a good sign," Brie said as her lips flattened.

"Yeah, we're okay. But Brie, you were upset, and I wanted to explain–" Renee started.

"Nope," Brie cut her off, "I can't. I don't need to know about the weird shit you do with him."

"It's not weird," Renee said in a low voice. Her eyes darted around them to the other members of the horde. She took a deep breath. She'd got Zane to open up and trust her. It was time to do the same with Brie, whether or not she wanted to. She grabbed Brie's arm and led her away from the horde to the side of the road.

"What the fuck?"

"It will only take a minute and I don't want an audience."

Brie huffed and crossed her arms. "Fine. What is it?"

"I need to talk to you. I know you're upset, and this is awkward, but you're my friend. I don't want things to be weird between us."

"Fuck my life," Brie said to the sky as her floral print skirt fluttered with the breeze.

"Brie, I know you're worried that my relationship with Zane puts the entire horde at risk. I used to think you were wrong... but you're not."

Brie turned those icy irises to her. "Okay, you've got my attention."

"You're right about a lot of things with Zane, but I am too."

Brie raised an eyebrow and adjusted her stance, but kept her arms crossed.

"He's a dick most of the time, especially where it concerns the horde, but it's because he's like, well… the rest of the horde. No one seems to notice or care when others die. Or even if they do, it isn't with the same concern humans would have."

"I guess that's kinda true. We live and breathe death. It's hard to get upset about individual deaths."

"But he tries to look after their basic needs. He and I disagree with what those needs are, but it's what decides where we go."

Brie's face twisted and Renee thought she was going to disagree with her, but she motioned for her to continue.

"With me he's different and I don't know why, except that maybe it's because we're together."

Brie huffed again and turned her head.

"And it does make him reckless if we aren't getting along. He gets confused and makes bad choices. Not because he doesn't care about the horde, he just," Renee paused, unsure how to finish.

"Is a selfish prick," Brie finished for her.

Renee wanted to argue the point but wouldn't, because he'd said as much.

"So, assuming this weird fucking that you do with each other keeps him in a better place, then everything is good? It doesn't work like that Renee. I get your young and probably don't have a lot of experience with relationships, but fucking doesn't fix things when you argue. If anything, it makes it worse."

Renee reeled from her words. She couldn't decide if she was more offended that Brie trivialized their relationship or implied, she was a child.

"I still don't understand how it's possible," Brie muttered under her breath.

"I don't think our physical relationship fixes anything. Sex is one part of a relationship, not all of it. If it is, then it's not really a relationship, everyone knows that. And stop saying it's weird!"

Brie stepped back and uncrossed her arms. "Don't say 'make love' I'll vomit."

"Why is this such an issue for you? You don't have a problem with the partners in the horde. I thought this was about the horde, but you seem... disgusted."

"You're a zombie, Renee! He's a zombie! You're both fucking DEAD! It *is* disgusting!" Brie yelled out.

Renee's eyes burned as her vision blurred. She stumbled back and bumped into someone. An arm came around her shoulder and tugged her against them. She blinked and peeked at who it was. Garren. His jaw locked as he stared at Brie.

"Renee, I didn't mean that," Brie started.

Garren glared at Brie and tilted his head at her. Brie flashed her teeth at him, but his expression didn't change. He gestured to the horde.

"You better not let our *king* catch you like that," she spat out as she passed them.

"Garren, I'm sorry, I..." Renee began.

He squeezed her to his side and shook his head.

"But you must've heard part of that."

He grimaced and let her go, instead taking her hand and led her into the mass of the horde. Renee tried to talk to him several times, but he politely declined and kept walking.

Finally, when she insisted, he stopped them as the sea of the horde trudged by them. He gazed at her a moment before he signed *friend* to her. To make his point, he gestured back and forth between them and then zipped his lips shut.

Recklessly, she threw her arms around him and hugged him before she whispered in his ear, "Thank you."

The rest of the march was blissfully uneventful. Renee was even more upset than she'd been when they started out. By trying to fix things with Brie, she'd made them worse.

Chapter 19 - Renee

Zane's fingers traced the scar on her stomach. Renee wasn't sure what his obsession was with it, but every time she was naked, he *had* to touch it, caress it at least once. She wanted to ask, but that would cause him to ask how she'd got it and she wouldn't go there. The idea made her nauseous, some things were better left in the past. She ran her fingers through his dark hair before he kissed her scar and laid his head on her stomach.

"I love you," he said as his eyes slid closed.

"Do you ever sleep around anyone else?"

"No. I don't have to, but I forgot how much I liked it until I slept with you," he replied with a soft expression.

"But you won't sleep tonight because it's not safe?"

"No. I don't sleep unless we're in a location that's guarded and never when traveling."

"And you just stare at me the whole night?"

"Yes." He smiled, but kept his eyes closed.

"That's boring and kinda makes you a creeper." She laughed.

"You're the most beautiful thing I've ever seen. I could stare at you for the rest of my life and it wouldn't be enough."

Renee was glad they were on the floor of a random shack he'd found because she was fucking swooning. "Were you this smooth when you were alive?"

"I'm not being smooth. I'm being honest. And technically, I don't think either of us qualifies as dead."

That got her attention. She hadn't told Zane about her awful conversation with Brie because she knew he'd overreact, but the harsh words had stayed with her.

"We're not dead? But we're zombies."

"Your words, not mine." He kissed her stomach again.

"Isn't a zombie a person who's undead and eats other people?"

"It depends on where you're getting the definition," Zane replied in a sleepy tone.

He didn't give a shit about what he was labeled as. Perhaps because he'd been like this for years, but Renee still cared, especially after what Brie said.

She stared at the top of his head. "Does anyone else's heart beat like yours?"

"Yours does too." He smiled against her skin.

He wasn't taking the conversation seriously because he was still relaxed from sex, but this was important.

"Okay like ours do," she corrected.

He opened his amber eyes and popped his head up. "I don't know. I haven't checked."

Her mouth dropped open. "You haven't checked?"

He moved until he sat, peering at her. "Why would I check?"

"You don't want to know?" She couldn't fathom in all this time he hadn't checked once.

"I don't think it matters. It changes nothing. We still have to consume. Our bite is still infectious and will spread what we are."

"But if our hearts beat, then we're not dead, right?" Renee sat up, leaning closer.

His brows pinched. "You told me a zombie was someone that was undead and consumed others. Why would a heartbeat make a difference?"

"Because doesn't that mean our circulatory system still works? That's the one for blood, right?

Zane touched the side of her face. "Yes, you've seen me bleed. Because I'm the host, my body functions more normally than many of the others. As yours does for whatever reason. It's why we're able to be together, like this." His hand slid to her neck and he pulled her lips to his.

Renee's heartbeat thundered in her ears.

"Don't think so much about labels. It doesn't matter because it won't change anything," he told her against her lips. Zane kissed her chin and then her neck. "Some people believe the undead came from magic," he whispered in her ear.

"Magic?" she breathed and scooted into his lap.

"Dark magic, but still magic." He wrapped her legs around his waist.

She moaned when she felt him ready at her entrance. This was magic. Them together at the end of the world, entwined together.

Zane's lips touched her neck and trailed kisses down her chest until he stopped at her scar. She grumbled because she wasn't ready to face the day just yet. Her hands rubbed his back.

"I don't want to get up yet. Can't we stay here for a little longer? We're both already naked," she teased.

"If I had my wish, we would find somewhere safe to live and never be apart. We would be naked all the time, if that's what you wanted."

Her eyes opened and found him grinning at her. "Don't tease me."

His expression changed to the melancholy one he wore so often. "I'm not."

"I didn't mean it like that. I only meant; we can't really have what we want. We shouldn't think about it." Renee had learned that painful lesson the hard way. Dwelling on things that would never be only hurt someone over and over until it destroyed them.

"I have to." He sat up and pulled his black t-shirt over his head.

Zane waited as Renee dressed slowly. She didn't want to face Brie.

"I have something for you," Zane said, and took something out of the bag he brought last night. "Close your eyes and hold out your hands."

She did as he asked and felt a light bundle. He held onto her hands longer than needed, but she didn't complain. "Can I look?"

"Yes."

"What are these?" Renee peered at the folded-up headphones. She tilted her head. Not headphones.

"Ear protection," Zane said with a smile.

"Like for shooting a gun?"

His smile broadened. "Yes. But that's not why I got them for you."

"Why did you get them?"

He tugged her to his chest. "The culling won't sound as loud."

Renee wrapped her arms around his torso and put her head on his chest, touched by his thoughtful gift. He kissed her temple as he smoothed her hair down.

"Does it start soon?" she whispered.

"At sunset. We need to get moving. There's an abandoned house for you to stay in a couple of hours away." His palms rubbed up and down her back.

"Okay." Her voice cracked, so she stopped talking.

Zane tilted her chin up. "Do you remember why it must be done?"

She nodded, blinking so she wouldn't cry.

"I'm sorry," he said in a rough voice.

Renee stared into his golden irises and recognized the despair, unlike before, when it reflected his sadness with his situation or the future, she knew in this moment, he felt guilty. Guilty because the act of the culling upset her. This type of remorse wasn't exactly what she wanted; Renee wanted Zane to care for the horde as much as she did, not because of, or for, her. She supposed it was a start.

He knew it was necessary, but it bothered him slightly. He felt unsure. Her fingers slid up his neck and threaded into his long locks.

"Thank you for the gift," she whispered and brushed her lips against his.

"Will you travel with me today? So, I can spend time with you before it starts."

Renee was conflicted. She wanted to avoid Brie, but also wanted to be with the horde, especially if she'd never see some of them again. Of course, maybe it would be easier if she didn't travel with them for the same reason.

He let her go and turned away. "It's fine. You don't have to. I know you prefer to be with the horde."

"Zane, it's not that. I want to be with you but," she paused and fiddled with the ear protection.

He faced her. "But what?"

"But it's important for me to be with them. It makes a difference to them. I don't really want to today because" — she swallowed — "it will be hard after. I'll notice who's not there." She blinked rapidly. "I always want to be with you."

"Then why won't you? I only see you at night." His voice was clipped. Did it hurt him that much that she refused?

"I told you it makes a difference to them. Makes me one of them."

Disgust twisted his mouth. "Makes you one of them? You *aren't* one of them."

"Don't start that again. This isn't about who is more functional or better, in your opinion."

"You are their *queen*. You need to act like it!"

Renee sucked in air. He'd twisted her own words and made them ugly. Damn him! "I *am* acting like it! You're the one being a tyrant king! You force your will on them! They're loyal to me because I earned their loyalty!" Shit. Shit. She wasn't supposed to say that. She wasn't supposed to reveal anything about her relationship with the horde.

He narrowed his eyes. "They're loyal to you?"

So much regret filled her. Damn her temper! No turning back now. She stuck her chin out and planted her feet. He closed the distance and grabbed her chin.

"After the culling we'll see who's loyal to who," he said through clenched teeth.

"What are you talking about?"

"We're almost to Albany. We'll see then." He released her face and stormed out the door.

Renee couldn't help but feel like he'd just threatened her. She didn't want his stupid, imposed crown. She stomped out of the shack and found Brie leaned against a tree, picking her nails. Her bright red lips formed a frown. She pushed off the tree and smoothed down her violet-print dress, crossing her arms.

"I need to get you to the house. Thanks for pissing him off right before a culling. I'm sure that's gonna go great for the rest of us."

Renee flattened her lips before she spoke, "I didn't mean to."

"Please shut the fuck up today. You and I are mad at each other. Apparently, you're picking fights with everyone. Let's just walk in blissful, fucking silence, okay?"

Chapter 20 - Renee

Blissful fucking silence — bullshit. It was silent, but not blissful. The walk to the abandoned house was the weirdest Renee ever had with Brie. No words were exchanged, but she huffed and puffed a lot. Twice she slowed but then realized her consideration, and sped up until they almost ran.

About an hour into the walk, Renee spotted Garren with the horde. He tilted his head and smiled. She was so touched by his concern. He only walked with the horde when he was with her, except today. Brie had made a point of keeping pace with the horde, but kept herself and Renee away from the walking mass.

"Can I ask you something?" Renee spoke when she couldn't handle the silence anymore. Perhaps if Brie yelled at her like the other day, she'd feel better and then they'd argue. She didn't want to argue, she wanted to make up and that wouldn't happen until Brie got whatever bothered her off her chest. Renee frowned; she had things to say to Brie, too.

"No. Silence, remember?"

"It's about you, your interests," Renee said in a sharper tone than she'd meant to have.

Brie slowed and turned to Renee. "My interests?"

"Yeah." Amused by Brie's sudden curiosity, Renee made sure she didn't crack a smile.

"You're so fucking silly sometimes." Brie shook her head. "Okay, what did you want to ask?"

Got her. Renee cleared her throat. "Since you can think more in-depth, don't you get bored just marching from place to place? I mean, at least the horde can't ponder too deeply, but what do you do when you're not walking or killing things?"

"Practicing killing other things?" Brie said with a laugh. "Are you really asking what my hobbies are?"

"Yeah, I mean we talk a lot when we travel but then you disappear into the cities or wherever. Do you look for cool things to collect? Or maybe that's when you go shopping for your fancy clothes and hair stuff?"

Brie stopped walking and put her hands on her hips. A wide smile stretched her red lips. "Are you seriously trying to make up with me by showing personal interest in stuff I like?"

"No. I'm still really angry about what you said. It hurt a lot. But we're still friends and I want to know."

Brie looked at the passing horde. "Damn it, Renee." Her icy irises turned to her. "I'm... sorry I reacted like that. I shouldn't have said that."

"Which part?" Renee crossed her arms.

"Most of it," Brie answered and dropped her hands from her hips. "I was hurt and overreacted, but I shouldn't have taken it out on you. You didn't know."

Renee's stomach twisted. "Didn't know what?"

Brie's eyes flicked to the horde. "I think you need to ask your boyfriend."

"Damn it, Brie!" Renee moved until she stood in front of her. "Stop! Either we're friends or we're not. You need to be honest with me. Trust me."

Brie stared at her. "It's not that simple. You understand that. He owns all of us. I can't do anything he doesn't want me to."

"Fine, but you're not even trying."

"I'm *trying* to be a friend. I've already screwed this up so much," she said miserably.

"We both have, but you're a good friend." Renee snatched her hand and held it. "Please be honest. I can handle it. We can manage it together."

Brie closed her eyes and sighed. "You won't like what I'm going to say."

"I figured."

"Fine." She huffed and sat on a fallen log, smoothing the violet-print dress over her legs.

Renee perched beside her and caught Garren, still in the mix. The horde went around him like he was a tree as he waited.

"It's not disgusting," Brie said in a low voice. "Maybe barf-worthy because it's so sweet." She chuckled. "I'm just —" her jaw locked — "I'm jealous."

"But you said it was barf-worthy."

"It is." Brie turned her watery eyes to her. "I told you before my boyfriend did this." She motioned to her shoulder. "I *meant* my ex-boyfriend."

Renee's stomach bottomed out. "You don't mean..." She couldn't finish.

"Yeah, I do. I might've been the first person he turned. That he's aware of, anyway. It pissed me off at first, but we worked it out," she said with a shrug.

Renee's arms wrapped around her stomach as she bent over. Shit. Shit. Anything but this. No way she could fix this. She didn't understand Brie and Zane's relationship the way it was to begin with. Now with this layer... how would she manage this?

"Hey it's okay." Brie put her palm on Renee's arm. "We're not together. It doesn't screw things up for you."

Renee blinked away her tears. It did. So many doubts raced through her mind, she couldn't keep one long enough to attach it to the hurt and anger that lurked inside her.

"Look, we weren't good for each other. Before I mean," Brie tried to reassure her.

"Before?"

"Yeah, before all this. We treated each other pretty badly, if I'm being honest." Brie's fingers touched the braid at the side of her head. "We were young and messed up people. I don't think we knew how to do anything other than hurt each other."

Oh god, that's why Brie knew so much about Zane. They'd been together before the end. He said he'd been around all this time, which meant so had Brie. They'd been traveling together the entire time. As horrible as the news was, the logical part of Renee screamed at her heart to shut up and get it together. She would have a meltdown later when she was alone. Brie was doing what she'd asked. She was being honest. Both Zane and Brie were trying to trust her.

"How did you hurt each other?" Renee heard herself say in an even tone that masked the chaos inside her.

"You sure you want me to answer that? You like who Zane is with you."

"I do, but I also see who he is with everyone else, and you keep reminding me that's who he really is." If Zane really was the monster everyone thought he was, she needed to see that side of him, to better understand his interactions with the horde.

"I never trusted him; always thought he was cheating on me. So, I was a bitch. He was like most young guys in the military." She paused, tilting her head. "I guess you don't know what I'm talking about. Not all, but a lot of the guys who enlist are arrogant, violent pricks. Some never grow out of it," she said with a twist to her lips.

Before you, this is all there was, violence, pride, pain. Zane's words echoed in her mind.

"Although, he didn't even want to be in the military. His dad made him enlist." Brie flipped her braid behind her.

"Why did his dad make him go into the military?"

"It was that or get locked up. Your boyfriend was wild, it was part of the appeal for me. Even when he started the criminal shit, I didn't care as long as he didn't involve me."

Zane had been a criminal? He'd only been around twenty-one when the world ended. Renee braced herself before she asked the next question. "How long were you together?"

"Not sure. It's been so long that we haven't been. Everything from before is like... almost like I'm just reading a book about it. You know?"

"Yeah." That Renee could relate to. Perhaps Brie had blocked most of the traumatic memories out like she had, so she wouldn't mourn the loss of everything that had been torn from her. Because of Zane, he was the one who'd killed both of them.

Brie scratched her head. "It was in high school when we hooked up. We fought all the time, were shitty and petty to one another, and then he killed me." She chuckled at the end.

Renee's eyes widened at Brie's lackadaisical attitude.

"Renee, it was literally a lifetime ago. I have zero interest in Zane, well anyone, for that matter. Zombies don't have urges like that. Unless they're pervy fucks like you two." Brie laughed at her joke.

Renee tried not to, but laughed too. "I didn't think you did. I just didn't want you to be hurt."

"I'm not hurt. I'm butthurt because he actually loves you. It's kinda hypocritical because I don't think I loved him, even then. It's just… I can't believe how much loving you has changed him and I guess it hurt my pride."

"He was stupid not to love you Brie, you're freaking awesome," Renee said as she wiped her cheeks.

"No, I was a total bitch then. Super-hot, but a card-carrying psycho. I might not be as sexy now, but I'm a better person." Brie crossed her legs like a lady and grinned.

Others are chosen and find a new existence in death. Zane's words filled her mind.

"He might not have been smart enough to love you, but I do." Renee threw her arms around Brie. She yelped, but returned Renee's hug.

"I love you too, you silly bitch. But I have a serious question." Brie paused and pulled back, narrowing her eyes. "How *do* you fuck? I don't need the details, but I thought those parts didn't work anymore."

"Brie!" Renee let her go, horrified.

Brie laughed until she wiped her pale cheeks.

"I'll tell you what. You tell me about your hobbies and I'll tell you what you want to know," Renee challenged.

"Shit. Can I start one now?" Brie stood up and twirled around gracefully. "Dancing?"

Garren approached and tilted his head down to Brie before bowing to Renee. Renee giggled. Brie crossed her arms.

"Garren, can't you see I'm trying to having a fucking hobby here?"

Garren gave Brie a smile and gestured toward the horde. The shamblers were almost in view. Renee bolted up. They were falling behind. Her brows pinched when she noticed how few shamblers there were.

"Play time's over kids. We gotta book. I'll have a hobby soon." Brie pointed at Renee.

They all took off and ran until they reached the center or the horde.

Chapter 21 - Brie

2010

Brie spit the blood from her mouth and stumbled to her feet, pushing her long, white-blonde bangs back, so they didn't obscure her view.

"What the hell are you doing, bitch?" the taller man sneered at her.

"Beating your ass," she spat.

He roared with laughter, almost doubling over. Stupid fuck. Brie used his elation to get the drop on him. Before he reacted, she straightened her posture, pivoting her rear foot and shifting her weight forward. She kept her left hand up near her face and her chin tucked as she landed a rear uppercut that knocked him back. No hesitation, she lifted her right leg, pulling her foot close to her lower belly before snapping it forward for a front kick. The asshole stumbled into the brick wall. Idiot didn't anticipate her next move and played right into her trap.

For weeks, she needed to blow off some steam. Impatiently she waited for Zane to return on leave so she could beat his ass instead. He cheated on her, but he hadn't returned yet, so she found someone else to punish. Honestly, it was more fun with thugs because they never held back. They didn't wrestle with hitting her the way Zane did. Sometimes he was such a pussy. Unless she made him so angry he couldn't control his inner-beast, he wouldn't hit back. Restrain her, push her off him, and sometimes smack her ass, but he had all these high ideals that women shouldn't be hit. Probably because of his prick of a father smacking his family around, including Zane.

They'd always had that in common. Both their fathers were very "hands on" with discipline. The difference being that Zane hated it and refused to be like his father. Brie decided when she was thirteen, she was done with her father's shit. Yes, she still let him beat her ass, so he felt superior and scary, but she wasn't afraid of her father anymore or any man for that matter. What would they do to her to cause more pain than what she already existed in?

Fuck them all. She'd never back down from any of them again. Once Zane was done with his tour, she would force him to marry her and move the hell away from both of their families. As screwed up as their relationship was, he understood her, accepted her, whereas if she showed her true colors to anyone else, they were scared shitless. He knew she was a monster, the same as him, and that's why they worked.

Eyeing the imbecile in front of her, she wondered if she could convince Zane to go hunting for assholes with her. They'd wreak havoc on people that society didn't care about to calm their demons and then have really hot sex after. The thought of it made her mouth water. As angry as she was at Zane for cheating on her, he had merits, too. He was a good fuck, and he remembered things about her that others didn't bother with. He could also be fun if they partied, and sometimes, when she let her guard down, they had real conversations that made her feel something. *Unsure of what the emotion was — it was pleasant and often compelled her to be around him more.*

The thug reached behind him, no doubt to pull a weapon on her. He didn't understand. No one but Zane did. She'd stared death in the face more than once and it didn't rattle her anymore. Part of her liked the thrill of existing in her last moments. She took the few, brief seconds to pick up a long piece of metal that had detached from the fire escape and rushed him as he raised a pistol, knocking it from his hand.

He screamed; the crack of his arm breaking was music to her ears. It made her heart race. A tiny whisper in her mind urged her to end him. To finally let herself savor death, jealous that Zane had taken lives due to his military service. He didn't like to talk about it, but once, when he was drunk, she got him to open up and admitted the rush of ending someone's life. She wanted that rush, too.

With a smile on her red lips, she hit the man several times in a row, sending him to the ground. She tried to stay focused on the alleyway to make sure there were no witnesses, but got caught up in striking him until he didn't move. It wasn't until she tasted coppery blood on her lips that she stopped and peered at him.

Had she killed him? She crouched down and studied him. A tiny, pathetic whimpering sound escaped his lips. Not dead. She frowned. She knew logically, it was wrong to kill someone, but she couldn't ignore the craving of destruction. However, given her attacker's state, it wouldn't be meaningful if she took his life now. His leg was twisted, she recalled striking his knee, but not when he got into the fetal position, he was now in.

She leaned closer and wiped the blood marring the pipe on his side as she spoke. "Next time you decide to mug a woman, do better. If I see you again, I'll end you." Brie raised herself above him and got to her feet. Not truly irritated that he attacked her, she was the one who went into a rough area late at night, and pretended to be drunk, hoping someone would be stupid enough to approach her.

He was just a different version of her. A hunter stalking its prey. The only difference was what he wanted versus what she did. He wanted her money and maybe her body. After all, she was a knockout, but he didn't expect what she wanted in return. Satisfied, she scanned the muted alley. Finding no one, she sauntered to the opening and returned to her car.

Once in her car, she glanced at the piece of metal she'd carried with her and wondered where she would keep it. Although it was only a length of metal, it now meant something to her, more so than the pile of jewelry she left in the glove box before exiting the vehicle. The maids couldn't find precious accessories in her room or it would raise questions.

Her mind wandered to all of her hiding places on the estate as she clasped her diamond tennis bracelet on her wrist and picked up her platinum and diamond necklace. She used the wipes she left in the seat to remove the splatters of blood. Perhaps the stables? Ester was good about keeping her secrets, even covering for Brie when she snuck off for her self-defense classes, telling Brie's father she was riding.

Brie rolled her eyes. Her father was an idiot as well. If he actually knew anything about her, he would have never fallen for that because her favorite horse was still in the stables, but he'd never paid attention to anything regarding her. Except for her appearance or how she presented herself to his asshole friends and their sons.

She turned on the ignition and slowly drove away from the curb. Her lips quirked into a grin. Her father's irritation was part of the appeal of dating Zane. He fucking hated Zane and considered him a bad seed. Although their prick fathers got along well and were considered frenemies, they didn't want her and Zane to be together because Zane was destined "for tragedy" as Brie's mother put it.

Good, because so was she. They just didn't know it yet. She played her parents' game and went on dates with rich twats that were just as empty as she was, but she wouldn't give up Zane. He was her ticket to freedom because he was the only one who didn't care about all the bullshit her parents did.

Her fingers tightened around the steering wheel. She just had to get him to stop sticking his dick into anything with a heartbeat. Zane swore he never cheated on her, but she wasn't stupid. She knew how most guys were. Her father wasn't even in the military but kept putting his cock into all manner of people and her mother turned a blind eye.

Brie grit her teeth. She had never turned a blind eye to that shit. Zane was lucky to have her. She was beautiful, dangerous, fun at parties, not stupid, and had a killer fashion sense. Sometimes she was even funny, although most of the time, too serious to cut jokes. She was still going to beat his ass when he got back, but taking a deep breath, she would make it until then. Now that she'd satisfied her own beast.

Chapter 22 - Renee

Brie stood on the porch of the abandoned house, her eyes roving over the structure. "Gotta be honest, this thing doesn't look all that sturdy. Thankfully, we're not starving yet."

"Are you worried we'll starve because we're not going south?" Renee asked.

Brie looked away.

"You said you'd be honest," Renee reminded her.

"I know. But it's hard with you. I like you being optimistic." Brie touched Renee's arm.

"Just because I know things will be hard doesn't mean I won't be optimistic."

"It's not that. It's this... living like this for years, always on the edge of death yourself. The only way to survive is to take the lives of other living things. Sure, humans hate us and want us dead, but it doesn't make it easier. It just makes it so you can sleep at night. Well, for those of us who sleep," Brie said with a chuckle.

Again, Brie made the comparison, that they were at war with mankind, except from the zombies point of view, they were the ones being destroyed. Renee clasped Brie's arm.

"I understand I'll change because it's impossible not to, but the core of who someone is never really does. I've always been silly and optimistic. I adore fantasy books. I'm the one who got everyone using cool titles," Renee said proudly.

Brie laughed before her expression darkened. "I understand this isn't the life you would've chosen, but I'm so fucking glad you're here." Brie yanked Renee into a hug.

Renee's eyes widened in shock. She was a hugger and made many of the undead uncomfortable with her physical contact. Brie let her touch her, hug her, but rarely initiated anything, especially more than once in a day.

"I hope you're wrong about people not changing. I don't want to be who I was before," Brie's voice cracked. She cleared her throat. "And I sure as fuck don't want Zane to be the prick he was before you showed up." Brie let her go and stepped back. "Get in the house. I need to check all the entry points to make sure once things get going, no one is stupid enough to try to get you."

"Okay. I'm sure you'll be okay. You always are, but be careful anyway, for me."

"For you, my silly queen, I'll be careful." She chuckled. "Should I leave the door open so you can talk to Zane before this gets started?"

Renee shook her head, she didn't want to see him, and she doubted he'd want to be around her. "No. I'll see him after."

Brie's brow furrowed, but she nodded, closing and barricading the door. Renee turned and peered at the decrepit house. She gathered the sleeping bag one of the horde had put on the porch, along with her traveling bag, and placed them next to a wall with no windows. The house was old. She had little architecture knowledge, but it had an old-world feel. She shuffled to one window and startled when Hatchet boarded it up on the other side. The glass was strange and appeared almost wavy.

There were stairs, but by the looks of them they would collapse if they bore any weight, so she decided to stay downstairs. She'd only be there for one night. The kitchen was odd — near the back door — and small. There were empty spots for appliances, but compared to newer houses built before the apocalypse, it seemed like it was added as an afterthought.

Exploring further, she discovered the very standard bathroom located across from the kitchen. She assumed this was an old house thing. In newer houses she'd squatted in over the years, the bathrooms weren't near the kitchen. Returning to her sleeping bag, she eyed the dusty furniture and decided against it. Every piece reminded her of the stairs, ready to collapse if any weight was applied.

She spread out her sleeping bag and got situated. Her stomach growled. Nope. She took out one of her collected books when a thunderous growl shook the house. Renee closed her eyes. No one needed to tell her who that was. She dug in a bag and found the ear protection, without hesitation, she fitted it over her ears and let out a breath.

She'd made it through the last culling and that time she was foolish and tried to run in the middle of the chaos before Brie saved her. Of course, the only reason she wasn't destroyed was because of Brie. Her body trembled. One of them. She was one of them now. She could handle this. It was different. She was different.

Why did it feel worse? Hot tears ran down her cheeks as she clutched the book Zane had gotten for her to her chest and rocked. Although the sound was muted, occasionally, she'd hear the fighting, the death. Hundreds of faces, some kind, some horrific and deformed, and others feral, like a wild creature, filled her mind. Hundreds of names whispered in her mind. They were her horde, and they were devouring each other.

She couldn't sense when they died, but it tore at her and even though she couldn't explain it, it seemed like part of her was dying with each harsh cry of pain. As if mystically, her soul was wounded when they were. She rocked harder. He was their king. How could he let them destroy themselves?

"This is all I want. You hate the violence and death and I hate all of it, except you."

Renee's eyes bulged. No. He wouldn't do that. Zane had explained why the horde had to be thinned. Winter was on the way, and he didn't want them to starve. He'd moved them around for months just to keep them fed. But he'd also told her numerous times he didn't want to be king.

Her fingers dug into the cover of the book. She had to stop the culling. Her people were dying. There had to be another way. She thought about Brie's reaction when she mentioned winter. She'd been worried too, and she cared about the horde. Brie always put the horde first.

The buzzing she had heard before suddenly returned and morphed into a ringing sound. Almost a relief because, along with the ear protection, it nearly drowned out the noises, the suffering. But even with the ringing, she sensed their suffering, their pain. The chaos and confusion in their minds. Was she going crazy? Or crazier?

Renee closed her eyes and kept rocking. Just a few more hours. She *would* make it. Her lips trembled as she sucked in air. A warm hand squeezed her shoulder.

"I know it's tough, but you're a queen now. Part of being queen is making tough choices and living with them," her brother's ghostly voice whispered. Somehow his calm cadence permeated the ringing, repressing the sound until it faded.

"I know. I remember you told me being a queen was hard. I miss you so much," Renee said through her tears. She felt like she might puke.

"I miss you too, Princess."

"I want to see you." Renee almost opened her eyes.

"Don't. Let me stay with you a little longer."

"Okay." She didn't want him to go. She never wanted Liam to leave. "I don't think I'm meant to be a queen, Liam. I'm trying. I am, but it's not like when we played make-believe, even our epic stories."

"Sure, it is. Renee, the secret princess, began a journey to become queen. Her story didn't turn out as she imagined, but she discovered her found family. She met her best friend Brie and the love of her life. It's arduous now because the story has to get grim first, before you get the happy ending where you rule over your kingdom."

"*You* were my best friend," Renee replied stubbornly. "And no one knows I was a secret princess."

"Of course, Zane knew. Why do you think he chose you?" Liam's voice was filled with amusement.

"Liam, he doesn't like being called king and—" Renee made the mistake of opening her eyes. He was gone. Damn it! She leaned against the wall. At least she wasn't shaking anymore. The nausea had subsided. Even dead, her brother was the best.

Chapter 23 - Renee

The door creaked open. She didn't want to be reassured when her gaze locked on him, but she was. Still angry but relieved, he appeared healthy and whole. His irises were bright in the darkened room. Behind him in the doorway, Renee could see it was sunny outside. After hours of forcing herself not to barge outside and attempt to stop the madness, she'd passed out and now wasn't sure what time it was.

She sat up but refused to let herself go to him. Her body tingled as their eyes met. Clad in black, it was difficult to tell what or who was on him.

She cleared her throat. "Is it done?"

He sighed. "Yes." Zane turned and closed the door before he sat against it.

"Is the horde..." Shit. She couldn't get her question out.

"The culling served its purpose. Winter will be more manageable." His expression was far away and forlorn.

"When do we leave for Albany?"

At her words, he turned his narrowed eyes to her. "Are you so eager to test the horde's loyalty?"

"No. It has nothing to do with that. I wanted to know if I had time to hang out with Brie before we left."

He turned his head. "Yes, there is time. We don't leave until after nightfall. She did well in the culling, found the weakest members of the horde and disposed of them. She has an eye for weakness."

Renee sat back, not sure if he was trying to hurt her, insult her, or make her angry. "Brie is the Knight Commander, so that makes sense. She's the defender and heart of the horde."

Zane laughed. Now she was insulted.

"You're such an asshole!"

"I don't understand how you got the impression Brie was a good person, that any of us are, but it's amusing," Zane said with a smirk.

Sonofabitch! Renee bolted up from the sleeping bag and stalked over to him. "Obviously you're a bastard, but don't you talk about Brie!"

Zane raised an eyebrow at her. "Are you now her knight commander who defends her honor?"

"If I have to be. Someone sure as hell needs to. Just because you knew her before you made her a zombie doesn't mean you can talk shit about her. I don't care who she was, it only matters who she is now."

He tilted his head and studied her. "What are you talking about?"

Renee crossed her arms. "I know."

He frowned. "I doubt you know the truth."

"Don't start with the vague statements. If you want me to know the truth, then tell me. Otherwise shut the hell up because I don't want you trash talking her."

"Renee, you've only known her for a few months. You don't understand who she is," he said in a reasonable tone.

Screw that. "I've only known both of you for months. I'm beginning to think I don't know either of you. The difference being I'm pleasantly surprised at how great Brie is. You, every day, it gets harder to be okay with your choices." She stopped when her voice wavered. Shit. Shit. She couldn't cry now.

He frowned. "Why do you pick fights with me about everyone else?"

Renee's eyebrows lifted. "What?"

"The horde, Brie, humans. You keep starting arguments with me about others."

"Because you treat everyone like garbage, except me."

His gaze intensified as he stared at her. "Then why are you upset?"

Renee's face scrunched up. He didn't get it. "You can't treat people the way you do, Zane. It's not okay."

"They don't matter. You do."

Renee looked at the crumbling ceiling in frustration and took a breath. "But you acting like that upsets me and you care about my feelings, right?"

Zane stood up and approached her now that she wasn't yelling. "Yes. I don't like when we argue." He stepped so close they nearly touched.

Renee picked up on the scent of flesh and blood and locked her jaw when her stomach twisted with hunger. Hated that. She would never be okay with her body's visceral reaction to gore now, it still made her anxious, but it also made her hungry. She swallowed.

"I don't like it either. I hate it."

His hand reached for her chin and tilted her head to look at him. God, he was gorgeous. His sensual lips begged to be kissed. His long dark hair, still mostly clean, beckoned her fingers to run through it.

"Then let's not fight anymore. Let me show you how much I love you." He lowered his mouth to hers.

She almost lost herself to the sensation of him. Renee clawed her way out of the endorphins that flooded her system, the chemical reaction that begged her to take her clothes off and push him to the ground. She broke their kiss and took several breaths.

"I know you love me, Zane. This isn't about that."

He touched her face. "Nothing else matters."

"I wish that was true, but it's not. Please listen to me." She put her hand over his and moved it away from her face. "I understand you're trying and maybe I'm not patient enough, but you can't... you can't keep treating everyone so horribly. I get you don't see it that way. But you don't listen to me when I tell you how to be better, either."

"You told me you accepted this life. Accepted me."

Shit. She had, and the raw pain in his voice cut through her. "I do. I don't mean it like that. Things are still muddled in my head for a lot of reasons." Renee paused as the ghost of her brother gestured from the corner for her to continue. Yep. Definitely mixed up. "Can you just not say crappy stuff about Brie?"

"Because she's your friend."

"Yeah."

He averted his eyes, but not before she caught the pain in them. "Okay. I'll attempt to be better toward her."

Renee stood still. She hadn't expected that to be so simple. He'd been all over the place for weeks. She thought he'd fight more about it.

"I don't want to test anything in Albany. I didn't say that right. Before, about the horde, I mean."

He narrowed his eyes at her again and his features shifted to a more feral countenance. His reaction confused her. His expression concerned her but also aroused her. She kept a poker face as best she could.

"You seemed up to the challenge before."

Renee couldn't tell if he was teasing or not. "I'm not. I was worked up because we'd argued."

"Then travel with me to Albany."

Her arms rested against his neck. She delighted at the vibrations skimming across her forearms, but her jaw clenched. They'd just made up, and he wanted to fight again. Damn it.

"We already talked about that." Her eyes drifted to the dirty floor.

He snatched her chin, knocking her one arm away, and locked eyes with her. "We did, and you were stubborn and wanted to stay with the horde because they are loyal to you. Either you still believe that or you don't."

She dropped her other arm beside her. "Damn it, Zane! You said you didn't want to fight!"

"I don't, but I want the truth. You lied to me. Now tell me the truth."

Unshed tears made her vision blurred. "I hate when you're like this."

"When I make you face the truth? You are their queen. They should be loyal to you."

Her eyes flicked to his face. He hadn't said that with malice. She was so confused.

Zane released her chin. "Brie may protect the horde. But she is not their heart. *You are.* For better or worse, you are a kind queen."

"But you were angry, and you said–"

"I said after the culling we'd see who was loyal to who," Zane interrupted as his fingers brushed her hair back from her face. "I am loyal to you and only you. Unfortunately for me, you are loyal to us all."

Tears slipped down her cheeks as she grabbed his waist. Fucking swooning again. "What does that mean?"

"It means, my heart, whether or not I want to be a benevolent ruler, with you by my side, I have to improve for *your* heart."

Holy shit, she was actually lightheaded from his words. When he sealed his mouth on hers, she was positive she was going to pass out.

Chapter 24 - Zane

Renee stood by a large, winding tree that branched out in all directions. Because winter was quickly approaching, there were no leaves left, leaving the twisted branches looking like claws reaching for her slight frame. Her fingers brushed the dark bark, not sensing his approach. His footsteps were always heavy. Over the years, he'd gotten them to be lighter, but his approach was never silent. If he was caught up in pursuing prey, he liked how it instilled fear—anticipating his arrival.

His steps slowed, caught in her beauty beneath the moonlight. Her long tresses danced with the breeze. He preferred her hair down, but understood why she often wore it tied back. She'd asked for a minute to collect her thoughts and he'd given her ten. Of course, she was never truly alone, but he didn't want her to know that. Zane wanted to give her more personal freedom, but wouldn't risk it. His growing paranoia that war was inevitable nagged at him.

Renee still hadn't fully accepted what she was, what they all were. She wasn't ready to learn about their enemies. It was better if she believed the only enemies they faced were the humans. Previously, he hadn't tracked her per se, but if one of his creatures spotted her or if he did himself, he'd lead his horde away or give her tiny human groups a wide berth eliminating any other random enemies that were within miles of her.

She hadn't been exposed to monsters as far as he knew because he'd done his best to shield her, allowing her to believe the worst monsters that existed were his species. Although part of him thought she might be more accepting of various creatures because of the books she'd read; he didn't want Renee to risk her life because of her kindness and acceptance of species different from her.

When Zane reflected, none of those thoughts had registered at the time. He only understood on a base level she existed and he needed her to continue to exist. His horde had battled all manner of creatures on and off throughout the years, the largest advantage being sheer numbers. He'd lost many, many horde members at the claws of werewolves, too quick-as-lightning vampires, savage ghouls that also consumed flesh, and resilient demons that healed too fast for anyone but him to deal with, but the toughest had been necromancers.

He fought other magic users, but in his opinion, necromancers were the most challenging because they lived and breathed death, the same as him. Zane's early memories were still foggy, but he recalled that in the beginning, the necromancers had more control of his undead. Over time, the control faded, leaving him and his horde victorious.

Thankfully, necromancers were a nasty, distrustful sort with many enemies, so over the years, less and less of them existed. He searched his memories, those that continued to resurface, to see if Levitt had mentioned necromancers at some point.

Zane's shoulders stiffened as Levitt approached. Technically, they were friends now, but even knowing that didn't necessarily make Zane feel safe around him. Sure, if there were enemies around, he trusted Levitt would take out the enemies with him, but the nagging thought that Levitt would turn on a dime never left him.

Perhaps it was because of how Levitt watched him for weeks. Almost stalking him and showing up in the weirdest fucking places when Zane felt the most vulnerable. The psycho showed up when he was showering and chased everyone else away. Why? Because he wanted to talk about his favorite band Disturbed. Zane liked Disturbed, clearly not as much as Levitt, but he was glad he knew most of their songs because he was pretty sure if he hadn't, that fact would have set Levitt off.

Zane lived around angry people his whole life, hell, sometimes nearly anything would set him off, he often didn't have to search for a reason to be destructive. But Levitt was next level. That bastard lived on rage, almost nothing else seemed to exist.

Of course, if Zane was honest, he had fun with Levitt doing stupid shit to unwind, even if it didn't involve taking out the enemy or beating the shit out of people. Levitt was a master at drinking games and could drive almost any vehicle, military or not. He was also smarter than he looked or acted and made difficult decisions in seconds, which made him a decent partner when they played pranks on each other in the platoon.

"Hey," Levitt greeted him as he lit a black cigarette. He rubbed his face. Zane didn't comment, but he didn't seem to have slept much again. It was rare when Levitt slept through the night and he usually had dark circles under his deep-set eyes, giving him an even more menacing appearance. From what Zane heard, no one would sleep near Levitt because he had violent nightmares and anyone within ten feet got hurt when he lashed out in the middle of the night.

"You eating?" Zane asked.

"Fuck, yes. I don't refuse food, even when it's the garbage they feed us here. I'm always hungry."

Zane nodded and shifted his feet to get more comfortable. He didn't need Levitt to tell him not to leave until he finished smoking. Levitt had been showing up for breakfast almost every morning for the past two weeks and talking to Zane until he was ready to deal with the "knuckleheads" inside the mess tent.

They never talked about the snake monster humanoids or what had happened. Colonel Stein never questioned or approached Zane, so Levitt took care of it like he said he would. Other than Levitt's paranoia, Zane didn't know why he decided to befriend him. Zane wanted to trust him, but couldn't shake the feeling something was off with Levitt, and it wasn't just his mental stability.

"Stop fucking brooding. Fuck. You've got nothing to brood over," Levitt snapped.

Zane stood straighter, changing his expression to a smirk. Unsure why, but if he slouched and his face didn't have some type of expression, it irritated Levitt. One time, Zane had been deep in thought about his prick of a father and had zoned out. Apparently, he slouched and had no expression on his face. Levitt smacked him on the side of the head so hard he fell out of the chair, hitting his face on the floor before he recovered. It only took once for Zane to get the message.

His father had been smacking him around since he could remember. It was strange, even though Levitt was hands on as well, the violence didn't register the same to Zane. The actions should have made him so angry he tried to beat Levitt's ass, but... they didn't. He figured it was because their motivations were different. Levitt didn't really mean anything by it. His violent outbursts weren't targeted at him like his fathers were.

"Listen" — Levitt yawned — "I have to go talk to Stein again. He's got his panties in a bunch over the last mission."

Zane's smirk grew into a smile. Levitt was the only one who called Colonel Stein just "Stein" or would make comments like that, at least amongst the cadets. He thought perhaps the officers made snide comments since Colonel Stein wasn't liked, but anyone else? Hell no. Levitt had balls the size of planets. Nothing scared him. Either that or Levitt had a death wish.

"Okay," Zane replied.

"It's about when I beat pussy-Preston to a pulp." Levitt chuckled at his clever words.

Zane didn't like Preston. He was an entitled prick who thought, because his family was all military, he should be treated better. He'd tried that posturing shit with Levitt, who put him in his place, but also broke several of Preston's bones. Zane knew Levitt was a favorite of Colonel Stein. The Colonel treated Levitt like a pet, feral wolf that only he had control over and to some extent it was true.

"He deserved it." Zane added.

"Yeah, he did. Not one of us is better than the other... well, that's not true. Most of these idiots make me ashamed to be part of the military, but some of these kids show some promise. They might actually be useful in the war someday." Levitt took a long drag of his cigarette.

Levitt always called this skirmish a war. Zane was starting to suspect he wasn't talking about where they were stationed.

"Anyway, I'm trying to get my shit together, so I don't fucking attack the good colonel or anyone else on the review committee. Who knew there'd be so much bullshit in the military? Fucking ridiculous."

"You going to be able to keep your temper under control?" Zane dared to ask.

Levitt shrugged. "I have to, at least for now. I can't... leave yet. Too much shit to do and I can't go back to... I can't go back yet. Not until things are right."

He'd made more than one comment that made Zane think Levitt didn't really want to be there, even though he'd signed up. It was a distraction because of something at home. Maybe he had an asshole for a parent too, although he'd never mentioned parents. Once he'd made a vague reference to an aunt and someone else named Andy. The only reason Zane even remembered Levitt's slip of the tongue was because he'd been drunk off his ass and seemed sad, instead of fueled by his typical rage. It was jarring. Even if Zane didn't want to remember, he couldn't forget. A lot like the snake monsters.

"Maybe you should drink something before you go before the committee, as long as they don't know," Zane suggested.

Levitt laughed and patted Zane's shoulder. It hurt a little, but Levitt had trouble not hurting people, even by accident. "That's a good fucking idea. I knew it wasn't a waste of time to keep you around. Come on before there's not enough bacon."

Zane grinned at the memory. The recollection hadn't been helpful because, as far as he could recall, Levitt must not have said anything about necromancers. But reflecting on it now, he realized that he'd been mistaken. Levitt *had* been his friend, and he'd proved that he cared by keeping Zane out of trouble, making sure Zane continued life as usual. And Levitt *had* conquered his rage — at least until the Colonel pushed him too far.

If someone, who was so tied to their anger found balance, grew to be less a beast and more human, then his sweet Renee had a chance too. The feral rage that she had shown in Springfield wasn't who she was. She still wasn't aware of how she had shredded the woman into pieces that were almost too small for the horde to consume, or the way she'd consumed the woman's heart. How her irises had been filled with confusion and madness. She hadn't responded to her own name at the time, much less recognized him. Renee had been reduced to her basest form, similar to the just-turned creatures he couldn't tolerate.

While his queen could be fierce when cornered, the aggression wasn't who she was. The reaction was a dormant part of her that only reared its head when jeopardized, or if someone she cared about was threatened. He didn't have a solution, but once he had more information, together they would figure out how to tame her beast.

Renee's head was tilted up, peering at the sky as her fingers continued to brush the bark. He approached, not keeping his steps light; he didn't want to startle her. Zane was rewarded when he wrapped his arms, circling her waist. She leaned into him and sighed.

"I missed you," he said before he stopped himself.

She raised the hand, not touching the tree, to the side of his head and caressed it. "I missed you too."

She squirmed and spun in his arms until she faced him. "I don't like when we argue. I don't mean to keep starting arguments with you. It's just that I get so frustrated because it doesn't seem like you're listening to what I'm saying. So many people have ignored me. I guess I'm sensitive about it."

He put his finger over her lips to stop her words. "Don't apologize. You're right. Sometimes I don't listen well enough. Your words are the only ones I want to hear."

Her eyes widened as her pupils dilated and her lips parted. He couldn't tell her how lovely she was when her green irises glowed at night, set against her pale face and long, dark hair. She looked ethereal. It was like somehow, instead of becoming a monster like the rest of them, she was one of the fae from her beloved books. Beautiful and not of this destroyed world they shared.

"Even if it seems I'm ignoring your words, I assure you I'm not. I hear you. I see you, always," he told her because it was true. "With you, I can pretend I have a choice."

He lowered his mouth to hers. She tasted sweet, like a delectable dessert. One of those tiny pastries that someone could only eat a bite or two of because any more than that overwhelmed their taste buds. Except he couldn't get enough of her, no matter how many times his lips touched hers. He wanted to be overpowered by her essence, his cells rewritten by her touch.

Zane wanted to absorb her lust for life and see everything through her eyes because it was magic. Somehow with her, when he viewed the broken landscapes, the beaten down state of things, he saw possibilities, not just the end of everything until nothingness. With her, he dared to have hope of a future.

She broke their kiss, but remained close. "Pretend you have a choice?"

He tilted her head to his chest and propped his head on top of hers. She wouldn't understand what it was like to be controlled, sabotaged by an invasive parasite that dictated much of who he was. If any god existed, he hoped she never would. He didn't want her to be tormented the way he was, so rather than talk about his seemingly literal and figurative internal demon, he chose a safer option.

"I've talked about it before. I don't want to be king. I want to spend my days and nights talking with you, learning things with you, showing you how much I love you." He lifted her head. "Cherishing you."

She put her fingers over his. "You can do all those things now, even with the horde."

He grimaced. "No. It isn't the same. Leading thousands of... troops takes a toll on anyone. Regardless if they are a king or not."

She frowned. "I guess I didn't think about it that way, but that is a lot of responsibility. It never seemed so bad in my..." she stopped averting her eyes as color dotted her cheeks.

He held in a laugh, guessing she was about to mention one of her books since most of the characters were some type of royalty. Those characters relished in leading a nation. However, her stories probably left out much of the mundane details that were tedious. And perhaps even the uglier parts when the leaders had to make hard choices and then have to live with them.

It had disgusted her how he'd dealt with the traitors from not long ago. She didn't need to say the words because her actions spoke volumes. Of course, she might feel differently now that she cared for the horde and it was the traitors' betrayal that had led to many members of the horde being needlessly killed.

Zane was still trying to figure out how to approach the subject of Miles, his rival. Her knowledge of Zane's horde was the best she had about their species, but it wasn't complete. There were other hordes of similar, but different creatures. He assumed by this point there were hordes all over the world, but the ones in Asia were likely different from those in Europe, just as the ones in South America were. It wasn't only genetics that gave marked differences, it was also regionally, based on the strain of infection they received.

"I meant that you're not alone now. I know I'm not as strong as you, but I want to be a good queen, and that means helping you with the horde. You don't have to lead them alone anymore."

He smiled. She always knew what to say to pull him from his darkness. As he'd told her, he could pretend, and it made all the difference.

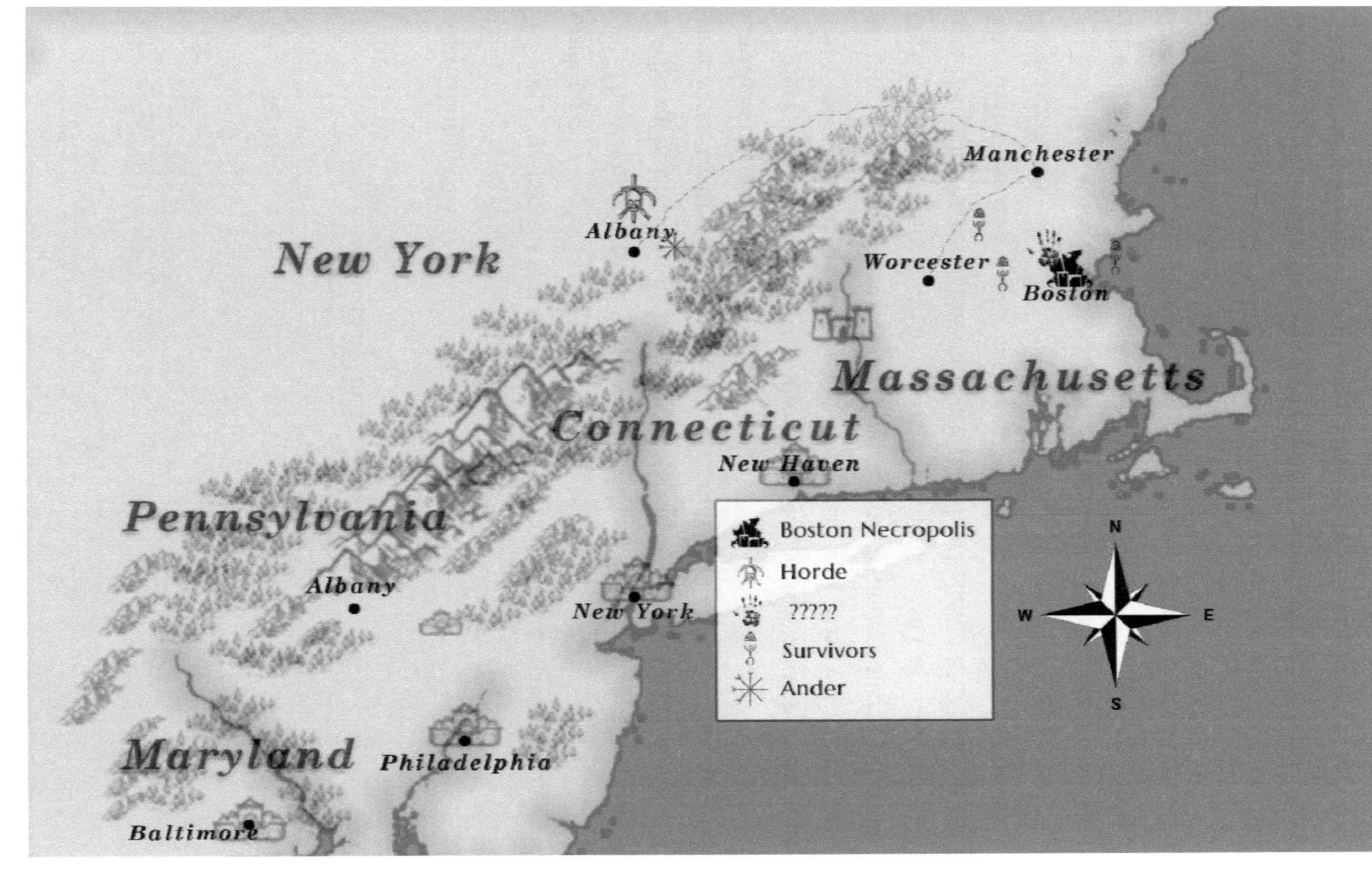

New York
Pennsylvania
Maryland
Baltimore
Philadelphia
Albany
New York
Connecticut
New Haven
Massachusetts
Albany
Worcester
Boston
Manchester
Boston Necropolis
Horde
?????
Survivors
Ander
N
S
E
W

Chapter 25 - Eric

Near Clinton MA

"I doubt your humans will allow us entry," Ander commented as they neared Brighton.

"They let us stay there. I told you they'll pretty much accept anything if it helps against the zombies. The other group that controls the islands and wastewater treatment plant... not so much. They don't trust anyone. Creatures or humans."

Since they'd entered their new agreement, Ander and the wolf were much more relaxed around Eric. Things were still tense with the others, because his group was worried that Ander had him under control somehow. He'd had to convince them four different times it wasn't the case, but each time they had the conversation, it felt like they believed him less and less. They didn't like how Ander and he talked often, not only as they traveled, but at night, too.

Eric had learned a lot about other creatures and magic. He'd wanted to tell Valen everything, but she was giving him the cold shoulder most of the time. He hated the distance growing between them, but couldn't do anything about it until they got back to Haven Port.

"Their rules for anything that isn't human are simple: just act as normal as possible. If no one makes a fuss over the person being a creature, then everyone turns a blind eye and doesn't talk about it." Eric lifted a shoulder.

"Chosen ignorance, extremely foolish. They could have a vicious creature living among them, waiting for an opportune time to then subjugate them all," Ander said with a contemplative expression.

Eric couldn't help but wonder if that was something Ander was already thinking about, but didn't comment.

"I will leave my minions outside of the boundary, if possible, but he stays with me."

Eric glanced at his wolf, that was a given. Ander wouldn't go anywhere without his wolf. "I figured. That's fine. Don't let him intimidate people." Eric glanced at the wolf. "You'll get some looks, just don't act like an evil wizard and it will be fine."

Ander's steps slowed as he peered at Eric. "Evil wizard?" The wolf huffed and then sneezed before it started breathing oddly. It was almost like it was laughing.

"You... you know what I mean," Eric said as his eyes flicked to Ander's markings to see if they'd changed. Relief spiraled through him when he realized he wasn't angry. Eric raised his gaze and noticed Ander's lips were twitching. Was that his distorted version of a laugh?

"A wizard, quite amusing." Ander started walking.

Eric was excited, they were only hours from Brighton. It wasn't exactly home, nowhere was home, at least not without his family. But it was where they'd settled down and tried to rebuild humanity, at least as best they could. It didn't matter that the horrible things that happened to them had changed them forever, awoken the dormant monsters inside of them. They still believed they were human, at least parts of them.

If it hadn't been for Valen and Lucy, the rest of them might have given up and turned into the worst versions of themselves. Zaila had zero issues being a werewolf, but considering how she'd been raised by a facility and was taught to use her abilities from childhood, it made sense. She was the one who helped Caleb accept what he was and not despise himself for it.

It hadn't been easy. After they closed the Hell gate and battled so many demons, they were exhausted. Not just physically, but mentally and emotionally as well. But his girl, Valen, had rallied them–inspired them to believe there was hope. She reminded them they still had each other, and that was all any of them really wanted. Eric admired her strength, powerful will and how she never gave up, even when they believed all was lost, that they were lost.

He glanced at Ander and his wolf. Perhaps that's why he didn't want to completely write them off and why he didn't understand why Valen did. Ander's and the wolf's steps slowed. Around them, all of Ander's zombies, which followed at their rear and sides, twitched. Eric swallowed. He knew what that meant after spending weeks with them.

"What is it?" Eric whispered to Ander, staring at his tattoos that increased in brightness.

Ander flicked his right hand, releasing his zombies, who took off running. The wolf let out a low growl. Thankfully, since the wolf and Eric had reached an understanding, it seemed to make efforts to not purposely intimidate him and directed its terrifying growl away from him.

"I sense them too," Ander told the wolf before his eyes drifted to Eric. "Demons."

Behind them, Caleb and Zaila handed their packs and supplies to Gina and Valen as they shed their outerwear. Seconds later, the telltale sounds of their bones breaking made Eric turn his head, knowing they were shifting. He checked his rifle and made sure his clips were easy to get to.

"It is unfortunate that most religious practitioners are dead. They were found to be quite useful against Hell's creatures with regard to weapons," Ander commented as he almost glowed.

Valen and Lucy clustered near them as Seth pulled his hood down on his hoodie.

"I got the rear," he said as his vocal cords became rough. His teeth sharpened as his claws made his fingertips bleed.

Caleb and Zaila, now in their wolf forms, padded in front of Eric. Seconds later, a cluster of demons, along with Ander's zombies, came into view, headed in their direction.

"Did you make your zombies bring them to us?" Valen exclaimed.

"Of course, I need their souls," Ander replied.

"You bastard," Valen grumbled, but raised her palms into the air and sent a gust of wind against the largest demon that had wings, making it stumble.

Eric raised his rifle and let out a breath. He squeezed the trigger and loaded at least twenty slugs into one of the demons. It dropped, but Eric knew it was only temporary and reloaded his weapon.

Ander's voice was hushed but carried by the wind and sent chills down Eric's spine. He understood a few words, but some, although familiar, were still gibberish to him. Eric squinted his eyes at the brightness surrounding Ander.

Caleb, Zaila, and Ander's wolf darted into the flock of demons. To Eric's surprise, Ander's wolf aided Caleb and Zaila by rounding up demons closer to them before it leapt up and tackled one of the larger ones. Blood sprayed up by the collective attack as they tore off limbs, tossing them to the sides. The wolves and demons ripped into one another, halting their motion toward the rest of them. Both species healed similarly, so as they grievously wounded one another, they'd heal and attack again. When the world first went to shit, it was the sheer number of demons that led to most of the werewolves' demise.

Seth made a grumble, it was difficult for him to resist violence, to push away his cravings for blood and flesh. He couldn't help it. It was part of who he was now, because of Pastor Cornell.

"Go. I'll watch our backs," Valen said and spun to face behind them.

Seth ran to the battle, gleefully knocking one demon over, and bit a huge chunk from its torso. A satisfied groan escaped his lips, and he removed another piece of the demon, consuming it.

Behind Eric, Valen started speaking, some words in Latin, some not, as the sky above them darkened. Damn, she was angry. He knew she wouldn't call down lightning near them, but it always made him nervous. It used a lot of her energy to cast and sometimes it got away from her and caused massive destruction.

Lucy, who was on his left, gasped. Several demons shrieked and started clawing at themselves, shredding their skin. Eric's eyes flicked to Ander, wondering if he'd cast some spell on the demons. Eric's mouth dropped open because although he couldn't *see* when magic was cast like Valen, he felt something oppressive flowing toward them—no, towards Ander. As it did, Ander's appearance changed.

His hands were out, fingertips extending toward the battle, and they were glowing. His skin gained color for a few seconds, his exposed arms grew in volume and looked less skeletal, and his cheeks and chin lost some of their sharpness—he almost appeared *normal*.

Another shrill cry from the demons drew Eric's attention back to them. Their appearance had morphed, leaving them looking greyish instead of reddish and thinner, like a husk of themselves. Eric drew in a deep breath. He knew necromancers drained life. He'd seen it in person. But not with so many and not all at once. The demons whined as they fell to the ground. Moments later, they stopped moving or making sounds.

Eric raised his rifle but didn't fire because the demon's souls now hovered over their bodies. They quickly clustered together, maybe to attack Eric's group — their souls — because spirits could do that, but they never had a chance as their collective souls zoomed straight at Ander and into his chest. The light of their souls brightened his chest before it faded.

Sounds of the fight continued. Thunder boomed in the sky, but Eric stared at Ander. It had only been demons, but he'd... absorbed them? Devoured them? Eric caught Lucy staring at Ander too, but he couldn't place her expression, only it wasn't disgust like he'd expected.

Eric forced his attention to the combat. All the wolves paused and then dashed away. A millisecond later, several lightning bolts crackled in the sky, slashing down and striking the largest demon with wings and any near him. They all screamed. The scent of burnt flesh filled the area and made Eric's stomach sour. The wolves finished off the rest of the demons.

As they destroyed them, their souls floated over their bodies. Ander didn't consume them but he held out several coins and whispered, "Laqueum."

Each time he said it, one of the souls would fly to his palm and, as far as Eric could tell, into the coin. Ander repeated the process until all but a few souls who escaped were gone. After he jiggled the pocket change in his hand, his lips twitched. Was he smiling about his actions?

"At least we helped the settlement," Valen said as she approached Eric. "We're close, which means they were probably headed for us, anyway."

"You're right, one less threat," Eric answered. Any time humans made an encampment that stayed in one place, it drew enemies. Sometimes monsters who wanted to destroy or eat them. Other times it was other human groups who wanted to take what they had worked for.

Ander titled his head and studied Seth as he continued feasting on the remains of demons, but didn't comment. Caleb and Zaila did a perimeter check to make sure there weren't any more enemies and Ander's wolf had disappeared.

"That was productive," Ander remarked. He didn't look as healthy as he'd had a few minutes ago, but he no longer resembled a skeleton anymore either.

Caleb and Zaila walked over to them, now in their human forms, putting their clothing on, and taking their packs from Lucy. Lucy wandered to Seth. She was the only one who could approach him when he was like this, at least without a fight. Careful and slow with her movements, she kept her distance but made her presence known to him. He growled but didn't make a move toward her.

"Seth, it's me. You've had enough. You have to stop," she told him in a soothing voice. "Come to me," she beckoned to him.

He growled and showed his jagged, sharp, bloody teeth, but once his eyes locked on her, he started to whine as he scampered to her on all fours, almost knocking her to the ground. She hugged him and brushed his long black hair over his shoulder, planting kisses on his bloody cheeks, healing him as she did. It was almost divine how she brought him back to himself, healing him simultaneously. Eric knew she was only healing his outside, but he couldn't help but wonder if she was healing his soul, too.

Seth resembled many of the monsters that destroyed the world, they all had to be careful and vigilant whenever they were around other people.

They wouldn't understand and would want to kill him. Heck, even after all this time, even Eric and the others barely grasped what Seth was, including Seth. All they knew was that Pastor Cornell had cursed them all in different ways, with Seth paying the largest price of them all.

"Remarkable," Ander said, transfixed on Seth and Lucy. His wolf appeared from a pile of debris and jaunted over to him, running its muzzle along his hip. Ander reached down to pet its neck. "I believe we are ready for your settlement now."

Ander grinned at Eric, but it didn't make him feel better at all. Ander's expression looked twisted and evil. Eric had been confident about this deal, now he was concerned that after they'd saved the humans, Ander might enslave them for his own purposes.

Chapter 26 - Renee

Renee adjusted her shirt, embarrassed by the numerous marks Zane had left on her. She wasn't sure why he'd put so many on her this time. It was like he purposely marked her for the world to know she was taken. Did he have to advertise to the entire horde they were intimate? Brie gave her the side eye but didn't comment on her hickeys.

"When we get to the city, you're with Garren, okay?"

Renee turned to her friend and asked, "Where will you be?"

Brie smiled, "Leading the charge, of course. Isn't that what knights do?"

"I think your title is going to your head," Renee replied with a laugh.

"Nah, our king handles any of the major threats. I just keep everyone else occupied." Brie said as she french braided her own hair.

"What do you mean?"

Brie's eyes slid to her. "He's unbeatable. No matter what any humans, or anything, for that matter, does—he doesn't die. Honestly, most of us don't think he feels pain."

Members of the horde agreed or nodded. Renee didn't reply because she knew that wasn't true at all.

"He's kept us from dangerous territories, unless there's no way to avoid them. I'm sure he's told you why we can't go south by now." Brie wrapped the elastic on the end of her braid.

Renee nodded again, even though she didn't know why they couldn't travel south. She didn't want anyone to know she was still in the dark about whatever the mysterious reason was. The irritation at herself for constantly getting distracted when she was alone with Zane bubbled up. *Stupid*, a harsh voice said in her mind.

From what Brie just said, it was to keep the horde from danger. She blew out. Again, everything Brie said made him sound like a good king who wanted to protect his horde. But only hours ago, he basically said they meant nothing. *Stupid*, the voice repeated.

"Why are we traveling at night? I thought it wasn't a good idea," Renee probed, desperate to shut up the nasty voice in her mind. She didn't need her internal dialogue sabotaging her.

Brie smoothed the top of her braid. "It's not that. There are too many other monsters that hunt at night and we're easy to spot."

"Because there's so many of us or because everyone's full?"

Renee peered at Brie; her icy glowing irises stared back. Renee turned her head, most of the horde also had glowing irises. Because they were well fed from the culling. Her stomach clenched. She was part of the sea of stars now.

Unsure why, but the realization hit her like a ton of bricks. Part of her was happy because if someone didn't realize what they were staring at, it would be beautiful, like a rare event that happened once in a lifetime. The whole sky at eye level, sparkling in the night.

It also signified that for the first time in her life, she was part of something bigger than herself—permanently. Once a human turned into a zombie, they would always be a zombie. But it also meant that this family, as icky as they were, wouldn't leave her — well, not by choice. It also meant they wouldn't intentionally hurt her, at least in an emotional capacity. They might try to attack her, if it was a culling, but not because they didn't care, it would only be out of instinct and that wasn't the same. At least not to Renee.

But it also meant she was undead and would never be part of humanity again. Although she had often felt like she didn't belong with the majority of people anyway, technically, she was human. She'd always hoped she would teach herself how to be as normal as everyone else and gain acceptance from her peers. Now there was zero chance of that. Part of her was still mourning the loss of the idea of acceptance from those who had been her peers.

"Both. Most groups aren't this large, even now. Well... that's not totally accurate. There are other groups that are larger, but they don't travel as much."

Remembering Zane's reason for traveling so much, Renee spoke. "But if there are larger groups of zombies, wouldn't they *have* to travel?"

"Nah, they just take out other territories." Brie's tone was matter of fact.

Renee kept the shock from her face. Brie, without knowing it, had given her a crash course on zombie politics that any humans would've gladly traded their lives for. If she'd known this before meeting them, she'd have used it to help in the struggle against the zombies.

Zane had already vaguely confirmed there were others. Brie mentioned other kings which Renee now took as other zombie kings that ruled other territories. And to top it off, they not only consumed humans, but each other. Not just for cullings, but also for old-fashioned land masses.

It must consume. It wasn't just about his parasite; it was bigger than that. When she talked about them eating themselves out of existence, she didn't realize until that moment how real that future was. Not just for Zane's horde, but for zombies as a whole. Shit. Shit. Her head felt like it was going to explode from the revelations.

"You, okay?" Brie's voice broke into her thoughts.

"Yeah, I just...do you think we could take a territory if we needed to?" Renee wasn't sure why she asked, but an unusual pressure behind her eyes eased up when she did.

Brie's pace slowed. "You want to go to war?"

As soon as the word war left Brie's crimson lips, Renee felt a spark travel down her spine. Excitement made her scalp tingle at the idea. What was wrong with her? The horde slowed their pace. Damn it, they were listening too.

"No. I don't want to risk anyone's life. I just meant; do you think we're strong enough?" Renee hurried through her words and wanted to take them back, but couldn't stop the exhilaration that still made her limbs tingle. Her steps seemed lighter, *she* felt lighter. Like someone had released a pressure value inside of her as butterflies danced in her stomach. What was happening to her?

Brie scanned the horde. "We haven't been to war in years. When we were before, it was out of necessity but" — she paused and grinned — "these magnificent monsters are always ready."

The horde turned their eyes to Renee and gave her nods, grunts and some moved their bent palms back and forth to sign the word *war*. Renee flattened her lips. The only reason she'd taught them that word was at Brie's request. Brie had told her it would be good for them to know when they took a city because, in their minds, that's what their life was. A war with the humans.

Her heart rate picked up pace as her face flushed. Renee struggled to catch her breath, feeling light-headed. Holy crap, talking about it was doing something to her. She reminded herself that she hated violence and bloodshed, she was tormented when she knew the horde had to be thinned. Why was her body reacting like this?

"That's good, in case things get tough in the winter. I want to make sure we have a back-up plan." Renee heard the confidence in her tone when inside she thought she might unravel.

"Good thinking, my queen," Brie replied and bowed dramatically before she chuckled.

Around dawn, Garren was at their side and declined his head to Brie.

"Alright, time to get set up. Don't be stupid," Brie told Renee before she turned to Garren and said, "Protect the Queen."

Garren gave her a stern expression and nodded. He led Renee away from the horde that trudged on. Oddly, Renee didn't want to be far from the horde. She understood she couldn't help when they took a city, but she felt guilty she was never there with her people when they put themselves at risk.

"I know we're not supposed to go anywhere near the violence but" — Renee paused and looked at Garren — "I need to... I need to be there, even if I just see the events. I get Brie, or Zane will kill you if something happens to me, but I swear it won't. I just, I *need* to be there with them." She bit her lip. "The horde I mean," she clarified.

Garren studied her for a long time. Renee didn't rush him; she was asking him to defy both Brie and Zane and she now understood it created a personal risk to him. He slowly nodded. Renee wrapped her arms around his waist and squeezed. He gave her a brief hug before releasing her.

Garren extended his pinkie and thumb to the sides, while keeping his hands positioned beside each other, and quickly brought them down at the same time. *Stay.* Then pointed at himself.

Renee had no interest in running from him. She nodded.

He cupped his ear. *Listen.* Once again, he pointed to himself.

She blew out before she answered him, "Yes, I'll stay with you and listen to you. I swear." She regretted letting him pick the words he wanted to learn first. Sure, they were the most useful, but she realized they were also a bunch of big brother words. Shit. She quickly turned her head to stare at a tree nearby.

His fingers lightly grazed her arm, bringing her attention to him. Learning forward, he raised his hand and curled in his three middle fingers, tapping his chin while he mouthed the words. *What's wrong?*

Because Garren, her Night Sentinel, was always looking out for her, of course, he noticed. She didn't want to tell him and felt bad for even thinking about him like a brother. Only *Liam* was her brother.

She blinked several times and signed it'd been a long few days. She threw in Brie and Zane's names and hoped he would think it was about the arguments and let it go.

Garren narrowed his eyes, but nodded and gestured to walk. Eventually they jogged to catch up with the horde but stayed to the side, hiding by broken down vehicles and piled up junk on the road. As they got closer, Renee picked up on the din of the attack.

Although her stomach was unsettled, it wasn't uneasy like it usually was. It was more like butterflies. They snuck into the outskirts of the city like they always did, but this time, instead of leading her away from the gunfire, they ventured toward it.

Time to find out if she accepted this life and Zane. She'd fought with Zane and called herself one of the horde. They might even regard her as their actual queen. But she couldn't call herself their queen, not when she wouldn't even face the most basic part of their life. She didn't protect them like Brie. She didn't lead them like Zane. Maybe she cared, but it wasn't enough. Brie told her before, she had to decide if she was with them or not. Tonight, she'd have her answer.

Chapter 27 - Renee

Renee was surprised at how smart humans were when they attacked the horde. Probably because the horde outnumbered them at least a hundred to one. It was only months ago when she was one of the humans fighting for her life against a now obvious, unbeatable enemy. Conflicted when she saw some of her horde cut down, she fought the urge to charge in.

Garren's fingers touched her arm, and he tilted his head to the right as he guided her into an alley. She wasn't sure where they were going, but he seemed to know, so she let him lead the way. Just as they reached the end, his arm stopped her and pressed her flat against the side of the building.

Renee's stomach bottomed out when a small girl, no older than eight, skittered into view. Her long, messy, dark hair whirled about as her eyes darted around in fear. Close to them, gunshots were heard and someone called out a name. The child didn't respond to any of the noise. Her tiny hands clutched a metal pipe.

The noise of struggle edged closer, but the girl still didn't respond. Instead, she glanced behind her and then scurried into the alley Garren and Renee occupied. No. No. Her eyes bulged when she spotted them. She raised the pipe as tears cascaded down her dirty cheeks.

Renee pushed Garren's arm away and approached her with her palms out. The girl's tiny hands shook. Renee sensed Garren behind her and she put one hand behind her to keep him at a distance. Renee crouched down to the girls' eye-level.

"We won't hurt you. It's okay," she told her.

The girl chewed on her lip and stared hard at Renee's face, zeroing in on her lips.

Renee spoke her next words slowly, "You don't have to be afraid."

The girl studied her mouth again. Renee sucked in her breath. She knew exactly what she was doing. It wasn't possible. How in all of this chaos had she found a deaf child? With slow movements, Renee raised her hands and signed they wouldn't hurt her.

The girl let out a breath as her shoulders dropped. She'd understood her. *But you're like them,* she signed.

We're not all bad. I won't let them hurt you. Renee signed back. *Can you hear at all?*

The little girl pointed to her head and shook her head no. It was then, through the girl's dark strands, that she saw the remnants of cochlear implants. The transmitter was still present, but the speech processor was gone. It was uncanny how much this child reminded her of herself.

Okay, where are your... people? Renee asked. She was afraid to inquire about family for fear her family was already dead.

I don't know. My dad and I got separated. I can't find him. The child continued to cry in earnest.

Renee stood, approaching the child, and tugged the pipe from her grasp, giving it to Garren.

We will try to find him or someone who can help, okay? Renee signed to her.

The girl nodded. *Why are you different?*

Renee gave her a sad smile. *I'm not sure. What's your name?*

The child raised both hands, touching her temple before she positioned them into a bent 'b' shape.

Hope, Renee signed, blinking to keep the tears away before taking her hand.

Given the girl's assumed age, her mom had been pregnant when the world went to shit. They walked hand in hand to the end of the alley. Before they cleared it, Garren moved in front of them and scanned the area. Her loyal Night Sentinel hadn't even questioned why she'd saved Hope.

Garren kept them right on the edge of the chaos for several blocks. He made them hide, scouting ahead before he'd let them continue. He signed it was safe by balling his hands, crossing his wrists over each other before he pulled them apart quickly. Hope's face lit up and she no longer looked at Garren with fear despite his more feral appearance.

Renee wasn't prepared for Hope's reaction as they passed a battle. She ripped her hand from Renee's and took off into the fray.

"Hope!" Renee called out and took off after her.

A man, in his late thirties, was fighting three of the horde at once, alongside a woman who fought two. He cut one down in front of Renee, which slowed her steps. They were hers, and he'd killed them. But he was Hope's father. It was obvious from the joy that flickered on his face as she ran to him. Ran right to where the zombies would kill her.

Renee let out a sound she didn't even know she could make. It reminded her of the thunderous growl Zane had made when she first saw him. The horde and humans stopped, temporarily stunned. Without processing what it might mean, Renee stalked toward the group.

"Back away from them now," she told the horde.

Confused, they retreated and gathered around Garren.

The man and woman yanked Hope to them and raised their weapons. Hope made a sound and tugged on her father's arm, frantically shaking her head no. With the speed only someone who used sign language daily would have, she signed to him that Renee was her friend. Her father turned his narrowed eyes to her.

"We won't hurt you, but you have to leave now. I can't keep them from you forever," Renee told him.

His brows pinched as he cocked his head to the side. "What?"

"The horde. You have to leave," Renee repeated, frustrated by his stubbornness.

"I can't... are you trying to talk to me?" he asked.

Renee's head jerked back. What was he talking about? Her eyes darted around to the horde. Their hunger and impatience gnawed at her. She couldn't ponder why she was so in sync with their motivations or instincts, but she was positive she wasn't wrong. She needed to wrap this up. Renee signed everything she'd said. *That* he understood. He pulled the woman and Hope close to him and backed away, but paused.

Why are you helping us? he signed.

Because not all of us are bad. Go, Renee signed.

His eyes widened. *Who are you?*

Hope stepped closer and hooked her index fingers together again, signing, *friend.* Renee smiled at her.

Do you have a name? he asked.

Renee, she replied.

Thank you for saving my daughter, Renee. We won't kill any more of your... zombies unless they try to kill us, he signed and turned.

Renee watched as they disappeared into the surrounding buildings. The horde stared at her expectantly.

"Thank you," she said in a low voice. Her hands signing the words simultaneously, *Go. Hunt.* They ran off. She turned to Garren, who was studying her.

He gestured to move. With a quick glance in the direction Hope had left, she hurried after Garren. She got turned around, as he made certain they didn't cross paths with another creature or human, by taking a haphazard route to what she assumed would be an apartment building.

Defeated, she kept her view on the ground. She'd failed the horde and had chosen humans again. She wanted to know where her loyalties lie; if she was their queen, and the truth cut her deeply. Renee wasn't worthy of them. How would the horde trust her when she continued to choose the enemy over them? Another failure.

Stupid! A voice in her mind screamed at her. But she wouldn't let a child be hurt or killed in front of her, not when she could do something about it. The horde had families, too. Wouldn't they understand? *Stupid!* The woman's voice yelled in her head and made her shudder. Shit. Shit.

Renee clasped her palms over her ears and stopped. Her eyes snapped shut as she tried to catch her breath. A tentative touch on her skin made her crack her eyelids open. Garren's glowing, reddish-brown irises were fixed on her.

A roaring growl reverberated off the surrounding buildings. It pierced through her and made her insides tremble. Even Garren winced at the sound. There was no mistake. It was Zane, and he was furious. Garren's face twisted as he dropped to one knee and panted.

Renee crouched beside him. "Garren, what's wrong?"

He grit his teeth, flicked his eyes behind him and got his hand in the 'k' shape, but couldn't complete the movement to his hip to finish the word *king*. Another loud howl of anger and Garren doubled over. Bastard! Zane was causing him pain somehow.

Renee stood and took off in the direction Garren had peered. She gasped when she got to where the noise came from. It seemed like everyone, undead and humans alike, had gathered in a parking lot in front of a row of stores. She blanched from all the death, both humans and zombies.

She stumbled forward as Zane ripped a human in two, tossing them aside like garbage. The horde surrounded him with bowed heads as three humans that were held by chosen struggled to get free. As she neared the massacre, two wounded people lay on the ground, dying. In the distance, she spotted Brie finishing off another person.

Renee's stomach twisted with hunger and it sickened her. Her mouth salivated at the sight of death. It repulsed her. Her hands shook as she continued closer. Zane yanked another one of the captive humans and tore their limbs off. It took everything in her not to scream.

Movement in the corner of her eye caught her attention. No, please, *not her*. It was the woman Renee had let go. Did that mean they got Hope too? This had to stop. All of it. Renee's own heartbeat made it hard to hear the woman's screams as a chosen dragged her to Zane. Blindly, Renee bolted to him.

She grabbed his arm, dripping with the blood of his victims. "Please don't." Her words were barely above a whisper.

A kaleidoscope of emotions played over his sharp features. First, he seemed almost delighted to see her, then irritation covered his countenance, shifting into righteous anger, and finally, resolve.

"Is this the human?" he barked at her. His words struck her like bullets. Normally when he spoke, she relished in the sensation, but this time it was as if he was wounding her with just the resonance of his voice.

Oh god. He knew what she'd done. She shook her head, for all the good it would do. Before she reacted, he turned to the woman and tore her head off. Renee opened her mouth to scream, but no sound came out. She wanted to hit him, yell at him. Do anything, but she couldn't move, couldn't react.

The horde, except the ones who held the humans and Brie, dropped to their knees like Garren had. Her eyes flicked to Zane's. Damn him! He glared at her and then gestured to the chosen holding the humans. Seconds later, they tore out the throats of the humans.

Finally able to move her limbs, she backed away and cast a quick look at Brie whose lips were in a thin line, before Renee turned and ran to Garren.

Chapter 28 - Renee

Garren had taken her to the safety of the apartment and refused to talk about what had happened. Not a single word about any of it. Renee was so frustrated, but he'd been hurt, or at least she thought he might have been, because of her, so she didn't demand conversation. He wouldn't stay once she was in the apartment, and she didn't blame him. She wasn't sure he would even be her friend anymore. She locked the door and collapsed on the couch.

She'd betrayed the humans for the horde, and now she'd betrayed the horde for the humans. Renee grabbed both sides of her head and hunched over, trying to catch her breath and keep her tears away. Her weakness was caustic, eroding any chance of happiness. She didn't have what it took to be anywhere, with anyone. But Zane told her he would improve. Of course, that was about the horde, not humans. He'd made it very clear they were the enemy. What was wrong with her?

"Nothing's wrong, Princess. You're trying to be a good queen. A good queen sees farther ahead," Liam's ghostly voice told her, his figure staying just out of view.

"How does a good queen betray her own people?" she snapped at him, seeming unconcerned that he'd leave. She couldn't make sense of the unofficial rules that kept Liam around anymore. More often than not, he and not she, seemed in charge of his appearances in her life.

"Because you're not. There's a bigger picture Renny, and you can see it. You're just afraid. Can't be a good queen if you are always so afraid."

Renee turned to her brother and to her shock, he didn't disappear. He stood in the corner lounging against the wall; he looked as alive as he had in life. Compared to Zane, he wasn't quite as tall, or as muscular, albeit, he was still fit. Liam had short, brown hair, and his deep-brown irises always looked like he was planning mischief.

"Don't pick on me Liam. I'm trying, but this world is scary, okay? It's gross and violent and bloody. I hate it."

"I don't think anyone wants to live during a war, but it is what it is. Look, you've got a good group around you and a way to end this madness," Liam said, pushing off the wall.

Renee perched forward. "End the war? What are you talking about?"

"Think about it. There's a reason *you're* the Queen. A reason you still feel connected to humans. The horde is loyal to you. They proved that tonight." He strolled toward the couch. "Other than the King, you think someone else could keep them from their food?"

Renee's lips pinched. Liam had a point. Damn it, she missed him so much. His image wavered like waves on an ocean. Nope. She had to believe he was there, or he'd disappear.

"The king only has one weakness, Renny... it's you," Liam said as he faded away.

"Liam, please don't go. Please!" Renee cried out, her hands grasping the air where his image had been.

She put her face into her palms and sobbed until she couldn't anymore. *Get it together,* she thought, wiping the moisture from her face. If she was going to get through this, she had to stop breaking down all the time.

Liam's words were still in her mind as she got up and changed her clothes, then she brushed her hair to waste time until Zane got there. She had to be ready to face him. She wasn't sure what she was going to say, she was still livid at his actions. Probably as much as he was at hers. She hated that her heart raced as soon as she heard his knock. It didn't matter how angry she was, she was always so grateful when they were together.

She unlocked the door and glared at him as he entered the apartment. Old thoughts from months ago clamored to the front of her mind. He was a monster. Murdered every human except maybe Hope and her dad. He glared back as he closed and locked the door behind him. Ready for the fight, she stepped toward him and squared her shoulders.

Annoyed at herself when her gaze drifted to his tight black t-shirt stretched across his chest. She noticed the shirt was still wet with the blood of his victims. So were his arms and neck. Disgusting. Her face felt hot when she forced her view to his handsome, sharp facial features. His cheekbones caught the flickering candlelight and made him appear more menacing than usual.

"You put the entire horde at risk with your behavior." His words stung.

"You put the entire horde at risk whenever you're in a shitty mood or we're fighting," she shot back.

"Do *not* try to turn this on me. You betrayed us. All of us!" he raised his voice. His words reverberated against her chest, causing it to warm in response.

"The horde wasn't fighting me! You were!" Renee shifted until their bodies almost touched. His words eviscerated her because they were true.

"That's because you're their queen and you betrayed them," he said through gritted teeth.

"No more than you have! You want them all dead so you can be free. Their lives mean nothing to you!" She shoved him hard. "They're yours and you're trying to destroy them!"

Renee hit his chest. He didn't respond, didn't even notice. Bastard. She hit him harder and shoved him again.

"How can I love you when you destroy what you created?" she screamed. She hit him repeatedly and then dug her nails into his chest.

Zane grabbed her arms and pushed her against the nearest wall. It knocked the air out of her lungs.

"You don't know what you're talking about," his voice sounded dangerously muted.

"You're wrong! I do." She took a breath and wondered how their relationship would survive. "I can't do this anymore."

His mouth slammed into hers and the kiss hurt. He kissed her even when she pushed him. When she kicked at him, he didn't let go, keeping her locked in place with his body. Against her better judgment, she stopped her assaults. She matched his brutal kisses with her own. She bit his lip until he hissed and bled from it before she drew it into her mouth, sucking on it.

He broke their kiss, his expression tormented. The blood colored his lips and pulled her gaze. She couldn't take her eyes off his mouth. She leaned into him and recaptured his lips, moaning into his mouth. Her fingers tugged on his blood-soaked shirt, ripping it open. She skimmed her fingers across his torso and lean muscles. His fingers dug into her hips as he tried to pull his mouth away.

Renee's fingers slipped into his hair, pulling it as her mouth dipped to his chin and neck. Her tongue flicked out and licked the blood off his skin. His surrender was obvious when he pulled her hips toward him by the waist. Zane undid her jeans, yanking them off. He slid out of his shirt and removed his pants. Without hesitation, she jumped up and wrapped her legs around his waist as he tore her shirt from her body, dropping the scraps to the floor.

For a heartbeat, they stared at each other. He shifted her along the wall, lining them up. With one harsh stroke, he slammed inside her. She gripped his shoulders and gasped. He'd never been that rough before. It hurt, but it was a delicious pain. Another brutal stroke made her see stars as she dug her nails into his shoulders, hot pain granting her satisfaction.

She dragged her nails across his back, tearing his skin open, but it only seemed to elevate his pleasure. She clawed at him as he savagely moved in and out of her, every inch of her skin prickling with awareness. Sex with Zane was amazing, it was like her entire body was coming alive from his rough touch. Each thrust pushed her to a heightened state. Zane moved her forward, gripping her thighs hard enough to bruise. Her eyes rolled back as her entire body vibrated. She called out, tightening around his shaft. He grunted but didn't stop.

Every inch of Renee was overflowing with fierce energy and hunger. So much hunger. Still coming down from her orgasm, she wrapped her fingers around his neck. His pulse raced, making the veins stand out. Pictures from the wall fell to the floor. A couple of knick knacks tumbled and broke near them.

He growled, pounding into her. Using the wall for leverage, he brought his right hand between them, stroking the sensitive bundle of nerves between her legs. The vicious motion combined with his touch pushed her over the edge and she came again as he thickened inside her. Renee gasped for breath, delighted as they danced with the edge of madness in their desire for one another.

Zane cradled her against the wall. She drew his throat to her lips and licked his moist skin. So good. The blood was gone, but he still tasted so good. It wasn't until he stiffened and winced that Renee realized she'd bit him.

Oh god. Something was in her mouth.

She was going to throw up.

"Shh, my heart. It's okay," his voice sounded, reassuring. Reassuring and in pain.

Renee shook her head, putting her palms on him, and pushed. She sobbed. Had to run — get away.

"Renee," his voice was so tender as he smoothed her hair down.

Her heart thundered in her ears. She barely noticed as Zane carried her to the couch, her body trembling uncontrollably. Even with blurred vision, she saw the blood, his blood. Her hand clamped over her mouth and she shook her head.

"I'm fine. I'm sorry," he told her.

Renee wiped her eyes with her other hand. Why was his voice trembling? He had done nothing wrong. She was the freak that just tried to... eat him. An awful whining sound filled her ears. It reminded her of an animal in pain. It took her a minute to realize it was her. Then that distant buzzing shifted to a ringing sound, and she worried her head was going to explode.

He drew her against him in a hug. "Renee. I'm sorry." How could he hold her when she'd just bit him? Is that what happened when someone was a zombie?

"Princess, you need to breathe. Let Zane help," Liam said from the corner of the room.

She frowned at her intrusive, older brother. It was weird he was there when she was naked, when they were both naked. Renee gave him the stink eye. He put his palms up in surrender and faded. She shifted and scanned for somewhere to spit out the chunk she'd taken out of Zane.

When her eyes fixed on the wound, it was awful and... familiar. Similar to her own, but worse. If Zane had been a human, he'd be dead. Blood still seeped from the wound. Her body shook again as she blinked rapidly. Zane pulled her hand from her mouth.

To her shock, he leaned over and kissed her. "Stay with me," he whispered against her lips. His fingers slid up to her neck and massaged it. "You need to swallow, my heart. Don't fight me, please."

Renee shook her head.

"It will make you stronger, more connected to me," he whispered.

Her heart slammed in her ribcage as the realization struck her. It was not the first time this happened. *Those words.* She squeezed her eyelids shut and swallowed before she choked. Renee sat back, wiping her mouth. "You... you fed me yourself when you made me."

"Yes."

Her throat was thick, but she got out the words. "Why didn't I remember that?"

He sighed. "Most don't remember when they awaken. Even Brie is still confused."

She flicked her eyes to him. "Then why do I remember?"

"I don't know. Maybe because you're the only one I've ever done that with?" he said with a shrug.

"Why didn't you tell me? Once I was okay with being a zombie." The taste of him lingered on her tongue. She wanted more.

He shifted on the couch. "You've never been okay with being what we are. If you didn't remember, I wanted to save you from the memory. I didn't know how you'd feel about it."

Disgusted by her actions, Renee forced herself to level her gaze on him, wanting to keep the conversation going because if she thought about what just happened anymore, she was terrified of what she would do. "You said the same things to me the night you found me in Baltimore. You called me 'your heart.' Why?"

"You have always been my heart. I've told you countless times there is nothing without you."

"But you didn't know me. I don't understand." Tremors cascaded across her body, making her twitch.

Zane scooted closer to her, reaching for her. "I shouldn't have been so rough with you; I'm sorry."

Her eyes pricked with tears. Her king might be a bastard, but the depth of his devotion and love disarmed her in ways her own issues never had. She just attacked him, wounded him, and he didn't care. Not only that, but he'd made her, when he hadn't made zombies in months, because he thought she was special. He'd fed her himself so she'd be strong. The memory was still fuzzy, but she knew he'd held her then too.

Renee wanted to keep arguing about the city and humans, but was exhausted by everything that had occurred. Arguing wouldn't resolve anything tonight, anyway. She'd saved Hope and her dad, or at least she'd tried to. She didn't protest when he carried her into the bedroom. They could argue tomorrow.

Chapter 29 - Brie

"How can we know we got our share if our queen lets the food go?" Flint grumbled.

Brie picked at her nails to keep herself from digging them into the soft flesh of his neck until she reached his spine. She imagined her fingers wrapping around the bone and breaking it so she could pull his simple head off his insignificant body. He was a selfish moron. Garren, Nail, and Hatchet tensed on either side of her.

Flint and his family were excellent at hunting herds of animals. They helped feed many horde members during tough times where there wasn't much to find to sustain them. Brie struggled to see the value in Flint's contributions as he continued his whining about not getting what he considered fair. Flint's entitled attitude had always irritated Brie. He seemed to believe, since he and his family had been integral to their survival for a couple of winters, his position in the horde was somehow elevated.

"Flint stop. I'm done with this," Brie snapped.

He sneered at her. "Of course you are, because you are one of the blessed ones who has the attention of our king. Your pack gets better food, better places to sleep, better–"

Brie didn't wait for him to finish his statement before she yanked him to her, digging her nails into his throat. The temptation to tear his head off was hard to resist. Pressure behind her eyes made her grind her teeth.

"Watch your words, Flint. Do not forget one of the betrayers came from your family. What you're saying sounds a lot like what they claimed."

Color drained from his face. Flint had cognitively advanced almost as quickly as she had, exercising leadership skills, but instead of being invested in the horde, he only cared about his family. He never accepted the concept that they all had to work together for their continued survival. He only helped when asked, when he couldn't refuse, and consistently tried to bargain for his family's gain. Not a team player at all.

"Does anyone other than our... rulers choose what the horde does?" she asked. It was odd using Renee's words, but she'd found that the horde responded well to them. Somehow, it made things easier for them to understand and accept, even the chosen. In a weird way, Brie enjoyed referring to someone *other* than Zane as a ruler. Garren perked up at her words and stepped beside her in a show of solidarity that Flint didn't miss. Behind him, his family members shifted on their feet and glanced at him, seeming every bit unsure as he seemed to be.

"No," he bit out.

"Then if our queen let the prey go, there was a reason." Brie didn't loosen her grip because the feral side of her wanted him to talk shit, give her a reason to end him.

"He never does that," Flint quipped. "Leave nothing but bones." Flint finished using Zane's order to counterpoint.

Brie tugged his face to hers, issuing a threat. No horde member put their face near another's unless they trusted them or they meant to destroy them. "It's not your place to question, only to obey."

"But... he must survive. She is... nothing," Flint said in a small voice.

Brie gnashed her teeth, attempting to keep from tearing into his flesh. Garren advanced without warning, snatched Flint's arm and snapped it. He cried out, but Brie held him using her preternatural strength. Garren hovered near his side, ready to strike, as he morphed into the hunter he was when he let his base instincts rise to the surface. Hatchet took Garren's place beside her, vibrating with energy, ready for Brie's order.

"She is our chosen queen, second only to our king. What is your purpose?" she growled at him before her gaze flicked to his family. "What do horde members do?"

Flint's partner, Levi, who hadn't renamed himself after his transformation, spoke up, "We serve the horde. Protect the horde."

She fixed her eyes on Flint's. He didn't want to say it. This fucker needed to go before he caused more dissention, but not like this. She had to time it correctly. Garren ground his teeth, barely holding on. If Flint didn't respond soon, she might have to deal with both of them.

"We are all part of the horde. We serve," Brie clarified. "Say it. Now."

Behind Flint, his family immediately repeated her words, but Flint — that prick — waited until they were done before he too, said the words.

"We serve the horde, we protect them," Flint said in a defeated tone.

Brie moved her gaze over his family one by one before locking them on his chocolate eyes. "We serve the King and Queen. We exist because of them. Do you take from yourself?"

"No," he muttered.

"How long do you think it will be before there is nothing left to hunt?" she asked, watching as Flint and his entire family blanched. Even Nail twitched near her.

"That's why we were confused," Levi piped up.

"Our rulers want us to survive. They will do anything to make sure we do. Don't question them or their choices again. Next time, we won't talk about it." Brie forced her fingers to loosen and then she released Flint.

Flint stepped back, which caused Garren to advance. Garren was still making threatening noises at Flint, even when Flint glared at Garren. Levi hurried to Flint's side and peered at his broken arm.

"You want a better position? A title?" Hatchet said, crossing her arms across her chest. "Then earn it."

"*My family* is the reason we survived two winters!" Flint raised his voice.

"N-no. Your family h-helped us s-survive, b-but l-like the culling, the s-strong would have s-survived," Nail chimed in.

Brie had to keep her expression impassive, but she wanted to give Nail a smile for speaking up. He was so shy most of the time. The only time anyone saw his monster was when he himself was lost to it.

"Your insubordination is enough to end you, even your family. Choose." Brie waited for his answer, as she enjoyed watching him squirm. "You quoted our king and his decrees." Brie's mind briefly thought about Renee ruining her with all the fancy titles from her books.

"Leaf," Flint responded, without hesitating.

That was disappointing. Brie hadn't actually planned on killing any of them, at least for now. She was trying to make a point. His family gasped and grumbled at his choice. He was usually so protective of his family; the fact he'd spit out Leaf's name so fast meant he was angry at them or didn't consider them useful anymore. Levi shot Flint a nasty glare.

Cowardly ass talking all that shit and offered one of his own to pay the price. "Leaf come forward," Brie ordered.

Leaf was of average height, with green irises and rich, tawny skin. Their hair was fashioned in coiled, golden-blonde strands that hung to their waist. They approached slowly, their hands trembling. Brie appreciated their obedience even if it was misguided by loyalty to an asshole like Flint.

"Nail, take them to the plaza. I'll deal with them soon." Brie's face tightened as she tried to control her bloodlust. Nail led Leaf away. Hatchet scooted further up, moving closer to Brie.

"Leaf will pay the price for your insolence. How many more of your family are going to pay for your mouth? For your bad choices?" Brie's eyes traveled over Flint's family, assessing their loyalty. Good. Him turning over Leaf so quickly had pissed some of them off. Brie almost cracked a smile when Levi's frown deepened. Flint was going to hear it later. It was always better to turn the enemy on itself before it struck.

The only reason she'd allowed this bullshit to continue as long as it had was because she had a gut feeling winter was going to be hard and they might need his group. If Zane had known about any of this, or that she suspected the traitors from months ago were linked to Flint's family — he would have ended Flint and his entire family long ago. She still couldn't prove that Flint or his family members had brought the traitors in and hid them, but her gut told her she was right, she just needed proof. Brie thought Flint was the problem, not his family. For the good of the horde, she had to save the ones she could. Those that continued to stand with Flint were as much an enemy as the humans they fought.

"You have forgotten Flint, we are *more*. We bear the burdens others can't. Fall in line or you'll be left behind," Brie said and backed away. Hatchet stayed close, moving with her. Garren snapped at Flint with his shark-like teeth before he finally shuffled away from Flint. He didn't look away from Flint, ensuring, at the very least, Flint knew Garren would be watching him. Given Garren's influence with the other Night Sentinels, it probably meant all of them would monitor Flint.

As they made their way to Leaf, once they were far enough away that Flint and his family wouldn't hear them, Hatchet asked in a hushed tone, "Are we using Leaf as an example?"

"Yes," Brie answered, but probably not in the way Hatchet expected. Maybe Renee's kind interactions with the horde were really screwing with Brie's methods because she didn't plan to kill Leaf as a public display as it would usually be done. Instead, she was going to have another of the chosen, Mace, take in Leaf to mentor them. Mace had been very patient with Toad in the past. He'd help fix the bullshit that Flint had poisoned Leaf's mind with. Brie wondered if in life Mace had been some sort of counselor.

"Garren, I know you like our queen, but I don't think our king is going to excuse what she did," Hatchet said with a grimace. Garren growled and snapped his teeth again. "Calm down. I'm not saying I agree, I just... I don't want you to die too."

"You think he should allow her defiance?" Brie asked, a little surprised by Hatchet's words.

"No, but... I don't know. We can't let humans survive. She doesn't understand yet, but I... I don't want her to be... gone," Hatchet struggled through her words.

Brie didn't comment because the horde didn't get it yet. She didn't think they would, perhaps Garren understood, but not the rest. There was no way in hell Zane would let Renee go or hurt her in some sort of public display. And he would absolutely *not* kill her, but understood why the horde didn't know that and why they'd expect him to maintain the status quo.

Garren started at Brie, wanting her to disagree with Hatchet and she might have if it was only the two of them. Instead, she plastered confidence across her features before she spoke, "Whatever he decides, we will follow his orders, as always."

Chapter 30 - Renee

"Renny, please don't die. Don't leave me with these assholes. I know I'm an asshole, too. I should've been there to get you," Liam's voice broke.

Renee wanted to open her eyes to tell him it was okay. She knew he hadn't meant to forget her.

"I'm sorry. Please don't die," Liam begged.

Using all of her willpower, Renee focused on her arm. Tiny tingles crept down her skin. She concentrated on her hand, and finally, her fingers. She wiggled her index finger inside of her brother's palm.

"Renny?"

She moved it again and felt a light hug.

"There's my princess. Stay right here. I'll get the doctor," Liam said.

Liam's footsteps faded before a door opened. Even with her cochlear implants, sounds were distorted. Probably from when she'd been kicked in the head. The door opened, and she listened for two sets of footsteps, but only heard a set of heavy ones she didn't recognize. Perhaps it was a nurse. She sensed the person as they neared her.

She almost felt the touch before it happened. A light caress touched her head, smoothing her hair down. Was it her dad? Did he finally care because she'd almost died? Her eyes burned with unshed tears. Warm lips pressed on her forehead. Her heart pounded in her chest and drowned out the machine noises. Did her dad understand she needed his love?

"I'll come back to you," a voice whispered, but it was also distorted.

Renee tried to open her eyes. Where was her dad going? Another business trip? She needed him. He couldn't leave now. She didn't hear his steps as he walked away. She was so stupid to believe he'd stay with her. Even her almost-death wasn't enough to make her dad want to be around her.

Renee's eyes flew open as she sat up, panting. Crap. She hadn't thought about the attack in years. Her fingers reached for the scar, tracing over the marked skin.

Zane sat up, brushing Renee's hair over her shoulder. "Renee?"

"I'm okay; it was just a dream."

His face tightened. "About what?"

"When I was alive. My dreams are how I keep my memories, good or bad. I mean, from before," she explained.

"I don't dream."

Renee peered at his face, unable to read his expression. "Not at all?"

"No, never have. Or if I do, I can't remember them." He lifted a shoulder.

Sometimes Renee wished she couldn't dream, so she didn't have to remember the terrible experiences. But other times when she dreamed about her brother, it was the only way to interact with him, even if only in the past. Her face scrunched up. Not entirely true anymore, but she wasn't sure what that meant. Maybe she was going crazy. She'd talked to him in her head for years. She assumed it was her way of relieving her own guilt about his death, but recently... nope, she couldn't handle that on top of everything else.

"What was your dream about?" Zane asked.

She was so happy he'd interrupted her thoughts before they suffocated her. She opted to focus on her father, because although his neglect hurt, it was far less painful than the loss of Liam. "My dad. He... wasn't around much."

"Did he travel a lot?"

Renee frowned. If only that was the main reason they didn't bond. "Yeah, he traveled a lot, but that wasn't why I didn't see him." She lowered her head, staring at the clean sheets under her.

Zane tilted his head to see past her hair that had slipped forward. "Why didn't you see him?"

"My parents weren't thrilled their child was broken. I was an embarrassment to them." Each word made her throat tighter and tighter as a lump formed.

He straightened as his eyebrows shot up. "What?"

"I was mostly deaf, remember?" Irritation filled her tone as she resumed her in depth, visual examination of the grey-colored sheets.

"That didn't make you broken. Is that what you thought?" His voice sounded melancholy.

"Liam didn't think so but..." She stopped. Shit. Shit. She wasn't supposed to say his name out loud. She couldn't have an emotional breakdown right now. Her eyes burned as she tried to swallow the lump in her throat.

"Liam didn't think so, but," he prompted.

"He was just being a nice brother," she mumbled and shrugged. Her fingers tangled with the sheets as she clutched them, trying not to cry.

Zane turned her face to his. "If your parents believed you were broken, they were wrong. It wouldn't matter if you couldn't hear now. It doesn't change who you are." His fingers traced the side of her face.

Renee didn't know what to say because she actually believed him. Although, since they had met, she was able to hear and speak, he accepted her despite her issues with being a zombie and her aversion to violence. He put up with her nasty temper and her pushing him to grow with her. He was supportive regardless of how angry he was and he tried to find things in a wasteland that were truly meaningful to her. It was the first time since her brother had died, that she felt truly safe opening up to someone about these old wounds.

"They didn't even learn sign language. I wasn't important enough to talk to." As a child, she'd hid the fact her parents were so put off by her impairment they hadn't bothered to learn how to communicate with her. If it hadn't been for Liam, no one would have talked to her for the first eight years of her life.

"My dad wasn't nasty and angry like my mom. He just never wanted to be around me," she whispered. "I got hurt right before all this happened. I almost died, and I thought... it didn't matter, he didn't want to see me then either." She stopped because even now, almost a decade later, her parents' neglect pained her.

"Renee." Zane tugged her to him, hugging her.

Renee felt so mixed up and the dream had reminded her she'd been working through her abusive past for a long time. Tears burned in her eyes, but she blinked to keep them at bay. She'd cried way too much and her parents didn't deserve her tears.

"Do you remember what happened?" he asked, his tone haunting.

Renee stiffened in his arms. Confused by his question. He had asked her that before, when he'd turned her. She pulled away and leveled her gaze at him.

"Remember what?"

His eyes drifted over her face before he answered, "You mentioned you almost died."

"Oh." She dropped her view to her lap and shook her head. "Not really. My parents were horrified because I had to go to therapy after it happened. The therapist said I blocked the event because of the trauma. At the time, the therapist suggested I finish high school and stay in therapy to address it in my own time. But then everyone ran out of time."

Silence filled the room. Renee knew she should pick up their argument from last night, but after admitting such personal things, she wasn't ready to go to battle just yet.

"What were your parents like?" she asked, facing him.

His eyebrows shot up at her question. "They were... My relationship with them was difficult. It was probably my fault. I was an asshole and an embarrassment to my father."

"What did you do?" She'd been curious about it since Brie's prior mention.

"The real question is, what didn't I do?" He gave a dry laugh. "I was a spoiled, rich dick that didn't enjoy being the baby of the family."

"How many other siblings did you have?"

"I had two older, perfect brothers. I was the black sheep and was content being so. My father, on the other hand, thought he could fix me." Bitterness crept in his tone.

Renee leaned forward, remembering Brie mentioned the military before. "What did he do?"

"None of that matters anymore. My history when I was human is almost pointless. This can't be interesting to you."

"Of course it is. We're a couple. I should know about your life. I know about your life now. It's travel, death, more travel, more death and... us. I want to know who you were, Zane. I shared stuff with you."

He clenched his jaw. "There's a difference. You were wonderful. I was a bastard."

"You're still a bastard, but I love you anyway. Knowing about you before won't change that."

"Don't be so sure," he replied in a clipped tone.

"Hey" — she made him look at her — "you thought I'd hate you when I found out you saved me and I didn't. I won't hate you because you're honest with me."

He frowned as a crease formed between his eyebrows. "I didn't save you. I took you because I wanted you."

Renee took a deep breath, trying to keep the frustration from her voice when she spoke. "When are you going to forgive yourself for making me?"

He shifted on the bed and averted his eyes. "How can I when you suffer every day?"

"If I suffer, it's because you're so unhappy."

Zane shook his head. "And because you are. This isn't the life you wanted."

Renee grabbed his chin and made him look at her again. "Stop. Nothing, since this all started, was what I wanted. But sometimes we don't get to pick how our lives turn out." She laced her fingers with his. "Sometimes you have to accept how things are and find the good in them. No matter how dark things seem, there's always light. Always hope, if you know where to look."

She leaned over and pressed her lips on his in a lingering kiss. He returned it with the same passion he always did. Renee smiled against his lips, delighting in his citrus taste. Unsure if it was a zombie characteristic or just Zane, but she was so grateful considering their diet.

"Now tell me about when you were alive."

He turned his head to the side and blew out air. "I agree on one condition."

She flattened her lips. "Which is?"

"Can we agree to disagree about last night? I understand you're still angry. I'm furious, but I don't want to spend the day arguing. I want to spend time with you." His fingers traced her lips before sliding to her neck and down to her collarbone.

"Can we argue later?"

He moved his touch to her shoulder and then down her arm. "If you insist."

"I'm pretty sure you're not gonna let go of what I did."

His face tightened as he paused his movement. "I want to, but you're right, I can't."

Renee considered his words before she replied. He wanted to let it go. Did the parasite demand retribution? She was curious and wanted to ask, but if she agreed to disagree for now, he'd tell her more about himself.

"Fine. We'll argue later. Maybe we can have angry sex again," she said in a playful tone, but then blanched when she remembered what she'd done.

His hand cupped her cheek. "No. I don't want to hurt you. I shouldn't have let that go so far. I'm sorry."

"It wasn't the sex that was bad, it was me, because of what I did." Her eyes drifted to his neck, which had healed but had faint marks, almost like scars.

"No." His fingers brushed the hair away from her neck. "I'm not upset about that."

Renee scooted closer to him and draped her arms over his shoulders. "Zane, I didn't mind that you were rough, really. I just can't let myself hurt you again."

"I should have realized. I can't control myself around you sometimes, and I don't want to hurt you," he said in a low voice.

Renee's lips twisted in confusion. She didn't think he'd been rough with her at all. The only difference was that most of the time, Zane liked to spend more time engaging in foreplay. "What do you mean?"

"I've never experienced anything like my reaction to you. You're everything to me." He stopped, sliding his palms to her thighs and pressing his fingers into her soft, yet muscular legs. "But sometimes... I can't be close enough, can't touch you enough; even if I'm inside you... it's not enough. It makes me crazy." His eyes darted away.

Renee understood what he meant. It was that weird thing that told her to jump on him as soon as she saw him. That pushed her to tear a piece of his soul from him and greedily tuck it away as hers. The part that reminded her she wasn't whole without him, that he was a shadow without her.

"And that's what made you so wild last night? Aside from anger?"

He nodded, but didn't look at her.

"I understand, I do. I literally tore a piece from you last night. As sick as it makes me, it kinda makes me feel better because... you're part of me." She bit her lip.

He flicked his amber irises to her, brushing his lips across hers before speaking, "I would gladly let you consume me if it meant you felt closer to me."

"Don't say things like that." Her tone was joking, but inside a shiver of desire, along with love, shot through her, because she understood he meant it. "Okay, tell me about your family." She adjusted herself on his lap and wrapped her legs around his waist.

He smirked. "It's going to be difficult to concentrate in this position."

"It just means once you've told me some stories, we can have really hot sex before we argue." She laughed.

"I love you," he told her, slanting his mouth over hers.

Both frustrated and eager when he pulled his lips away, she ran her fingers through his long locks as he talked about his family.

"Having wealth solves nothing. Many believe it's the answer to their problems, but in reality, it only creates different ones." His eyes stared in the distance at nothing as he talked. "My father was very concerned about our family's image, or rather, *his* image."

"So, he wanted you to act a certain way?"

"Yes. Dress a certain way. Act exactly as he wanted. Truthfully, he didn't want any of us to have independent thoughts. He was a tyrant."

Renee averted her eyes, taking a shallow breath. She didn't want to point out the similarities of how Zane ran the horde, that it sounded shockingly similar to how his father governed his family.

"When I was younger, I wanted his attention. So, I acted out so he would see me. I didn't care if he was screaming at me. At least he noticed I was in the room with my golden brothers."

When Zane talked about his father, it was eerily similar to her own problems with her dad. All she wanted was her father's love and attention, and it seemed like Zane was the same. The only difference was that he tried to get it by acting out.

When it didn't work, he just kept escalating things until he ended up being a petty criminal. Mostly stealing, destruction of property, and brawls. That must've been what Brie was talking about; she liked he was a thug. Zane wasn't aware of how sorrowful his expression was, but Renee couldn't help but notice.

"Eventually my father got tired of my bullshit and made me enlist in the military. It should have straightened me out, but it made me worse. Then all of this happened." He put his forehead against hers. "I thought I deserved to be a monster — until I understood."

Renee's chest tightened. "Understood what?"

"That I wasn't like the others. I was the host. That *it* wouldn't let me die." He spoke so softly she almost didn't understand his words.

"But you weren't happy about that. I mean, when you talked about it." She was confused. Zane had never presented the fact he was immortal, like it was a good thing. When he had said that he couldn't die after she killed that woman in Springfield, she thought he was just trying to reassure her.

He sat back and gazed at her, taking a deep breath. "I should have died before all of this."

Her brows raised in surprise. "What?"

"I was sick. I had cancer," he whispered, his expression tormented. His fingers tightened on her waist.

Renee wasn't sure what she had expected him to say, but cancer definitely wasn't it. "But then it's good it happened, right? I know you hate the parasite, but now you can't die." Her head spun. Zane was sick with cancer at twenty-one. Holy crap.

"Only because you are here." He released her hips, trailing his fingers up and down her back.

Shit. Shit. Again, he attributed his existence to her. Something wasn't right. She knew he'd wanted to die before. He hadn't said those exact words, but he had told her his plan. Since he couldn't escape the parasite, then he would just lead his horde on a never-ending journey to consume everything until there was nothing left and then they'd all be dead.

Renee recalled her conversations with Brie. Perhaps his desire for death wasn't completely accurate? Maybe freedom was what he really wanted, but she didn't think it was possible. If the parasite cured his cancer, then she was pretty sure he couldn't live without it. But when Zane talked like this, her heart twisted in her chest because it made her doubt anything had changed. She knew Zane didn't want to be king, but he *did* want to be with her. Did he still wish for death?

She cleared her throat. "And I want you here with me, always. Even if we fight. I need you too." She gave him a feathery kiss.

He grinned. "I don't think you need anyone, my queen."

Renee pinched her lips because he was trying to make fun of her or start a fight. With a quick breath, she reminded herself she agreed not to fight. "Only you, my king," she teased.

"I would give anything for you to need me the way I need you," he told her before he sealed his mouth on hers.

Chapter 31 - Renee

Brie pushed off the wall outside the apartment door as Renee stepped into the hallway.

"Took you long enough. Must have been some make-up session," Brie said with a smirk. "And before you tell me it wasn't like that, don't, because it was."

"I was going to say we haven't made up. Not exactly. We called a truce for the day," Renee said as she stepped toward the stairs.

"A truce? How the hell does that work? You ignore the problem and screw so you can fight later?"

Renee opened the stairwell door. "Something like that. I needed to talk to him about other stuff. We won't agree about what happened last night."

"You're damn right you won't. Gotta be honest, I'm pretty pissed too. The only reason I didn't raise hell was because Garren and the horde told me why you did what you did," Brie explained.

Renee stopped on the stairs and turned to her friend. "Why I did what I did?"

She was nervous about what Brie's response would be because she was certain any good rapport she had with the horde, including Garren, had been ruined by her actions.

"Yeah, the girl. I'd have hesitated too." Brie lifted a shoulder.

"You would've?" Renee tried to keep the shock from her face.

"Fuck yes, you really think I'm that much of a monster? Wow." Brie started down the stairs.

"Wait no. I didn't mean—"

"I'm fucking with you, Renee. I know you don't think I'm that awful. You're probably the only one who doesn't believe that about me." She chuckled.

"Damn it Brie," Renee grumbled, but followed her willowy friend out of the stairwell and into the lobby.

Numerous chosen milled around. As soon as they entered the area, many of them stopped and stared at her. Shit. Hawk's whole body moved in that weird way again—like his metaphorical feathers were ruffled. His slender, pointed nose twitched when he twisted his mouth in what seemed like disgust. Hatchet just stared at her with a contemplative expression and Nail wouldn't meet her eyes. Renee hustled up to Brie as they walked out of the doors into the night air.

"What's the rush?" Brie asked.

"Why were they all staring at me?" The distant ringing in her ears had returned and made her pause her steps. After her recent dream, the sound somewhat reminded her of when she was kicked in the head when she was human.

Brie put her hand on her hip. "Last night, duh. They figured Zane would rip off your limbs or straight out kill you."

"This is bad, isn't it?" Renee's eyes darted around to the horde milling about outside of the apartment building. They didn't seem to pay attention to either of them, but despite the annoying ringing in her ears, Renee picked up on the general unease from their gait. Not exactly stiff, but something about the way their bodies moved when they passed her seemed off.

"It's not good. They're confused. Zane should've made a show of punishing you. Or he needs to. Otherwise, it's gonna be a mess."

"Brie!" Renee's mouth dropped open as she stumbled back.

Brie strolled along the sidewalk away from the horde and gestured for Renee to follow. They walked in silence until it appeared they were alone. Renee wasn't fooled by Brie's casual posture or pace. She understood it was a show for the horde, to keep them at ease.

Brie faced her and put her hands on her hips, eyeing Renee. "Don't act dumb. You get how this works. If he's in charge and you don't fall in line, then he's *not* in charge."

"You *want* him to hurt me?" Renee's stomach turned over as panic made her limbs hot. Brie *was* still upset despite Renee believing they had made up. The ringing in her ears became louder.

"No dummy. Of course I don't. But do you have any idea what a wild group of undead is like? No king to lead them?" Brie cocked her head and waited.

Renee pinched her lips and spoke softly, "I don't know."

"You remember how things were in the beginning, the chaos?" Brie tapped her foot.

"Yes," Renee whispered.

"So, what do you think happens when a horde this size believes their king is weak?" Although Brie was trying to keep the condescending tone from her voice, it wasn't working well.

"Nothing good."

"Why the *fuck* do you think I'm here with you right now? Why I've *always* been by your side?" she snapped.

"Because you're my friend?" Renee said, sounding hopeful.

"I *am* your friend Renee. And yes, that's why I'm here, because if I wasn't, I wouldn't bother to follow Zane's orders anymore. You know why? Because he showed weakness. The horde doesn't follow him out of loyalty, you understand that."

"But he's always looked after them and—" Renee began.

"Because he *has* to. He owns us, but that's not the same thing as caring. You were just bitching about that."

"But you and the horde agreed he wasn't terrible, not as bad as other kings!" Renee implored.

"He's not, but he can't show weakness, not like that. Not with our enemy." Brie crossed her arms.

Renee couldn't help but remember the night he stumbled into the apartment bleeding out. The parasite let him show her weakness, but he'd been right. Anyone else was forbidden, even Brie. Everything was a mess.

"She was just a little girl. She wouldn't have hurt us."

"No, but her father did. He killed one of us in front of you." Brie narrowed her eyes.

How did Brie find out about that? Crap, probably the horde members that she'd sent off told Brie.

"I know!" Tears welled up and made her even more angry at herself. "I tried to stop him. I stopped the horde. I made everyone stop. I didn't want anyone to die. Why does everything have to end in death?"

The ringing intensified, and she reached up to touch her right ear, pressing on it to see if it made a difference. Was she going to lose her hearing, or was it just in her mind?

"Because we're zombies, Renee. I told you that you'd have to pick a side and you did, *yourself.* You need to figure out where you're at in your head because..." Brie adjusted her stance. "Either through Zane without meaning to, or by your own actions, you're going to kill us all."

Renee stared at her friend in shock. Brie was gorgeous, as always, with the moonlight highlighting her pale, blonde locks, but her expression was grim. She was like a beautiful angel of death, prophesying the end. But this end would be Renee's fault.

"I-I couldn't go back on my word. I told her I'd help protect her. When we found her dad, I made them all stop. He told me he wouldn't hurt anymore of us unless we attacked him," Renee tried to explain with a shaky voice.

Brie's eyes bulged as Renee spoke. "Wait. You understood the humans? You *talked* to them?"

"Yeah, the little girl was deaf and knew sign language. I tried to talk to her dad but he," Renee paused and remembered his confusion when she tried to speak to him without sign language.

Brie uncrossed her arms and approached her. "You *understood* what the father said?" she asked again.

"Yeah." Renee flattened her lips. Something wasn't adding up, but her thoughts were scattered, unclear. She dropped her hand to her side as the ringing finally faded.

"And you talked to him directly?"

"With sign language, he didn't seem to understand me when I spoke." Renee studied Brie, unsure why she was so invested in their conversation.

"Holy fucking shit," Brie said and looked up, staring at the sky for a long time.

Renee's brows pinched together. She didn't understand what she was missing, but Brie's reaction made it obvious she was missing something important.

"What?"

Brie leveled her gaze at her. "Renee, you are the silliest and luckiest friend I've ever had." She shook her head in disbelief as she stepped closer. "I was freaking the fuck out because I couldn't figure out how to fix the shit storm you caused." Brie's fingers wrapped around Renee's shoulders. "You were *not* getting how bad it was, how disappointed I was because you didn't choose us again, and how afraid I was that you were gonna be gone." Brie tugged her into a hug.

Renee hugged her, but didn't know what to say or do. Nothing Brie said made sense to her, except as she'd feared, her impulsive actions had hurt both Brie and Zane.

She cleared her throat. "I'm confused."

"Of course you are. Let's take a walk. Do you need something to eat?" Brie asked in a conversational tone before she strolled down the pavement.

"Umm no I'm good," Renee answered as the memory of Zane's flesh in her mouth surfaced. A tide of sensations rippled through her. Desire, hunger, disgust, and longing hit her in rapid succession.

Brie's eyes darted around before they settled on her. "We can't talk to humans."

Renee almost laughed. "What? I just did."

"Yeah, *you* did, but *we can't*. None of the horde. Hell, even Zane. We can't talk to them because we don't understand them and they can't understand us," Brie explained.

Renee stopped and stood completely still, unsure how to process Brie's words. She thought back to every time she'd been around both humans and zombies. She'd always understood humans, and most of the time, she got what the horde was saying. She recalled when she'd tried to escape. She had even understood the more feral members of the horde.

"I don't understand," Renee whispered. The realization that she'd been speaking various forms of "zombie" all this time and not "human" made her head spin.

"Yeah, I don't either, but it doesn't matter. Is that why he didn't punish you?"

Renee frowned; she didn't like how casually Brie talked about Zane punishing people. It was disturbing. "No, we haven't talked about it yet. I told you we called a truce."

"That means you fucked. I mean, had sex, all day. Barf."

"Brie."

"Sorry you made," Brie sucked in the air, shaking her head. "Can't do it. I just can't say 'make love' and *not* make fun of it. Plus, it still freaks me out."

"I know that's why I try to not talk about it, but you keep bringing it up," Renee said, exasperated. As she spoke, she listened to her own voice, the syllables, the cadence, and pronunciation.

"Because you haven't explained how all that even works." Brie laughed before her expression grew solemn. "Okay, so you did whatever, and called a truce, so he doesn't know?"

"No. I'm not even sure what it means."

"What it means, is for the first time we can understand humans, our enemy. We can find out how they're planning to kill us. You could save the horde because you understand them." Brie's icy irises lit up with excitement.

Renee felt the blood drain from her face as she focused on Brie's words. Although Brie's voice was higher pitched than hers, there was no way to mistake Brie's words for human language — it had never been human language. Zombie was more guttural and harsh sounding. All the words were clipped and tonal. Renee hadn't really noticed before because everyone sounded the same — mostly. When the horde spoke, they did so with fewer words and more sounds. When the more feral zombies spoke, it was more growling and grunting.

Renee didn't want to be some sort of spy for zombies. "*Or* I could try to talk to them. Maybe we could call a truce with them."

Brie laughed. Doubled over and laughed like Renee had said the funniest thing in the world. Renee frowned again. Was Brie laughing at her or just the idea?

"Is Garren okay?" Renee snapped.

Brie tried to stop laughing to answer her. "Garren? He's fine."

"Zane... did something to him. Made him double over in pain," Renee said slowly. Now that she heard herself, it was hard to talk and not dissect the sounds.

Brie stopped laughing and averted her eyes. "He didn't tell me that. I guess he feels lucky Zane didn't kill him."

"What did Zane do?" Renee wondered how she'd learned to speak zombie. Did someone just wake up and talk like a zombie? And why didn't the horde speak as well? The feral zombies were the closest to animals, so it made sense language would be an issue for them. Perhaps the chosen's brains had healed? Or at least the area that handled communication.

Brie's words cut into her musings. "What he could do to any of us, including you. I keep telling you this: he owns us, all of us. You do what you're told or you pay the price."

Renee wanted to scream in frustration. Her conversation with Brie was all over the place and she didn't have the patience or energy to deal with it. Plus, her mind was on overdrive translating the sounds into words. It was like the more she thought about it, the harder it was to understand any type of difference between speaking zombie or human.

"I didn't do what I was told, so I guess I need to pay the price," Renee growled, turning back toward the apartment building.

Brie grabbed her shoulder. "Before you go picking a fight with Zane, I need to tell you something."

"What?" Renee barked.

"I know I always make Zane sound like a dick because he is, but he's done good things too. Other than keeping the horde healthy."

Renee spun around to face Brie. "Like what?" Odd when her tone softened, she could almost use the same sounds to make different words.

"I said I understood why you hesitated, because I did too. Only in the beginning, and only a few times. It took a couple of times because I'm stubborn, but trust me, humans are our enemies. They can't tell friend from foe regardless if you try to help them or not."

"You tried to help humans," Renee said not as a question, but as a statement because she now knew without a doubt, Brie had.

"Yeah. It was because of kids. Zane should have killed me or let me die when they captured me, but he didn't." Brie lowered her gaze and stared at the ground. "The horde wasn't as big then. There were a lot of people still alive and fighting us. I disobeyed and the human kids betrayed me."

Renee's stomach rolled with worry over what Brie was about to confide to her. "What did Zane do?"

"He..." She paused and swallowed. "He sent in some of the chosen to save me. We killed all the humans, but we lost most of us and..." Brie's lips flattened.

"And what?"

"Because he showed me mercy and sent in chosen, some of the horde rebelled. He had to decide what was more important, keeping the few chosen that had survived or me, the betrayer." Brie's voice shook as she spoke.

"He chose you," Renee said in a low voice.

"Yeah, and he told me every time I thought about betraying him again, to remember what happened, the lives lost, because they were on both our hands. Mine for the betrayal and his for executing them." Brie blinked rapidly.

"But couldn't there have been another way?"

"No Renee, it doesn't work like that with us. Weakness is a death sentence." Brie wiped the corner of her eyes.

Shit. Shit. Renee's actions hit her like a ton of bricks. There were so many members of the horde present when she'd done what she did. Would Zane execute them all to keep control? He didn't even want to be the King, but the parasite would never let him leave.

"What am I going to do, Brie?" Renee barely noticed the clipped words. It just sounded like talking again.

"You need to tell Zane you understand the humans. I get you want to fight with him, but you can't like you're hoping too, anyway. The only way the horde will accept what happened is if they understand you're special and can help in the war." Brie paused and took a breath. "Otherwise, it doesn't leave Zane any other choice. Punish you or punish the horde."

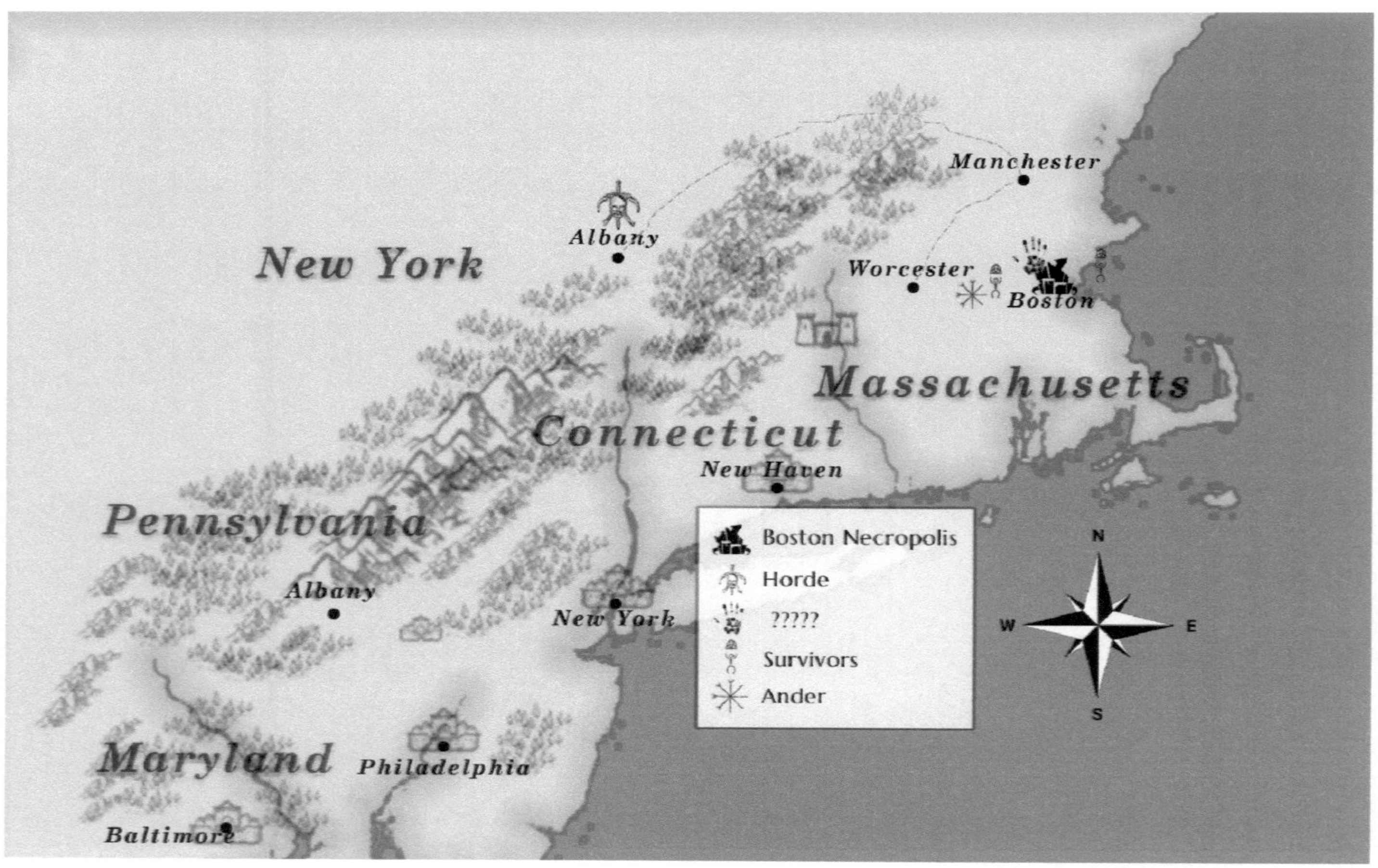
New York
Albany
Manchester
Worcester
Boston
Massachusetts
Connecticut
New Haven
Pennsylvania
Albany
New York
Maryland
Philadelphia
Baltimore
Boston Necropolis
Horde
?????
Survivors
Ander
N
W
E
S

Chapter 32 - Eric

Eric approached his group, admiring how well Valen dealt with their questions. Caleb's posture told him his friend was nervous about going into their large encampment. Zaila and Caleb had scouted ahead and discovered their encampment had doubled in size and could be referred to as a town now. Not only because of the population but also the way people had taken up residence in a more permanent way.

According to old maps, they were actually in Boston. But since the zombies took over, and the humans referred to the settlement as Haven Port, they considered it separate from Brighton. He glanced at Ander before he took a deep breath.

"You appear nervous. Are you concerned your humans will attempt to destroy us?" Ander asked as he studied Eric.

"No. I'm more worried you'll think they want to and then you'll destroy them," he answered honestly.

Although Ander's expression didn't change, his mismatched eyes twinkled with mirth. "As enjoyable as that might be, we have other business at the moment. So, I suppose, for this introduction, I will access my previous skill set to make the exchange go smoothly. However, I will not continue to do this."

Eric wasn't sure what that meant, but hoped everything didn't blow up in his face. He didn't want anyone to die, and he wanted his family to understand what he was trying to do, especially Valen. He was showing her he meant it when he promised to support her in reestablishing society.

Eric was still stunned at how well the meeting went. Ander kept his fake smile on until they reached the house, they all shared. It was a two-story, four bedroom that was in decent shape. Caleb and he had done a few repairs before they left on their most recent trip to gather things. Valen had been right; it was nice to have something to return to, even if it wasn't forever. Having a house, they called home was better than the endless traveling they'd done for years until settling there.

"This is your living quarters?" Ander asked, his visage back to its blank expression.

"Yeah, we have a room you both can crash in." Eric gestured for them to enter. "You made... a really good impression on Maggie. She's happy you're here."

"Yes, although the other male, Nathan, was present, it was easy to understand she makes the final decisions," Ander replied and moved his gaze around their living room, taking in all the details. His wolf padded to the couch and climbed on it, letting out a satisfied breath. The damn wolf took up the entire couch.

"Of course they don't know about your... minions," Eric reminded him and used 'minions' because Ander liked that better than 'undead.'

"I mentioned I had some creatures under my care but did not provide specific information. It is not relevant... yet. Once we choose the manner, we attack the undead, I will be more forthcoming. However, in the meantime, as I agreed, I will send several creatures to gather information from the undead in the enemy's territory. Even if they perish, I will still own their souls. They will be called back to me. If needed, you will speak to them to obtain the details."

Eric nodded. "Right. When do we start?"

"First, I must know their patterns. You told me the undead guard the borders of their area within the city. Is it always the same creatures? Are there shifts?"

Caleb grunted and for a second, Eric thought he might say something, but he didn't. Instead, Lucy spoke. "They didn't when we were here before, but that might have changed. We've been gone for a while."

Seth moved to stand beside Lucy, lacing their fingers together, careful to keep his claws from touching her. "I'll go watch for a few hours. I can find out what you need. They don't notice me."

"Indeed. I doubt they would." Ander's eyes flicked to Eric before they landed on Seth. "It is unfortunate I will not be able to discover your inner workings, but I suppose I can learn enough by observation."

Eric pressed his lips together, wishing Ander didn't say stuff like that. It sounded sinister and kept everyone on guard around him. Eric wondered if he'd been this creepy before he lost whoever Maeve was.

"I will rest. When you return with your report, we will plan the next move." Ander turned to Eric. "Where is the room?"

"It's down the hall, here." Eric gestured for Ander to follow him.

There was only one room downstairs, all the others were upstairs. The one downstairs had been the primary bedroom, but they all chose upstairs because it gave them more time to react if zombies flooded into their house. Heights weren't an issue for them, but ravaging zombies were. So, they used the bedroom downstairs as a guest room if they needed it.

Ander and his wolf entered and appraised the furnishings. "This is satisfactory. I will speak with you in a few hours."

Eric backed out and shut the door behind him. He wasn't prepared when he entered the living room—everyone was still there, waiting for him, for an explanation, a plan. He'd hoped at least a couple would gather water so they could bathe. Resigned, he lowered himself to the chair with an ottoman.

"He shouldn't be here. We could find a different place for him to stay in. Why is he here with us?" Valen demanded.

"We need to monitor him. We're the ones who brought him to Haven Port. If things go badly in the next week or two, they'll blame us." He tried to keep his tone reasonable.

"Exactly! We've already done enough. I don't understand Eric, why are you being so... I don't know... nice isn't the right word. Why are you keeping him around? Did something happen during the trip?" His fiery beauty, Valen, approached him.

"I know you don't believe me, but I'm doing this for Haven Port, and for us. Sometimes when things are like... well, how things are—we're living in an apocalypse—we have to make alliances, we normally wouldn't; *do* things we don't want to." Eric had already explained his reasoning, but Valen wouldn't accept it.

"Sounds a lot like what we were told by GI," Zaila commented. "It was usually right before they did something fucking horrible. Or made *us* do something fucking horrible."

Greystone Industries, also known as GI, was the global organization that had created Zaila and many others like her. Sometimes they "found" creatures when they were young and forced them into their program. From what Zaila said, the initiates were brainwashed to think what they were doing was protecting humans, but ever since the zombie apocalypse, GI had receded back into the shadows and weren't helping humanity like they claimed to. Zaila told their group GI's disappearance was a good thing because if they showed up it was game over for everyone. From what she explained, if the world got to a specific threat level, the only reason GI would show up in full force is to wipe a town, city, or whatever, off the map completely.

"He's not wrong," Seth said as he lifted a shoulder.

Eric hadn't expected Seth to back him up.

"I don't like him, but I think Eric's right. Keep your friends close but your enemies closer," Lucy said in her typical quiet voice.

Both Caleb and Zaila snorted and shook their heads. Valen put her hands on her hips and tapped her foot. Eric guessed she was counting backwards to calm down. She'd worked hard to control her temper once her powers grew in strength because she didn't want to accidentally hurt anyone by losing control of her abilities.

"I'm gonna go," Seth said and hugged Lucy. He whispered something in her ear, but Eric didn't hear it, although Zaila and Caleb probably did.

"Do you need anything?" Eric asked as Seth released Lucy.

"No." He removed his customary hoodie, placing it on the edge of the couch. His long, thick, straight black hair fanned out before he stretched his shoulders and arms. For someone so small, Seth was all muscle. Eric wasn't sure if it was his condition or naturally how he would have ended up if things had been different. Seth brushed his lips against Lucy's before he started toward the door. "I'm going to fit in. I'll be back." His voice shifted to a gravely tone as his vocal cords and outward appearance turned monstrous, like the other zombies. He flashed them his now, jagged, sharp teeth and left.

"I'm putting a ward outside of the door. Don't debate me. We can't let him stay here without one," Valen said in a clipped tone, referring to Ander.

"That's fair," Eric responded and shuffled closer to her. "Can we talk? Alone?"

"Yes, but not right now. I won't feel okay until this is done. I get your logic Eric, I just... We can't let another evil thing use us." Her tone was still angry, but he saw wetness gather in her eyes and finally understood why she was so opposed to Ander.

"We aren't kids anymore." His fingers brushed her cheek. "We won't allow something like that to happen again. We closed the gate."

"More than one," Zaila added.

Eric kept his irritation from his face. This was why he wanted to talk to his girl alone. While he loved his family, he didn't always want them around when he was with Valen. Not only that, Valen wouldn't ever truly let her guard down, except with him.

"But he... he wants destruction. The same as Father—"

"That doesn't matter." Eric cut her off. "That's not what we agreed to and I think" — he swallowed and peered down the hall, hoping Ander was asleep or zoned out so he didn't hear his words — "he wants his own destruction more than he wants the world to stop existing."

"Doubt that. Necromancers are the worst," Zaila inserted herself into their conversation again.

"Trust *me*. Trust my judgment," Eric implored.

"I do." Valen stepped closer to him until their bodies touched. "I do. I'm sorry."

He gave her a small smile. "I know you don't like that I've been spending time with him, but I needed to understand how much of a threat he was. I needed to know what he was going to do once we got here. He's going to help us." Eric softened his tone. While he was confident in the agreement he struck with Ander, he was unable to stop the nagging doubt that lingered in his mind.

He *was* positive Ander would help, but how much, and for how long, before he turned on someone? He reminded himself he'd made friendly with the gigantic wolf and attached ghost. They might not save his life, but there was a possibility he could strengthen the good will between them all. Eric didn't believe Ander would go against their deal, so if things went to shit, his family would make it out.

Valen nodded. "As long as we have each other, we can weather any storm."

Chapter 33 - Brie

Brie wandered around the streets, the dread from Renee's choices weighing her down. She understood why Renee had wanted to help. She'd made the same mistake too, been just as naïve and hopeful. To this day, she couldn't understand why she ever tried to help humans. They wouldn't ever accept the undead, not that she blamed them. They were the monsters that had destroyed their world. They hunted humans to consume them, even if it eventually caused their own extinction due to lack of food — eventually, they'd wipe out all the humans on the planet. Her life was now a twisted version of what she thought she wanted it to be as a human.

She huffed. How spoiled and stupid she'd been then. Perhaps it was her young age or her desperate need to be the hunter instead of the hunted. Even as she aged as a human, she still had to play the part of prey in her home to keep her father from discovering her plan to escape. So many times, when she was almost an adult, she could've knocked him on his ass, but she'd let the abuse continue. It was how she controlled her father, kept him blind to the changes that were happening, not just her self-defense training, but her mind as well. Changes that empowered her soul.

Reflecting on it, perhaps Zane wasn't as much of an asshole as she'd always made him out to be. Sure, he craved bloodshed like she did, but she wasn't sure if it was because it was all they'd ever known versus them both actually wanting it. At the time, it got both of their libidos running, but... Brie grimaced and slowed her steps. If she was being honest with herself, there had been subtle shifts in Zane's behavior near the end of their relationship. Signs he didn't want the violence anymore, he'd grown too, but not in the same ways she had.

It was confusing because once they'd both become zombies, they were nothing more than animals for a long time. Killing anything with a heartbeat for years. She couldn't remember specific things from that time, but even then, when she'd had rudimentary thoughts, she didn't think past her next meal. Brie frowned.

She had no idea how many children she'd slaughtered during the early years, when she had no control over her body or any of the choices presented to her. The only thing that drove new zombies was hunger. Hunger to drive the pain away. Hunger to satisfy the need to consume. Even when she was a human seeking trouble, looking for bloodshed, it never included children and it never would have. That was a line she didn't want to cross.

Brie leaned against a building, thinking about her time with Renee. By coincidence, or perhaps it was the natural progression of things, she had so many more thoughts plaguing her now. Not just instinctual ones that required she use her intellect as she made better decisions or strategized for the horde. Actual deep thoughts that caused her to analyze her actions and her words, and it was driving her crazy.

Gone were the days of marching with silence and surface-level thoughts. The horde communicated, but the only words spoken were basic things needed for survival or shouted orders when they took a city. As far as she knew, the horde as a whole spent little time pondering anything.

The chosen thought about the health of the horde, survival against the elements, their personal units or families if they had them and finding prey. Only Zane seemed to think and plan for their well-being. Did Renee even understand the impact of her presence?

Brie shuffled alongside the other chosen, stealing a quick glance at him, wondering if he was still upset with her for her mistake. She couldn't be sure when, but it seemed not that long ago that she'd let a human boy go and almost

lost her life because of it. Maybe it was an un-life? Were they dead? Were they alive? She shook her head. It hurt to think about it too much.

She smoothed her matted hair back and had a strange thought: she should brush her hair. Brush. It took her brain a few seconds to picture what a brush looked like. She wanted one of those. But how would she keep it? Her mouth twisted as she concentrated. A backpack! Her lips widened as a smile tugged the corners up.

Brie was proud of herself. She'd remembered two things today. A frown wiped the smile from her face when she realized she didn't know where or how to get those things. As they covered many miles, she kept repeating the words, hoping she wouldn't forget them. Backpack. Brush.

The scouts barreled toward them, growling out they had found humans. Her stomach twisted with hunger as her mouth salivated. They filled in the chosen with the details before Zane held his hand up. The horde stopped moving. He barked out orders loud enough for the mass of the horde to hear before turning to the scouts.

The scouts perked up waiting for their reward and practically jumped up and down when Zane told them they would have hearts of two humans. Brie pouted. She wanted a heart, but that was a rare treat, only reserved for those Zane deemed worthy. Hearts or livers, but most of the time, the chosen were given the livers for their additional protein.

The horde split into several smaller groups. She took her pack members and headed to the east as instructed. When they attacked the group of humans, it was pure joy to chase after them. Watching them scramble as they tried to get away sent tingles all over her body. A short human darted just out of reach. She followed close at its heels.

Brie scrambled up onto a pile of junkyard vehicles and got ahead of the human, dropping in front of it as it rounded a corner of garbage. The tiny human let out a shriek as Brie's fingers wrapped around its shoulders. Wet, brown eyes stared up at her as its lips trembled. The sight familiar, but usually she wasn't looking down at a human, unless she'd knocked them to the ground. This one's body was also tiny, with not a lot of meat on it.

Her brows pinched. Something wasn't right. The tiny human muttered something with its mouth, but Brie couldn't understand. More tears streaked *over its cheeks. This boy reminded her of the other one she'd let go. Her fingers pressed into the human's sleeves and drew blood. She wouldn't let another one go. If she did, she would be chained up and left for dead.*

An odd sensation made her chest feel like something stood on it. Why wasn't she ripping the human apart? None of the others even distinguished a boy from a man. Why could she? Her hands shook against its arms.

Child.

That was the elusive word she couldn't remember, but that is what the tiny human was. Once the word had invaded her mind, it wouldn't leave, and it made her chest hurt more. Meat was meat. But as the boy trembled, sobbing in her grip, it seemed wrong *to hurt him. He was food. They had to consume. She flashed her teeth in frustration at her hesitation.*

Unsure of what to do, she scanned the area and realized she was separated from her pack, but she heard the screams as they continued, which meant the horde was feeding. A tiny shadow from behind another car drew her attention. Another tiny human, a girl. Another child.

Brie froze when the girl waved and smiled at her. Her eyebrows drew together as the girl motioned for Brie to come to her. She flicked her eyes back to the boy, who bobbed his head up and down. She snapped her eyes to the girl, and watched as the child tiptoed from behind the car, her small hand holding another tiny hand, and waved again. Three children?

Brie dragged the boy with her over to the other children, expecting them to run, but they remained rooted to the spot, waiting for her. Warmth replaced the pressure on her chest. They were afraid but... wanted her near them. Her lips titled up as she approached. She loosened her grip on the boy's arms so she wouldn't hurt him.

The girl who had waved her over said something, but Brie didn't understand, but the girl's face had a sweet expression. Brie shuffled the boy in front of her, presenting him to them. The way the horde would present their trophies to each other.

Something smelled delightful as Brie stopped in front of them. The scent made her mind foggy, and she almost bit the boy, but then another child stepped out from behind a tall vehicle holding out a heart. Brie's eyes widened before she let the boy go and snatched it, devouring the heart in seconds. It was a pig's heart, she knew from the taste, but still it was delicious.

The boy had scrambled beside the girls, still shaking. The girl who had spoken to Brie before opened her mouth again, but it was all just sounds to Brie. The girl's face twisted because she must have realized Brie didn't understand and she started to make more gestures with her hands and arms. The girls peeked at the boy and then faced Brie.

The girl lifted her hand to her mouth, gesturing like she was feeding herself, which Brie understood as food, and then pointed behind them. Were they telling her where more humans hid? Brie tilted her head to the side and pointed in the same direction. The girl clapped her palms and nodded. Brie glanced over her shoulder in the horde's direction before turning back. The girl had put her hand out for Brie to take. It shook just a little, but Brie was impressed at the tiny human's bravery.

Maybe they could stop eating the tiny ones. They had little meat on them anyway and they seemed to want to be... friends? Was that the right word? Brie slipped her hand into the child's and followed her to where more food waited.

Brie shook her head. Those crafty shits had been cunning and duped her with their fake innocence to trap her. Once she was trapped in the human encampment, she'd tried to understand the humans' words to figure out why they'd picked her. As the humans tried to figure out more about zombies, they'd done terrible things to her, but Brie never complained because it was her own fault for being stupid enough to trust humans.

She'd tried several times to interact with the children who'd tricked her, but only the boy seemed genuine in his actions. Odd because he had been more scared than the others, but he was the only one who didn't like when the humans hurt her to learn about zombies. Even though her thoughts weren't as well developed at the time, she wanted to spare him when the chosen arrived to rescue her.

Lead filled her stomach as the guilt ate at her. It hadn't at the time, guilt apparently, or at least understanding what it was, didn't come until later, but they had lost many good chosen because of her. She accepted Zane's decision and understood why he'd done what he'd done, but it didn't remove the guilt. Whether or not she executed them, she was the cause. Her mistakes had weakened the horde. She had taken from herself because she was selfish and, much like when she was still alive, had escaped consequences. Others paid for her mistakes.

She wanted to be worthy of the horde's loyalty, to be the Knight Commander Renee believed her to be. But fuck, she was an awful person and not a great zombie either. However, if she had to pick, as much as she sometimes got caught up in the nostalgia of being human, especially with Renee around, she was a better zombie than she ever was as a person.

Brie recalled Zane talking about evolution at some point when he spoke of the chosen, and she wondered if she'd actually accomplished that. Had she grown as an individual? Was she finally something more than good looks and surface qualities?

Her senses picked up on Garren's light footsteps as he approached. He was always nimble on his feet, more so than most of the horde. Although most of the Night Sentinels, as Renee liked to call them, were. It was part of why they were assigned to night watch. They didn't just protect the horde's borders; if there were threats, they snuck up on them and ended them. Several of the Night Sentinels were also scouts because they were swift, smart and deadly.

Garren was an interesting chosen. Although he couldn't speak, Brie suspected he'd been having deep thoughts for a lot longer than most of them. The way he watched everything, how in tune he seemed to be with his environment and the other horde members. He didn't need speech because he got his points across with gestures and expressions. Brie hadn't known him in life, but since he'd joined the horde, his expressive features made it clear what his thoughts or feelings were.

"Hey," Brie greeted him.

He declined his head in greeting before he scanned the area.

"You worried about our king finding you?" she asked.

He grimaced before he straightened and shook his head. Interesting. He was worried but also didn't regret his choice to aid Renee.

"I guess if you die, at least it will be for supporting our queen," Brie offered, mostly to see his reaction.

He pushed his shoulders back and nodded. Brie's eyebrows shot up. She hadn't read that wrong. How in the fuck had Garren managed to be more loyal to Renee than Zane? Holy fuck, things really were changing because of Renee being a part of the horde—but why? Brie knew Zane had turned Renee, and like herself, that meant Renee would be a stronger, better version of a chosen. The closer a horde member was to Zane, the more functional, smarter, and deadlier they were. Their physical bodies were better and healed faster and their minds could work more like a human's would, even if it wasn't right away.

"I'll talk to him, try to convince him not to rip your head off. I know we can't allow weakness or disobedience, but it was for our co-ruler, that has to count for something, right?" Brie kept her tone light, but she wasn't sure she would get Zane to agree not to kill Garren. Zane was already jealous of Garren's relationship with Renee.

Garren's clawed hand reached out and wrapped around her arm. Brave fucker knew that action alone would start a fight if she took it the wrong way. It was part of why the horde members were so careful about how they touched each other. Even the more dignified chosen might misinterpret a touch and attack the person who only meant to comfort them. For all of their growth, their behavior resembled wild animals more than people. He shook his head and then brushed his palm down the length of her arm to show his concern.

Brie's fingers grazed over the surface of the skin on the back of his hand. All this touching had to be Renee's bad influence on them. "I told you before Garren, I don't want you to die... again. You know what I mean."

He gave her a sad, resigned smile that still appeared creepy because of his wide mouth and sharp teeth, but regardless, it made some tender emotion swell up, causing a lump in her throat that confused her. Garren's expression fell as he let go and stood stiffly.

Brie sensed Zane approaching. Most of the horde always sensed his approach, it was impossible not to sense him. It was like they were hardwired to know when he was near. Tendrils of awe and fear crept over her as they seemed to for all horde members. The urge to bow and show fealty surged, but Brie shoved it away. There was a time and place where she'd do that and now wasn't one of them. She had to be brave, for Garren.

Chapter 34 - Renee

Renee burst into their apartment. Her eyes darted around for Zane, but she found only empty space. Where the hell was he? She knew she was being unreasonable because he always went off and did whatever it was, he did with the horde while she hung out with Brie. But after her conversation with Brie, she was terrified he was out executing members of the horde to maintain control.

Once positive he wasn't there, she left the apartment and thundered down the stairs. When she got to the street outside the building, she was surprised not to see Garren anywhere, but then, perhaps Zane already killed him because of what she did. Shit. Shit. She didn't linger, avoiding the chosen in the lobby area before hurrying out of the door.

She started running like a madwoman, trying to find Garren, Brie, or Zane. A few chosen outside stared at her as she passed, but didn't approach. They were probably afraid to even talk to her or they'd die, too. After a couple of blocks, she rested against a brick wall and took several steadying breaths.

She was exhausted, reasoning it was all the events that had occurred recently. The encounters drained her emotionally, but she discovered the confrontations killed her energy levels physically, too. Her fingers reached for her scar, it itched again, most likely because of the dropping temperatures and drier air.

"Princess, calm down. You've got yourself too worked up. You're going to hyperventilate," Liam chastised with a smirk.

Glad to see him, but also annoyed, she gave him a sour expression. "Shut up Liam. I'm freaking out. I can't find him and he might be..." Renee stopped and swallowed her tears, refusing to bawl again.

"You're not thinking clear sis. He wouldn't do that, not without telling you."

"Bullshit, he would. He'd say something like he didn't want to upset me or argue about how he runs his horde. Damn it, this is my fault. So stupid!" Renee raised her voice to herself.

"Don't!" Liam raised his voice and shifted beside her.

Her eyes snapped to him. He wasn't leaning on the wall anymore; he stood next to her.

"Don't say that about yourself. She was a bitch Renny. You can't let her win."

"But I've made so many mistakes," Renee admitted, even though it pained her to speak the words. Finally, she understood the harsh woman's voice was her mother's. She'd forgotten how often her mom called her 'stupid' when she was little, because she couldn't hear.

"Making mistakes is part of learning, remember?" Liam's dark eyes appeared as soft as his voice.

She remembered. He'd told her so many times when she was little and she would call herself stupid. Her heart hurt again. She missed him so much. His image wavered. No. No. She'd ruined it by thinking about him not being alive.

"Please don't leave me," she sobbed.

"I won't. I'm always with you," his voice responded, even though she couldn't see him anymore.

Renee leaned her head on the wall and closed her eyelids. No need to worry that a zombie wouldn't try to eat her anymore. She just needed a minute to get it together, to think.

Renee huddled under the pile of debris. The sounds outside of the junk she'd burrowed under would have made her piss her pants if she wasn't so dehydrated. Her group had been in the process of collecting water to boil so they could drink and bathe when the zombies attacked.

These zombies were so much worse than the ones before them. They were faster and chased people more efficiently. She was almost toast twice before she got under the piled-up crap above her. She was terrified that if something knocked into it, the hill of garbage would bury her, killing her in a different way.

Growls filled the air. Even with her one implant acting up for the last few weeks, there was no way to miss that terrifying sound. It ripped through her and caused her to gasp for breath. Ice raced down her spine as her entire body froze. That growl—not a zombie. At least she'd never heard a zombie make that sound before. It sounded like an animal, a gigantic wolf?

Linny and Ricardo swore they'd seen werewolves before, and Thomas had a claw he claimed was from a demon. Even Rachel, who was pretty level-headed, told Renee that she'd met vampires. Renee wanted to believe all of those creatures existed, well perhaps not demons. If vampires and werewolves existed, then there was a possibility that fae did too — holy crap, maybe even dragons!

"Not the time, Princess," her brothers whispered in her good ear.

His voice was the only clear one she heard, at least since her batteries died in her right processor. Her hearing had always been better in her right ear than her left, but she hadn't moved the batteries over yet. Both of her processors were damaged and fragile now, so she was extra careful when handling them.

The growl came again and her chest seized up as sweat broke out over her skin, her teeth clenched to the point she worried her jaw was locked. She wanted to move, to scream, but was completely frozen in fear. It didn't matter, she couldn't see anything.

Seconds later, sounds she was more familiar with cascaded over her, smothered her. Discord, screaming, grunting, cracking bones, the odd clicks some on the undead made, and the moist sound of flesh being rendered from bodies. Bile rose in Renee's throat. Her group was dying—again.

"It's okay Renny, just don't move," her brother told her, his voice coaxed her to breathe.

Still paralyzed, she squeezed her eyes shut and dug her nails into her palms. No mistaking the awful noise of the zombies feasting, but there was also more... fighting. And more growls, not the same kind that had her immobile in terror, but what wolves or feral dogs would have sounded like when attacking.

A pack of wild dogs had attacked one of her other groups. It was terrible and left her depressed for weeks. One of their group had died, but they had fended off the dogs, killing three of them and then later ate them, because they were starving. Because Renee hated the idea and objected to eating them, the group had mocked her and told her there was no place for animal lovers.

More snapping of jaws and crunches signaled the animals might be killing her group as well as the zombies. Shit. Shit. What should she do? She couldn't fight, not really. Yes, she'd attacked zombies and killed a few, but each time it was only when there was no other choice and every time, she'd hadn't thought about anything — she just took action.

As she debated things in her mind, silence blanketed the area for a few heartbeats until slow steps milled around. Not shoes or boots of any type, which meant it wasn't any of her group. She cracked her eyelids open but didn't see anything. Renee tried to discern if there was the telltale shuffle of a slow zombie or the loud slapping of feet of the fast ones. Recently she'd noticed some of the fast ones had shoes too.

But it was a steady pace of several feet. They padded around as snaps and growls filled the area. A crease formed between Renee's eyebrows as she homed in on the sound. A small whine with a huff confirmed to her it was feral dogs, a pack. A tiny part of her wondered if she left her shelter, could she make friends with the dogs?

She'd always been good with animals. Animals got her, and she understood them most of the time. The corners of her lips dropped. Things weren't the same anymore. She'd thought the same thing with the other pack and still had a scar on her leg from when she'd been bitten. Renee was lucky not to have contracted rabies.

More sounds from the dogs broke her thoughts. The longer she listened, the more it sounded like conversation only in "dog" language. Her eyes widened. Had dogs always talked, just never in the presence of humans? But now, in the end times, they didn't have to hide it anymore? Stupid!

Renee winced at the hateful voice in her head. Okay, perhaps her thoughts were dumb, but she was panicking. Dogs had great senses of smell. She was probably about to die. She rolled her eyes at herself, irritated that her last thoughts would be about unrealistic fantasies, *as her mother called them.*

There wasn't any place for her daydreams about the possibilities of the world if it hadn't lost all its magic.

She needed to believe there was still magic in the world, somewhere — anywhere — because she was living in a nightmare and hungry murder machines were eating humans out of existence. The din of the dogs faded until silence filled the area. The stench of metallic blood, innards, and general rot made her nauseas.

After waiting for as long as she could stand to be in the same position, she wiggled her way out of the pile at the speed of a snail because she didn't want to cause the heap to topple. She slowly rose, her eyes darting in every direction, but nothing was standing.

Her fingers flew in front of her mouth as she swallowed back vomit. Bodies littered the ground. At least she assumed what she saw were bodies. It was more like... piles of meat. She identified fingers, elbows, feet, and a couple of limbs... pieces of everything. She couldn't tell what chunks had been her group and which ones were the zombies.

The dogs had done this. How large had they been to do this much damage in such a short span of time? The pack must have been large to take down her entire group, along with what she thought might have been over a dozen zombies. She tiptoed through the remains; her body shook, but she forced her steps to be light.

Alone. But the only other choice she had was to fight and die like her group had or hide and try again. She'd made a promise to him and no matter how much she wanted to give up, she wouldn't. She had to keep going until she discovered a way to kill all the zombies, a way to wipe them off the planet. It wouldn't bring him back, but at least he wouldn't have died in vain.

Renee set her jaw and jammed her hand into her pocket, pulling out her knife, opening it. She'd find a new group. She wouldn't stop until she ended the zombies.

Renee chuckled at the memory and wiped her eyes. How young and foolish she had been. Now she was having a breakdown trying to save the zombies, her zombies, for her mistake. Past-Renee would have stabbed her. But past-Renee didn't know what the future held or how things would change.

Past-Renee didn't have compassion in her heart, or rather it was being chipped away by existing in a world like this. Compared to others, she was still a softie, most individuals had turned into the worst versions of themselves. Perhaps if Zane hadn't found her, saved her, she might have gone down the same path.

She clenched her jaw. He believed he was still a monster, that his path hadn't changed, except for her, but he was wrong. He didn't have to pretend. One way or another, Renee would show him he had a choice. Unsure how, yet she was determined to help him not be a slave to the parasite. Renee pushed off the wall, even more determined to find Zane.

Chapter 35 - Zane

Zane moved through the lobby, ignoring the assault of awareness that always threatened to overwhelm him as he maneuvered through his chosen. The din in his mind was worse with the chosen versus the horde. Perhaps because they were capable of more, thought more like humans, or at least what he remembered it was like to think as human.

The chosen and horde were still predators, most of their conscious thoughts revolved around food. The pursuit of sustenance, concerned with being without it, and planning their next meal. He couldn't discern their thoughts, but their connection with him made their presence obnoxious and loud in his mind.

Inescapable.

Smothering.

Renee's appearance had woken him, dragging him back from the depths. For the first time in years, something other than the din of the horde occupied his mind. He remembered *himself*. Not human anymore, he hadn't been for years, but he somewhat recalled more humane thoughts and motivations. And unlike the times before—when he had brief moments of clarity—it didn't fade. Her presence kept him present.

He hadn't been prepared for the tumult of emotions when he caught sight of her after believing her dead. His monstrous gaze locked on her ethereal form, causing his heart to pound so furiously he worried it would break his sternum. Zane assumed it had always beat in his chest, but that was the first time he'd been aware of his own pulse in years. Renee was as perfect as he remembered her, only older, a woman instead of a girl.

Zane left the building, searching for Brie. He could find any member of his horde if he needed to. It only took seconds to focus and home in on their location. Of course, the strongest connection was to Renee, due to his emotions and how he created her.

The memory of Renee's touch slowed his steps and made his chest ache with longing. It had only been a couple of hours since he saw her, but after not being with her for years, and also believing she was dead, he hated to be apart from her.

His lips curved into a smile at the thought of her beautiful, large, curious, green eyes, her joy filled laughter, and the kindness she extended to others, even him, even when they quarreled about the horde. She had always been strong and brave, and whether or not she realized it, always ready for battle. Zane was grateful she agreed to stay at his side. He'd almost lost her twice. Nothing would ever take her from him again.

He shook his head to clear his musings about Renee before he approached Brie. Garren almost jumped out of his skin when he saw Zane. Without words, he ordered Garren to leave.

As Garren passed, Zane purposely restricted Garren's movements with his will. Reminding Garren how lucky he was, he still lived after his choice to aid Renee in her betrayal. Garren lowered his head. Brie narrowed her eyes at Zane and crossed her arms as Garren hurried away.

"You don't have to do that. Garren knows he fucked up," Brie said in a hushed voice.

Zane didn't respond. Garren had made a choice, and he chose Renee. His loyalty was to her. Zane was proud of Garren, but wouldn't tell him that. It wasn't time yet. Renee wasn't ready.

"We need to talk." Zane motioned for her to move.

They walked to a more secluded area. Zane used the time to make sure none of the horde were near them before he spoke.

"We need to talk about us," he stated.

"What?" Brie responded with a poker face.

Zane sensed her surprise because of his connection to all of his creatures. "I need to... apologize. I'm sorry... for a lot of things."

Brie's poker face disappeared. "What the fuck?"

"I haven't treated you the way I should have."

"I don't." She paused and scrunched her face. "I don't understand. Why are you saying this? I thought this was about Renee."

He shrugged. "I guess, in a way, it is. Things are different now."

"Because of her," Brie snapped.

"Yes." He didn't see the point of lying. He wasn't in front of the horde and Brie knew him better than anyone other than Renee.

"Holy shit." Brie ran her palm over her hair. "Shouldn't you *not* show weakness by apologizing to me?"

"It's not weakness, it's leadership. I don't need your fear or your loyalty," Zane told her because it was true. Brie was loyal to the horde, always. It was why he didn't exert his will on her. It wasn't necessary. She'd always do what was best for them.

"Leadership?" Brie said, full of confusion. "You don't need my fear *or* loyalty?"

"Yes. No."

"You don't need me..." Brie cleared her throat. "Leadership looks good on you."

"I didn't say we don't need you. You know the horde needs you. You're the Knight Commander." Zane's body temperature rose at the thought of Renee.

Brie's lips quirked. "Whatever that's supposed to mean."

The corner of his mouth tilted up to a small, lopsided grin. "I like it. The title suits you."

"Yeah, you're saying that because you're the King."

Zane grimaced at his title. He would never feel comfortable with it. The parasite stirred, as it always did when it heard the title, which only made Zane dislike it more. "No, because you protect the horde at all costs."

"I learned that from you, Zane," Brie said in a softer tone. "She's really changed you for the better."

Zane tried not to smile at her words, but couldn't help it. Renee was his heart, and only with her would he ever be more than a monster. His smile faded when the parasite seemed to have found joy in Brie's words. That made him more on edge than he already was.

If Renee asked him to explain how he and the parasite communicated, he wouldn't be able to because he didn't understand it himself. It was more like an empathic connection versus a mental one. Although occasionally, usually in battle, or when it was having a vehement reaction to exterior stimulus, it would *move*. It was partly how he knew it was located in his skull or spinal column near his head.

"She sees the best in everyone, even us," Brie continued.

"Maybe she sees what we want to be," he offered.

"Rather than what we are," Brie grumbled and took a small step closer to him. "You don't have to apologize. You've mostly been okay since we've been dead." She chuckled. "And before... we both hurt each other. We weren't good together."

"It doesn't matter. I could've treated you better." He didn't like to recall what a selfish asshole he'd been when he was human.

Brie stepped toward him. "Zane, stop. We both could've treated each other better." Brie's fingers grazed his arm.

"The only thing we understood was violence, pride, and pain. We shouldn't have inflicted that on each other."

"It's okay. We were both fucked up and, honestly, we got lucky. What other world could we live in that it would be okay to have violence with no repercussions?" She laughed before lips twisted and her brows drew together. "You really don't like it anymore, do you? It bothers you. Not like it does, Renee, but you don't want the violence anymore."

His eyes flicked to her palm that rested on his arm. They hadn't touched each other in years and even then, it was brief. A flash of the last time she'd touched him when they were human crept into his mind. The memory echoed with pain, cascading into other memories of violence. Unable to control her rage when she was human, Brie had wounded him more than once. He had tried his best to bear her wrath and disgust for the world, but eventually he too, lost his temper.

Was the parasite trying to get him angry at Brie?

"We cared about each other, but we didn't love each other, not the way you two do." She squeezed his arm.

Zane didn't reply, but sensed her honesty.

"We're better friends. I like us being friends," she told him.

"You do?" His voice was softened by her honesty.

"Yeah, you're not such a prick." She laughed. "Seriously though, we make better friends. We treat each other better."

The memory of her abuse faded from his consciousness. "That's true." A grin stretched his lips across his face.

"Listen, you may be my friend and king, but if you hurt my girl, I'll kick your ass." Brie's tone was still playful, but her eyes betrayed her.

"Your girl?" he replied in a playful tone, all the while he admired her devotion to Renee.

"Yeah, Renee is my best friend and I care about her. Don't fuck things up with her," she warned.

Zane placed his hand over Brie's. "Thank you for being loyal, for being my friend."

Brie's eyes widened at his earnest words. She swallowed before she cleared her throat. "You're the King I have to, right?"

"I haven't forced your loyalty in years, except where it concerned Renee."

"I know," Brie said with watery eyes and moved closer, keeping her hand on his arm.

"Winter is approaching faster this year and we can't go south." Zane averted his gaze.

"You fear him." Brie kept her voice level. He assumed it was an attempt to keep him calm.

Zane snapped his eyes to hers. "No."

Brie's expression shifted as realization filled her mind. "It's not him, it's *her*. You're worried about her."

"Are you willing to risk her safety?"

Brie shook her head. "No."

"Then we stay north. It will be difficult for the horde." The winter had weighed on his mind for weeks, with no good resolution.

Brie shifted on her feet. Her eyes darted around before she spoke, "Renee wants to go to war."

Brie was lying. Why would she make up such nonsense? Zane narrowed his eyes and yanked her close to him as he spoke through clenched teeth, "What?"

"She... she said if things were bad... She wanted to know if the horde could take another territory."

Despite the fact that he and Brie were friends, and closer now that they'd talked, fear still lurked in the depths of her eyes. It made him pause. When they had been human, she'd been the aggressor, left him with multiple wounds over the years and even then, she'd been afraid of him. He wouldn't blame the parasite for her fear. It was him. He'd always been a monster. He loosened his grip and thought about her words.

"I'm sorry." He adjusted their stance, so he held her more versus restricting her movement. "Do you want to go to war?"

"If it's go-to-war-to-survive-the-winter, then yes. We do what we have to do to protect and take care of the horde. You taught me that," she said resolutely.

Brie's devotion to the horde made him lightheaded. Zane forced a neutral expression. He hadn't taught her that, not really. She'd learned that when the parasite controlled most of his actions. He pulled her into a quick hug.

"I'll think about it and let you know," he told her.

"Don't worry, I won't tell the horde you've gone soft. Your secret is safe with me," she said in a joking tone, but he sensed her loyalty as it reverberated through her and over him. The parasite was pleased, and it made him nauseous.

Chapter 36 - Renee

She'd been searching for Zane or Brie for what felt like hours. Her stomach was churning with worry. Renee was still winded from running around concerned. No matter what she did, she couldn't seem to catch her breath. She rounded the corner and froze.

Zane and Brie were hugging each other and whispering like lovers. Maybe it was because her heart pounded in her head. She couldn't hear them. No. They shouldn't be like that. She stumbled backwards, shaking her head, trying to clear the image.

Zane wasn't killing anyone. He was with Brie, hiding from the horde. Numb, she turned and fled to the apartment building. Bolting past everyone and taking the stairs two at a time until she reached the apartment.

Renee paced the room with fast steps, smacking her ear. The annoying ringing was louder again. She kept yanking at her hair, probably appearing feral as many times as she pulled at it or ran her fingers through it. He would return any minute, and she was ready for battle. He shouldn't have touched Brie like that. He shouldn't have touched her at all.

Zane was *hers—only hers.*

She was stupid to run away. She should've said something then, but she was too hurt. Now that pain had morphed into a blazing fury. They would both pay, but first she'd teach him a lesson. Her chest vibrated and made her glance down. It was only then she heard the low rumble emanating from her. She was fucking growling like an animal.

The door opened, with Zane pausing when he spotted her. His eyes widened before his eyebrows drew together. "Renee?"

"Bastard!" She rushed him and knocked them both into the door, shutting it. She scratched at him, screaming incoherent nonsense.

He grabbed her wrists. "Stop!"

She showed her teeth, hissing at him. Her fingers curled into claws as she tried to scratch his face. He would *not* touch others. His chin trembled. Good, he should fear her wrath. No one touched her king. No one—but her. She snapped at him, trying to mark him, make him bleed.

"Renee," his voice shook.

She pushed her arms forward and kicked with her legs. The next thing she knew, she was flat on her back with him holding her down on the floor, her arms pinned to her sides.

"Stop. Please." He swallowed and stared at her. "Do you remember what happened?"

Renee stopped struggling. Unsure if it was his desperate tone, or that he asked her if she remembered, but the red dissolved in her mind. In its place was Brie's flawless beauty and them holding each other.

"You touched her!" she screamed. The sound of her own guttural voice assaulted her, disrupting her thoughts.

Zane let out a breath. "You're talking about Brie," he said, more to himself than her.

"Of course I am!" she snapped and became fixated on her voice's shift in cadence, the lack of enunciation. She wasn't speaking chosen, she was speaking a variation of horde.

"I don't know what you think that was, but it meant nothing," he told her in a reasonable tone.

It made her want to scratch his eyes out. The anger eclipsed her thoughts again. "Bullshit!"

"Stop!" He squeezed her wrists until it hurt. "I did that for you," he spoke through clenched teeth.

"What the hell are you talking about?" She fought him again and tried to knee him. Renee growled when he blocked her.

"You wanted me to be better to Brie because she's your friend," he reminded her of their conversation only days ago.

The memory surfaced in her mind. Shit. Shit. He was right. Even so, violence swelled inside her, screamed for blood, retribution. What was wrong with her? She took several breaths and closed her eyes. Renee tried to focus, making every effort to go to her happy place, but it didn't work because her happy place was with him now and he ruined it.

"There is no one but you. Nothing without you."

His words cut through the haze of rage. Destroyed it like a bullet to the head. Finally, her body relaxed under his. The ringing disappeared, and the bloodlust dissolved.

"Renee, there has been no one but you in my heart. Even before." He loosened his grip on her. "I never loved anyone but you, only you." His fingers released her wrists and smoothed down her knotted hair.

She cracked her eyelids open, almost afraid to look at him after her behavior. "You had feelings for Brie."

"Not like this. I cared about her, but I didn't love her. I've only ever loved you." His bloodshot, amber eyes were filled with the love she feared had just been her imagination.

"Why?" She turned her head and stared at the trim that ran parallel with the carpet. She was so broken and so mean. Every time he made the smallest mistake, she was horrible. Said terrible things. Did worse things. Her entire life she hadn't seen herself as a selfish, violent person, but dying had made it crystal clear.

"Because you are my heart."

Renee brought her teary eyes to his gorgeous face. "How? I can't be anyone's heart. I'm so terrible to you."

"Shhh." He kissed her cheeks and forehead.

It made her cry harder and caused her body to go limp. He moved off of her, scooped her up off the floor and carried her to the couch. Zane settled them with her still in his lap.

"You aren't terrible. You were jealous. Anyone can be jealous." He rubbed her back.

"Not everyone attacks someone because they're jealous," she replied stubbornly.

"Not everyone is like us."

She raised her head off his shoulder and peered at him. "You think that's why I acted crazy?"

"You saw my very controlled reaction about Garren." He paused. "I only controlled my behavior because I understood you would be… upset if I ripped his head off."

"You literally wanted to rip his head off?"

"He touched you," he said through clenched teeth. "More than once."

Renee glanced at the clenched fist in his lap. She wondered how he'd react if he knew that she and Garren hugged. Crap.

Zane took a deep breath. "We aren't human anymore, Renee. I understand you don't want to accept it, but we're violent, bloodthirsty creatures by nature. Our first instinct is always death."

"I didn't know it would be so hard. That those instincts would evolve the longer I was like this." She wrapped her hand around his.

He unclenched his hand and moved it to hold hers. "It's worse?"

She nodded. "Yeah. At first, I still felt human. I didn't even know I was like this. But lately it's" — she swallowed — "hard. I notice things now and want things and I…" She buried her face in his shoulder.

"What is it?" His tone was strange, like he didn't want to ask her.

"I don't know, but it's like I crave the violence and blood now. It used to make me sick and now I… I want it." Her voice broke, and she shoved her face deeper into his shoulder.

His arms wrapped around her as he held her in silence for a long time. "When did you notice the difference?"

Renee lifted her head. His voice didn't sound right, but she wouldn't look him in the face. "I'm not sure, the last couple of weeks? Why?"

"I'm just trying to figure out if something caused it."

She sat back and peered at him. "What do you mean?"

He averted his eyes. "We've argued on and off about the horde."

Renee pinched her lips. "That wouldn't cause me to be crazy."

He faced her and touched her face. "Don't say that."

"That I'm crazy?"

He winced at her words. "Yes, I don't like it."

"Why?" Perhaps because she understood it wasn't just the irrational anger or lust for blood, she'd been talking to Liam a lot more than usual and the odd whining and ringing noises she kept hearing had to mean something.

"Because it's not the truth. No one should say that to you." His fingers tangled in her hair.

Her chest tightened at his words. Not only because he meant them, but because, despite her actions and her admitting she might actually be losing it, he refused to see her that way.

"I won't touch Brie again. I'm sorry," he vowed.

Damn it. Now that she was thinking clearly, she felt like a jerk. "It's okay. I overreacted. I didn't mean it." She grabbed his hand. "It's good you and Brie are getting along. I don't like when you two fight. Aside from concerns about the horde, you don't agree much."

"I thought you and Brie agreed on the horde and I was the problem," he replied with a smirk.

"Don't start a fight with me. I guess she kinda agrees with us both, depending on what's specifically going on. No matter what, with Brie, the horde is always first." Renee couldn't help but think about when Brie told her Zane sent the chosen to save her.

"As it should be. She's the Knight Commander, right?" He grinned.

"Are you making fun of me?"

"No, my queen." He brushed her hair behind her ear. "At first I thought you were too caught up in the fantasy books you love so much, but now I think you were right all along."

His words made her perk up. The negativity vanished. "So, you want to be king?"

"No. I should have never been their king, but you were meant to be their queen."

Chapter 37 - Renee

Renee burst into her older brother's room and put her hands on her hips. The other two boys in the room with him didn't even glance at her. Typical. Everybody ignored her, but Liam wasn't supposed to. He was her best friend, her only friend.

He signed to Renee to give him five minutes, but she shook her head. He sighed and said something to the other boys, who cast a quick look at her before they walked away. She stuck her tongue out at the boy with tanned skin and dark brown eyes because he made an ugly face at her.

I waited for you! *Renee signed at lightning speed.* You were supposed to save me! *She stomped her foot to show Liam how mad she was.*

"Maybe you should've saved yourself," Liam snapped out loud. "You need to practice talking out loud," he reminded her.

Renee wanted to tell him how mean he was but when he actually spoke to her, told her she should talk, it hurt. It's what her mom and dad were always telling her... and she was stupid. She wasn't stupid and she could talk now, mostly. She just didn't want to. When she and Liam spoke, they almost always signed to each other. It was like their secret language.

Her parents hadn't learned sign language because they didn't talk to her unless they had to. Liam learned because he was the best brother. Her best friend. Best everything. But he didn't want to do it anymore. Didn't really want to play with her anymore, either. Did he think she was stupid now, too? Hot tears ran down her cheeks.

"Renny don't cry. I'm sorry. I didn't mean it. My friends are gone. We can play now." Liam pulled her into a hug. He knew how much she needed to be hugged. "Go on back to the tree house. I'll rescue you, Princess."

Renee pulled out of his arms and signed, You like them better than me.

He sighed. "No. It's not like that, it's just different. I'm a lot older than you, Renny." Liam looked out the window for a long time. When he turned back to Renee, he appeared happier. "But not so much older that I can't play with the best sister in the world. Come on Princess." He held out his hand.

Renee wanted to be mad at him, but couldn't be. Liam was the best, always would be, and he said he was sorry. She knew she wasn't supposed to be born. She'd been a mistake. Mom told her all the time and Dad just acted like she wasn't there, but not Liam. Liam said she was a miracle.

He told her she was secretly a princess in hiding and that's why everyone but him had to pretend she didn't exist; it was to protect her. One day she'd be a powerful queen, but not if he didn't do his job and protect her until it was time for her to take the throne. Until then, he would be her knight commander and keep her safe.

Renee's eyes flew open as she sat up, dazed. She scanned the unfamiliar room blinking, because the image of her brother's room was superimposed over the room, she knew she was supposed to recognize.

"Renee?" Zane's voice enveloped her, making her skin tingle. His fingers touched her shoulder.

She closed her eyelids and pulled him to her. Her chest ached. Liam had been there. It'd been like it used to be when they were kids. Zane pulled her into his lap and cradled her.

She had to stop talking to Liam. Between dreaming about him and seeing him all the time, it was like his death was recent. Every time reality reared its ugly head, she was devastated all over again.

"Was it another dream?" Zane asked.

She nodded but couldn't make herself talk. Zane held her for a long time and rubbed her back. She was floored by how much he loved her, how he was always there when she needed him. Renee pushed her face into the crook of his neck and held on tighter.

She was delighted by how good he smelled. She sniffed at him before her tongue flicked out and licked his neck. Renee adjusted in his lap so she straddled him. For a heartbeat, she admired him, tracing the blue and purple lines on his skin. She pushed on his shoulders until he fell back to the mattress. Her fingers trailed over his chest and stomach as she kissed everywhere she touched.

"Renee, are you sure..." he began.

She hissed at him and nipped at his stomach. His fingers gripped her shoulders and hauled her face to his. His eyes moved over her face with concern. Annoyed, she slammed her mouth on his and moaned when she tasted citrus and sunshine.

Renee nibbled on his lips, teasing them with her tongue until he opened his mouth. The grip on her shoulders lessened. Renee rolled her hips against his. His growl rumbled in his chest all the way up to his lips. The vibrations made her skin dance as tingles crept over her. Zane slid his palms down her arms, to her sides, her waist, and settled on her hips.

She kissed his jawline and then his neck as she rubbed herself on him shamelessly, coating him in her wetness. He hissed and made a weak attempt to lift her pelvis from him, but Renee licked his neck, as his excitement pressed against her core. She pushed her heated center down, sliding herself over his length as a tiny moan escaped her lips.

Renee knew she'd won when his hands lifted her, but only to line them up. She set her palms on his shoulders as she lowered herself onto him, a shiver running up her spine as her nipples pebbled. Leaning over, she kissed his lips and bit his lower one until the flavor of his sweet blood tantalized her tongue. Their movements picked up speed and became more frantic.

So hungry.

He gripped her ass, pulling her forward as he thrust up. It created friction against her pearl, which made her head spin. Renee dragged her lips up his neck, nibbling his skin until her teeth sunk into the meat of his shoulder. He winced, but raised his hips, sinking deeper inside of her and groaned. God, he tasted so good. She swallowed and tore off another piece of him. He grunted, slamming his hips up ferociously as he tilted hers, hitting the spot that always lit a fire inside her.

Renee threw her head back, crying out as pleasure exploded through her. Her breath was stolen as the grip of his fingers tightened, rocking them together. Seconds later, he growled and came, warmth filling her. She licked his blood off her lips and gazed at him.

Her king, the other half of her soul, stared back, panting, his golden irises filled with love and... fear. Fear? She blinked, that couldn't be right. Her fingers touched his cheek. Why was he afraid?

Movement on his shoulder caused her eyes to flick to it. He was bleeding. His shoulder consisted of a messy grotesque wound, like a wild animal had gotten ahold of him. Something with sharp teeth. His collarbone was visible from the missing chunks of muscles, tendons, and skin.

Panic filled her. She wanted to scream but couldn't breathe. Obnoxious ringing blasted in her ears. It had never been that loud before. Her head spun before everything went black.

Chapter 38 - Renee

Renee was freezing, but he was here. He held her like she was precious. She gazed up at his gaunt, handsome face and wondered how she could be so lucky to be loved at the end. Blood choked her as she coughed. It dribbled down the sides of her face.

His gold irises were tortured as he stared at her and smoothed her hair. "Shh my heart. It's okay. I won't leave. Never again."

Her vision tunneled. It was hard to keep her eyelids open. The last thing she saw as they slid closed was him.

Everything hurt.

Everything burned with pain.

Agony.

She couldn't think, she had to make the pain stop. Anything to make it stop. Something pressed on her mouth. She gnashed her teeth in annoyance, but then she picked up on something that smelled delicious. Hungry. She was starving.

Fingers slid up her neck and massaged it. She snapped at them as she tried to pry her eyelids open. Arms held her as her lips were on something soft. Her tongue flicked out and tasted skin. Yes. She opened her mouth and bit down. Blood ran over her lips as she tore into the skin.

Savage lightning hit her. The shock invigorated her and made the pain stop. Finally, she could open her eyes, but she didn't want to. Nothing had been this amazing. She wouldn't stop. Nothing would take her food from her.

When powerful hands pulled her mouth away, she hissed and clawed at the offender, snapping her teeth. Her eyes flew open.

"Stay with me," the bleeding man whispered.

She snapped her teeth at him again.

"Stop," he commanded.

She stopped struggling and blinked.

"Don't make me do that, not to you." his voice shook as he spoke.

His words confused her and made little sense. She wanted to listen to his commands but didn't understand them. She stayed still as his fingers traced the side of her face.

"One more should be enough for now. Sit up," he told her.

She did as she was told and waited. Her mouth salivated at the idea of more food.

"One more and you stop. I have to protect you," he said and brought her closer to him.

She didn't know what his words meant except that she would get to consume more of him. Sensing his unspoken command, she lunged at him and tore off a large piece of his shoulder. She hissed when he pulled her off, still chewing what was in her mouth, she already wanted more.

"Don't fight me, please."

She paused her movements and stopped chewing. The haze of hunger receded. Everything sharpened around her. The colors brightened. Every ambient sound sounded like a trumpet. Her skin tingled. The man's scent enthralled her. Her fingers moved up to her mouth as she blinked.

Where was she? What was in her mouth?

"You need to swallow, my heart. It will make you stronger, more connected to me," he whispered.

Renee shook her head. She was trapped in some hellish dream. Nausea made it hard not to throw up. He was a zombie. Why was a zombie talking to her? Her eyes darted around the room as panic filled her. An odd ringing filled her ears as her vision tunneled.

"Damn it. Swallow now," he commanded, but sounded so sad.

Renee swallowed what was in her mouth and swayed. The zombie caught her as she crumpled to the side, falling to the ground. He put his forehead against hers. Her eyelids closed. It was just a bad dream.

"Stay with me, there is nothing without you."

Chapter 39 - Renee

Renee coughed and opened her eyes. Zane's expression was haunted. Haunted the way it had been the night he created her. Even when they'd talked about it before, he hadn't told her the truth. The horrible truth that he had to use his powers of control to make her stop devouring him. All this time, she thought she was different from the others, both in good and bad ways. Perhaps she was, but Brie had been right—he owned all of them, including her.

Zane could control her if he wanted to. He just didn't. That made every awful thing she'd said or done to hurt him even worse, because he could have easily stopped it if he'd wanted to. She wasn't sure if she would have allowed his cruelty if she could've controlled him. When she thought about all the arguments they had about the horde, it was sobering because she knew without a doubt, she would've forced him to do what she wanted.

Even if she was right and he needed to care more, the fact she knew if she could have controlled him, she would have, which said a lot about how little character she had as a person. Especially considering how terrible she'd been toward him about controlling the horde. Her eyes dropped, and she didn't know what to say.

He tilted her chin up and peered at her with worry. If she were him, she'd be worried too. She was just as feral as some of the other horde members were. Renee wondered if the only reason she hadn't gone full zombie was because of Zane. Had he commanded her not to? Would that work?

"Renee."

Most of the time, the way he said her name made her heart melt. This time, his pain was so obvious it gouged her heart.

"I'm sorry," she whispered.

"You don't need to apologize, my heart."

Her eyes filled with tears. How could he say that to her when she tried to rip his throat out no less than three times?

"I made a mistake," he began and paused.

Her vision distorted, her heartbeat thundering in her ears. She was going to pass out even laying down in the bed. A mistake. She'd been a mistake. Her fingers clutched the sheets as she tried to breathe.

"Renee," he sounded scared.

She panted. Mistake. She was a mistake, just like her mom told her all the time.

"Please stay with me." His arms were under her as he held her pressed to his chest.

"Zane," she croaked out his name.

"I can sense something's wrong, but I don't know what," he sounded panicked. "You need to eat. You're still hungry."

God no. She could not bear hurting him again. "No."

"I made a mistake. I was distracted and didn't realize you hadn't consumed enough."

"No. I'm not hungry." Why did her voice sound weird?

"You are. I can always feel the hunger of the horde."

Renee blinked to focus and peeked at him. He was serious. "Because of the parasite?"

He grimaced. "Yes."

"If you tell me more about it, I'll eat," she offered.

He raised his brows. "You'll eat if I talk about *it*?"

"Yeah." She gave him a weak smile.

"You're bargaining with me when you're sick?" His tone was so full of shock she couldn't help but smile.

"That's the deal." She chuckled but was lightheaded and nauseous again.

He laid her on the mattress and stood. "Don't move."

Renee pondered what might be wrong with her and then dozed off when Zane left the room. Her mother's now recognizable voice told her in no uncertain terms she was a stupid, pitiful mistake who was not only crazy but also broken. It was obvious what was wrong with her. She wasn't meant to survive, and this was nature's way of fixing it.

Renee gave a mental middle finger to her dead mother's condescending voice. She couldn't deal with that bullshit on top of everything else. Her mother would just have to wait in line to ridicule her.

When Zane returned with some kind of cooked meat, her body immediately reacted. She might be sick, but apparently as a zombie, nothing would come between her and her next meal. She sat up and snatched the meat on a stick out of his hand before he'd even sat on the bed, devouring it.

Afterwards, she leaned on the headboard, scratching her scar. Zane studied her and scooted closer. All of her nausea and dizziness dissipated and her breathing felt normal again. Weird.

"So, the parasite gives you intel on everyone?" she asked in a playful tone and licked her fingers.

He frowned. "Something like that. It's more of a sense of the hordes' wellbeing."

"What do you mean? Like you read their minds? Or you can feel their feelings?"

"Nothing quite that informative. It's a silent communication, a sense of their physical health and general location."

She leaned forward. "Can you tell if someone's hurt?"

"Yes. I can sense their pain, their death." His tone was grim.

"You feel every death? Even the ones you cause?" she whispered.

"Yes."

Renee sat back as his words sunk in. So, when he punished them or destroyed them, he felt it too. "Do you feel the exact pain or more like you can just tell?"

"It depends how close they are to me, which is determined by how they were created. If what you're asking me is, is there pain? Yes, there's always pain. Just not identical to what they're experiencing." He turned his head away.

"But how can you function when we take a city? Wouldn't their deaths be too much?" Renee scratched at her stomach and legs. Why was she so itchy? Crap, perhaps she was allergic to whatever she'd eaten. Did zombies have allergies?

"I've learned to deal with it over the years. I don't want to talk about this anymore," he said with a sour tone.

"But you haven't told me about the parasite," she complained.

"Yes, I have. I'm able to perceive things because of *it*." He turned to her. "We need to discuss your health."

Renee flopped against the headboard and twisted her lips. She was fine, better than fine, although the low whining in her ears had returned. Zane had dressed when he left, back in his head to toe black. She wanted him to be naked like her. Sitting up, she scooted to him and tugged on his shirt. She began to reminisce at how amazing their skin felt pressed together, lost in the throes of passion, how his kiss set her on fire. He put his hands over hers and peeled them off his clothes. She pouted.

"I can't let you do that again," he said in a gentle tone.

His words were a slap to her face. She moved away, guilt nagging at her for hurting him. But her thoughts were less riddled with hormones and clearer than they had been seconds ago. Renee was certain if he'd allowed, their bodies would have been locked together again. Her abdomen fluttered at the idea, even as the sharp blade of remorse cut through her.

"Renee, no. I didn't mean..." He shuffled until they touched. "I meant I can't let you seduce me because I'm worried about you. I told you I can sense something isn't right. We don't have doctors because we don't get sick, but you aren't well."

She wasn't sick, she'd just felt crazy because she hadn't eaten enough. "I'm not sick. I feel great. Don't worry, I just went too long without eating. Is that how we get before we turn into shamblers?"

His face tightened. "No."

"Oh." She chewed on her lip. A nagging voice that sounded a lot like her mom kept repeating she wasn't meant to exist. She wouldn't acknowledge her inner dialogue and she wanted Zane to stop freaking out. The only choice was to change the topic. "I'm good now, I ate. We need to talk to the horde. There's so much to do."

"No. You'll rest until we leave."

Fine. If he wouldn't cooperate, then she'd have to pick a fight with him. "Only if you promise not to kill any of the horde for my choices." She held his gaze even as she watched the anger flare in his eyes.

Zane's face tightened. "You aided humans. I don't have a choice."

"You aren't killing our people because I helped a child!" Renee got out of the bed and put her hands on her hips. The logical part of her brain tried to tell her to put clothes on because she looked silly yelling at him naked, but she was too irritated to listen to it.

"You didn't just help a human child; you helped her father and mother." Zane slid off the mattress and stood.

"You wanted me to let a child go without her father? How would she have survived?"

"That isn't your concern. You aren't human anymore." His face shifted to that monstrous expression, leaving her conflicted. It pissed her off and turned her on simultaneously.

She stepped back and picked up her shirt on the floor, yanking it over her head. So many ugly words swirled in her mind. Dressing kept her occupied enough, she was able to hold her tongue. Her jeans were uncomfortable. She had to fight to get them zipped.

"You are so short sighted!" she yelled, stomping by him and into the living room. Her intent was to find her bag she'd tossed on the ground and get her other, more comfortable, jeans, but she stopped when she saw Brie waiting by the door.

"Did you forget we're monsters?" Zane's voice was snippy as he exited the bedroom.

"You choose to be a monster! You don't have to be!" Renee spun and pointed her finger at him.

"You don't know what you're talking about." His eyes flicked to Brie.

"I'll just... come back." Brie said and left the room.

Renee wanted to stop her, but had to finish with Zane first. "Yes, I do." She moved until their bodies almost touched. "You told me about *it*. What *it* makes you do, but you're in there too, Zane. It's why we're together." She put her palms on his chest and slid them up to his neck. "You told me you weren't really you until I was here."

"I wasn't."

"But you are now. *It* doesn't control you anymore. *You* control it. It hijacked your body, but not your soul. You're not a monster." Her fingers brushed his sharp cheekbones.

"I've always been a monster." The resignation in his voice hurt to hear.

Brie had known Zane when he was a human and yes, she had said he had been an asshole, but never that he was evil, that he was a monster. He'd been a petty criminal, spoiled and violent. Perhaps during his time in the military, he experienced something or did something awful and that was the guilt he carried. Her frustration with his inability to open up rose, but she shoved it back down. It wasn't the time.

"Why would you say that?"

"You weren't around me before. I've only ever been different — better — with you." His amber eyes softened at the mention of her.

"I don't understand."

"I don't want you to." His tone shifted to the remote sound it got sometimes, and he pulled out of her arms, turning his back to her.

Renee felt like she had no choice but to poke at him. Get him to open up, even if he was vague. At least then she'd know what she was dealing with because, when he was like this, it devastated her.

"Is that what Brie was talking about when you were together? She said you were terrible to each other."

Zane's back tensed at her words. "Somewhat."

That wasn't helpful at all. Renee circled him so she could study his face. "How were you awful to each other?"

Zane's gaze dropped to the carpet. "It doesn't matter. We've made peace with it. It's in the past."

She frowned. "I don't think you like anything from before. I mean, when you were alive."

"That's not true. There were things that made it worthwhile." He raised his gaze to her.

"Then why don't you ever want to tell me about your life? Who you were?"

"Because I was a bastard. All the time. Every day. I excelled in the military because they wanted animals, not men. I'm not proud of anything I did there. I'm not proud of anything I've ever done, except—" He stopped when his eyes got watery.

"Zane." She pulled him to her and hugged him. Still not positive, but she thought maybe something happened when he was enlisted that now caused him so much shame.

"Why do you keep asking me who I was? The past doesn't matter. I don't have to be that. With you I can be better, what I wanted to be," he said in a quiet voice.

Renee said nothing. Zane didn't understand who he was still influenced his decisions now, making him so cold at times. It wasn't just the parasite, it was him. Maybe the parasite pushed his buttons and brought out his inner demons, but as long as they plagued him, he would never escape the cycle of pain.

Chapter 40 - Eric

Seth waited while Gina aided him, healing his injuries as well as the cells that had broken down when he'd allowed himself to be more of a zombie than person. Ander still hadn't come out of the guest room and they were all back in the living room.

"We have a problem. The zombies are being controlled by another," Seth rasped out.

"Another zombie or a necromancer?" Valen asked.

"Another zombie." Seth's vocal cords were smoother again.

Eric furrowed his brow. He'd wondered about that ever since they started migrating in large groups. It didn't make sense they would stay together for long periods of time if something or someone wasn't in charge of them. But how was a zombie smart enough to lead a group? He'd seen some that were more intelligent than most of them, it made them more deadly and better hunters. But if one of them was in charge... how would that even work?

"Most of them didn't know I wasn't supposed to be there, but some of them seemed to talk to each other," Seth explained as Lucy sat beside him. He took her hand, now that his claws had receded.

"Wait. Talked to each other?" Zaila perched forward on the couch. Caleb shifted beside her with a frown.

Seth nodded. "I didn't understand anything, but they expected me to. When they realized I didn't, I had to hide. Some other zombie, a big bastard, came out and was yelling at them, smacking them around."

"Did you understand what that one said?" Zaila asked.

Seth shook his head. "No, it was the same kind of sounds. It sounded like nonsense to me, but I could tell it was about me from the gestures."

"This is bad. Fuck, this is shitty news," Valen grumbled near him. "Zombies were bad enough, but now they talk to one another?"

"How did you know he was in charge?" Eric asked.

"I followed him after the others left." Seth picked up his hoodie and ran the tips of his fingers over it.

"Why didn't they find you?" Eric knew that some zombies over the years, the fast ones, had better senses than the others. They were better at tracking.

"He covered himself in their stink," Zaila complained.

"It got me far enough in there to see he was the one calling the shots. After I watched him order zombies around for a while, I left."

"What did he have the other zombies doing?" Eric wasn't sure what complications it would cause, but it definitely was going to make things harder.

Seth's face scrunched up. "All kinds of things. Labor tasks like carrying things around, patrols, and some went in and out of buildings. They'd take things into the buildings but come out empty-handed."

"What were they carrying?" Valen asked, scooting closer to him.

Seth shrugged. "Clothes, water, dried goods? I wasn't close enough to get more details."

"Water? Dried goods? Why would zombies need either of those?" Valen mused.

Eric balled his hand. It made no sense because zombies didn't need clothes, water, or dried goods. Something wasn't right. Damn it. Worse, he would have to tell Ander because it meant they would have to approach the situation differently.

"This is good info, Seth. I'm not sure what it means yet, but thanks for doing this," Eric told him. He acknowledged when his friend did things to help them. It was important to Seth because he wanted to be seen as helpful and he'd made it clear that he was loyal to a fault with his family. The least Eric could do was appreciate his actions.

"What are we going to do, Eric?" Lucy asked, uncertainty in her big eyes.

"I need to think about it and talk with Ander." His view slid to the hall. Valen's lips pursed at Ander's name, but she didn't comment. Eric rose to his feet and brushed Valen's long hair over her shoulder. "I'll let you know soon. Get some rest."

Eric padded down the hall, keeping his back straight so he didn't appear frightened, but he was, uncertain how Ander would take the news about the zombies. A good portion of the reason he'd agreed to help was because he wanted the zombies, or at least some of them. Eric understood he'd take the souls of at least a few of the humans in Haven Port, but Eric had agreed to that for Ander's help. Knowing that one of the zombies was ordering around others meant they may be the kind Ander couldn't control, and that was a problem.

With a deep breath, he raised his hand and brought his knuckles against the wood door panel. Seconds later, the door opened and Ander stood there with all his glowing marks on display. Eric tried to wipe his expression from his face, but he'd never seen Ander with only pants on.

Not only did the glowing marks make him want to squint, he realized he hadn't imagined how *many* there were. It was hard to see Ander's actual skin because it seemed more glowing symbols than anything else. But he'd been correct. From Ander's waistband all the way up to his face, he was covered in sigils.

Eric had known Ander was thin, near skeletal, but it was almost repulsive because he was little more than bones covered with skin. How could he wield the strength he did? Perhaps at one point Ander had been human, but not now. A human couldn't live like that, wouldn't still be breathing.

Eric cleared his throat as his eyes flicked to the floor behind Ander. He'd drawn a bunch of symbols on it and created a circle. Crap, he was using magic in the house. Valen wouldn't like that. "We need to talk. I have information."

Ander stepped back and gestured for him to enter. Eric grit his teeth and entered the room.

Chapter 41 - Zane

Zane hovered in the kitchen area, waiting for Brie to return so they could discuss what happened when they took the city, they currently occupied. The horde was restless and wanted answers. He couldn't read their thoughts, but he sensed their restlessness. The corners of his mouth tilted down when he recalled Renee's words about being intuitive about similar things.

Had he somehow cursed her even more than the rest? By trying to strengthen her more than his other creatures, bonding her more to him because he was selfish—had he created an even more dangerous predator? His jaw clenched. The idea of burdening Renee with being more like him versus his chosen made Zane want to throw himself out of the window above the sink that he was currently staring out of.

He let out a breath for all the good it would do. He still wouldn't die. The parasite would simply hijack his body and force the movements to break his fall or soften the blow as he hit the concrete. His bones might shatter, but the parasite would protect his head and force him to suffer until he healed enough to move. Then it would encourage Zane's appetite because he needed to heal and rebuild his body, which would cause him to go on a rampage, consuming any living thing in his path. He closed his eyes. Immortality was a bane.

Watching her gasping for breath was agonizing, the light slowly leaving her eyes. He'd wanted to stay with her so she wouldn't die alone. It was all he could give her.

Except he refused to accept a permanent death for her.

The moment her fingers brushed his cheek, everything stopped. The chaos in his mind, the noise of his horde, even the presence of it, faded. For the first time since he had become this creature—he felt like himself. It was as if she'd breathed life into him again.

He understood he would not return to who he was and part of him was relieved. He didn't want to be that person, he never had. It was only with her he could be more.

She hadn't changed, even after the hardships she must have suffered over the years. Terrified and bereft, she still sought to comfort others. Her motivation had been to ease his sadness. The monster who would destroy her, devour her, the reason her world had been ruined and yet...

Zane had never watched one of his creatures die and reawaken. He'd never had any interest in witnessing it. For her he would do anything, even if it meant he had to bear her hate when she rose. At least she would still exist. If she existed, there was a chance.

She shivered, and he drew her closer, smoothing her hair back, wanting to do more, but didn't know what he could do to ease her transition. "Shh my heart. It's okay. I won't leave. Never again."

As the words left his lips, an expression of relief covered her face and her eyelids dropped shut. Moisture collected in his eyes. He understood she would return to him because he'd cursed her to his existence, but still, his heart twisted in his chest.

Unsure how long he held her before small flickers of movement caused her appendages to twitch, before she made pained noises and trembled in his arms. Her skin lost all color as her body temperature cooled. He rocked her and tried to focus on the surrounding sounds; he tried using his horde-sense to see if the city was safe for her yet.

When Renee woke, she would be ravenous, as they all were. None of the other undead he had spoken with recalled when they rose or their first meal.

However, Zane had witnessed enough fresh creatures to understand their primary goal was food. He frowned. That was always their goal—it was tedious.

Renee shook in his arms and made adorable, animalistic grunts and growls. Others may have not found them endearing, but everything she did made his heart flutter, it also meant she was coming back to him, where she was always meant to be.

Zane repositioned them so she sat in his lap. She was his and he would fill her needs, no matter what they were. Her movements grew more violent. She hissed at him. He lifted his hand to massage her neck, coaxing her to him.

With her eyes still closed, she snapped at his fingers. He almost chuckled, guiding her lips to his neck, close to where he'd bit her. Her tongue flicked out and licked him. He knew she was tasting him to see if he was edible, but it still made him lightheaded.

He grit his teeth as she tore into him. It wasn't as gentle or precise as he'd been. She was in a frenzy and ripped several chunks out of his soft tissues. Despite that, her satisfied sounds made him happy. He braced himself as she ripped another piece of him off. It would strengthen her, make her more connected to him. Even if she hated him when she regained her senses, they would be more united than any of his horde. If it had to be only that — it would be enough. She would live and he would have a basic awareness of her. He wanted more but would settle just to have her still breathing.

Renee clung to him and dug her nails into his flesh as she consumed more of him. Part of him considered letting her continue, but he had to deal with the horde and wouldn't allow them to see him like this. He gripped the back of her neck and tugged her away when her mouth was full.

She hissed, clawed, and snapped at him. Her glowing, green irises were full of fury. Moments ago, he was confident in his decision, but seeing her in this state broke his heart. Had he damned her? Destroyed the parts he loved most by turning her into this?

"Stay with me," he whispered.

Her response was to snap her teeth at him again.

No. He wouldn't allow her to lose herself to the violence. Drawing on his innate ability to control the horde, he spoke, "Stop."

Renee stopped and stared at him, waiting for his next command. When he didn't give one, she blinked. His fingers traced the side of her face.

"Don't make me do that, not to you," his voice shook as he spoke. He didn't want to control her like the others. He wanted her as she'd always been compassionate, fiery, with her head in the clouds and her heart open.

"One more should be enough for now. Sit up." He wanted to get this over with so she would rest and heal. She hurried to obey him. "One more and you stop. I have to protect you." He tugged her closer to him.

She lunged at him and tore off a large piece of his shoulder. He pulled her off while she chewed his flesh and she glared at him. His beautiful, feral queen.

"Don't fight me, please," his voice was barely above a whisper.

Renee stopped chewing and froze in place. Her eyes became clear and her expression sharp. He assumed her senses were already more acute. She was advancing much more quickly than the other creatures, even his chosen. Her fingers moved up to her lips as she blinked. Confusion scrunched up her face. She almost looked like his Renee.

"You need to swallow, my heart. It will make you stronger, more connected to me."

Renee shook her head as horror replaced confusion. Her eyes darted around the room. Her shaking hands balled up as she sucked in breath, her lips trembled with each breath.

He wouldn't let her have a panic attack. No choice but to command her. He clenched his jaw before he spoke. "Damn it. Swallow now."

She immediately swallowed and swayed. He caught her as she crumpled and put his forehead against hers. Her eyelids slid closed.

"Stay with me. There is nothing without you."

Chapter 42 - Renee

"So, are you done? Did you" — Brie made a gagging sound and then laughed — "make up?"

"Brie," Renee chided and shook her head.

"I'm trying to lighten the mood. That motherfucker looks as grim as death." Brie scratched her head. "Of course, to some people, I guess he is death."

"Brie," Zane said in a tone that made Renee think of a dad chastising his child.

Renee giggled, but then stopped when they both turned to her. She wasn't sure if it was the tension she held from being disoriented, but she was struggling to control her outward reactions. The urge to run and search for... something made her twitchy. Her legs bounced in front of her and she couldn't seem to make them stop.

Zane rubbed his forehead before he lowered into a chair near the couch. Renee frowned. Why didn't he sit with her? Her gaze wandered to his neck. It was healed, but a faint scar that hadn't existed before was there.

"We need to talk about what happened with the humans." His tone was strained.

Brie sat on the couch with Renee, but far enough away that they didn't touch. She glanced at Renee's bouncing knee. "Are you going to punish her or the horde?"

Renee's eyes widened at Brie's words. It bothered her how comfortable Brie seemed about punishing her. Renee flattened her lips and crossed her arms.

"I will not publicly punish Renee," Zane said with an unreadable expression.

Publicly punish her? What in the hell did that mean? He'd spank her in private? Renee's stomach bunched as her knees picked up speed, going up and down.

"So, it's the horde then," Brie said in a despondent tone. "Do you need me to round them up?"

"Wait. Wait. Wait. We're *not* doing that. I helped Hope! I'm the one that gave my word to her, only *I'm* responsible. The horde only listened to me because…" Renee stopped because she wasn't sure what to say next.

"Because you're their queen. They obey you the way they obey me," Zane finished.

Renee couldn't get a read on his tone, but he didn't sound irritated or like he was mocking her. It was just him stating facts. After her decision to help the humans, she didn't feel much like a queen.

"Did you tell him how you could communicate with them yet?" Brie asked.

Shit. Shit. She'd meant to as soon as she saw him, but then she found Zane and Brie hugging, and then she was hungry. She swallowed. Too much had happened in a short amount of time. It was making her scatterbrained. Her legs slowed their movement as she tried to figure out how to explain the exchange.

"Communicate?" Zane prompted.

"Yeah, it was how I knew that Hope's dad wouldn't attack us unless we attacked first," Renee said, rubbing her stomach, feeling nauseous anew.

Zane pitched forward in the chair. "What?"

"Renee can talk to the humans. She *understands* them and they understand her. Well, kinda." Brie crossed one graceful leg over the other. A smug expression filled her face.

His eyes widened. "You understand when humans speak?"

Her legs stilled. "I thought everyone could, and you just didn't care." Renee lifted a shoulder. "I tried to talk to her dad. He didn't understand what I was saying, but since his daughter was deaf, he understood what I signed to him."

Zane let out an exaggerated exhale and sat back. He stared at her for a long time. Brie busied herself by picking at her nails. Renee rubbed her upset stomach and tried to ignore how lightheaded she was. A tiny fire of panic grew in size each minute that passed.

Was she sick? Of course, she'd be the one zombie that was damaged and would be ill. She'd been broken her whole life. Her eyes dropped to the floor, she had to pull it together, she refused to have a breakdown in front of them.

"So, I was thinking with Renee's help, we could finally know what they planned. Figure out their next move." Brie leaned forward. "Of course, our queen isn't interested in that. She wants to make a truce."

"A truce?" Zane's voice was loud and drew Renee's attention. It was like the resonance reached into her chest and demanded her focus on him. His rage spread like an invisible force that permeated the space between them. Most of the time, it would unnerve Renee, but at the moment it made her body heat.

Brie flicked her hair over her shoulder. The movement broke Renee's fixation on Zane. "Yep. She got that guy to agree to not kill us when he left, so who knows?" She gave Renee a small grin.

Zane gnashed his teeth. "The scouts confirmed he and his daughter made it to safety. And now he's aware not only that we are capable of thought, but we communicate!"

Renee startled when he raised his voice again. From how Brie made it sound, he should be happy she understood humans, but perhaps it was because she wanted to make peace, not war. A nudge in her mind, almost imperceptible, pushed back as the word "war" repeated in her mind. As it did, warmth spread throughout her chest.

She flicked her eyes to Zane and sucked in her breath. He looked the same, but his appearance reminded her of when they first met, more a monster than man. Shit. Shit. He was barely controlling his anger. His reaction was terrifying but also urged her to be near him, to soothe him, which made no sense.

"Do you know how this horde has survived? Maintained its size despite the challenges?" His bright, amber irises locked on hers.

"No," she whispered.

"Because we don't leave any humans alive!" His fist struck the chair. The chair made an odd cracking sound and shifted under his weight. "They can't destroy us because they know nothing about us." He leaned forward in the chair. The light from the windows made his cheekbones and chin more pronounced. "They understand shamblers, perhaps even zombies, but not *us*. Not *my* horde."

The way he'd said zombies with such disdain... And when he'd called them his... he *was* their king. Zane might not be aware of it, but he did care. Holy shit, he cared a lot. She pinched her lips. Or was it the parasite? She blanched. Was she talking to Zane or the parasite?

"She made a mistake, but she also understands them. It changes everything. Our horde is different because of you. *He* doesn't have anyone who understands them," Brie said pointedly. "It might change the winter for us. If we planned well, we could take the city from him."

Zane's head snapped to Brie. He growled at her, fucking growled at her, but Renee shivered when she understood what he meant. That sound meant he was confirming Brie's words. He agreed with her. That didn't make sense, it was only a sound. But she understood it like he'd used words.

Was that horde language? Maybe it was parasite language? Her head hurt. She knew Zane didn't want to accept her emotional instability, but she was pretty sure she was having a mental break. Unlike when she discovered she was a zombie, this felt different. She supposed her humanity was rejecting what she didn't want to see, but this... it was like drowning.

Renee tried to ignore how the nausea and lightheaded feeling evaporated and was instead filled with excitement. Bone tingling elation at the idea of going to war with a rival to take a city. Her chest once again blossomed with warmth. *What?* Her hand shook as she raised it to her lips. She hated violence. Except... perhaps she didn't anymore.

Her mind continued racing. Barreling down a synaptic road so quickly, the signs were blurred. It didn't matter, all the signs would tell her she was on her way to crazy or maybe Hell. She couldn't process everything that had happened. Zane's reaction confirmed there was a rival. How in the hell did she understand that?

Brie turned to her and winked. She was giving Renee what she thought she wanted. Everything was backwards. Renee's eyes darted around the room. Was this a dream?

Liam lounged in a corner near them, his dark irises filled with mischief. "It's okay Renny, queens go to war sometimes. Don't be scared; it's for your people."

She shook her head no and glanced at Brie and Zane. They were having some type of weird, silent conversation and weren't paying attention to her. Liam's appearance unsettled her. He had shown up around Zane before, but those were extreme circumstances; him being there now was too much.

Liam moved closer, standing next to Zane like a loyal advisor. "Bigger picture, remember?"

"Not now, I c-can't think," she whispered.

"Don't be like that. I have some ideas. I'm the Knight Commander and am supposed to help plan." Liam said before he strolled over to Renee and sat between her and Brie.

She blinked at him, but his image never wavered. He seemed solid. Renee shook her head no again. "I don't want to talk about this right now."

"I know, but it's getting cold. We need to plan, Princess," Liam said in a tender tone.

Renee slapped her palms over her ears. "I said not now Liam!"

Brie's head snapped to Renee; her ice-blue irises filled with confusion. Liam's image wavered and faded with Brie's sudden movement. Shit. Shit. Renee didn't see Zane staring at her, but she sensed the weight of his gaze. She forced her stiff arms down to her side and stood.

"I'm tired. We can talk later," she mumbled, turning away.

Renee took a few shallow breaths before her hand clasped the bedroom doorknob to enter the bedroom. The room spun around her, but she forced her feet forward and into the bedroom, closing the door. She let go of the door, stumbling forward before she crumpled to the floor. Everything went white.

Chapter 43 - Renee

Her eyelids cracked open to find both Zane and Brie hovering over her. She reached up, scratching her head, and then cleared the sleep from her eyes.

"Renee!" Brie leaned over; her pretty features pinched with worry.

"What time is it?" Renee croaked.

"You've been out a full day. You scared the shit out of us. Why didn't you tell us you felt like you were going to pass out?" Brie demanded.

"I didn't know."

"The fuck you didn't. You acted really weird, then said even weirder shit, and then we heard you hit the floor. We don't pass out. Why did you pass out?" The edge in Brie's voice could have cut through steel.

"I was just tired," Renee offered with a small, sleepy smile, ignoring her mother's shitty commentary in her mind

"I need you to find something for her to eat," Zane's voice said beside her.

The sound of his voice drowned out her mother's and made her insides stop shaking. The timbre of it caressed her and caused her limbs to relax under the sheets.

"Right. Okay, but only because I need you to get better." Brie grabbed her hand, squeezing it until it hurt. "Please don't fucking die." Brie's voice cracked.

"I promise I'm not dying, Zane would know," Renee answered and turned her head to Zane. "Right?"

"Yes, I would know. Now get the hell out. Renee and I need to talk," he barked at Brie.

Brie frowned and leaned over to hug Renee. "I'll be back soon." She got up and cast a nasty glare at Zane. "Don't be an asshole to her."

As soon as the door closed, Zane scooped Renee into his arms and held her. With a gentle squeeze, he laid her down, stretching his body beside hers, facing Renee His fingers traced over her body, like he had to keep touching her to make sure she wouldn't disappear.

Fear eclipsed his features and tightened the corners of his eyes. "You aren't dying, but you're sick. I don't know what to do."

"Is that why you're not yelling at me about the humans?" she asked.

"Damn it Renee, I don't care about any of that. You're all that matters to me." He kissed her cheeks and gave her a feathery kiss before he settled on his back beside her.

"You were pretty angry earlier." She bit her lip. Why couldn't she ever keep her mouth shut? Perhaps this was the real reason she had trouble making friends. She never knew when to stop talking. The thought almost made her laugh because the only reason people believed she was "quiet" or "nice" when she was younger was because she rarely spoke out loud. Not because she couldn't, but at the time she was more comfortable signing. Once she grew more comfortable hearing her own voice after she got implants, she never shut up.

"You can't be serious." He blew out a breath. "Why are you trying to argue with me?"

"Was that you or *it*?" she challenged him.

Zane rolled onto his back with a frown. "I don't want to talk about this."

"Yeah, I don't either, but I need to know who, or what, I'm dealing with when you're not worried, I'm going to die."

He turned on his side and pulled her against him. "Don't say that. Don't ever say that." His panic and desperation filled the sliver of space between them.

"You said you'd know if I was going to cease to exist," she reminded him.

He grimaced and tightened his grip on her. "I should also sense what's wrong and I don't."

"I'm not dying. I just don't feel great, well sometimes I don't. I won't leave you," Renee stated with confidence, because it was the truth. He was hers and nothing would separate them.

His fingers drifted down her sides as he gazed at her. "Why were you talking to Liam?"

Shit. Shit. She chewed on her lip. Unsure how to answer him, she didn't want to tell him she was unstable. He was already worried enough. She also didn't want to admit how bad things in her mind had gotten over the past weeks. Although she missed Liam, and wanted him near, he was appearing more and more often when she wasn't thinking about him. "I... miss him sometimes."

Zane's fingers touched her cheek as he studied her. "Does he answer you?"

She blinked rapidly, but the tears came anyway, before she averted her gaze. "Sometimes."

He put his forehead against hers and closed his eyes. His fingers trembled on her neck. "Do you want to go to war?"

Renee pulled back at his question; it wasn't what she'd expected. Again, lightning traveled down her spine to her toes at the idea of war. Warmth blossomed in her chest and raced down her limbs. He opened his eyes, staring at her. She tried to turn away, but he wouldn't let her. Their eyes locked.

"Why?" he choked out.

Renee tried to wiggle out of his arms, but he kept her immobile. She wanted to break eye contact, but was compelled not to. Was he doing that? Her lips trembled as he saw through her—into her soul. Something shattered in his eyes, broke him into pieces. It reminded her of when they briefly broke up and he sunk into the depths of despair.

"You want the bloodshed, the violence, the victory," he said in awe and then released her.

Renee recoiled from his words. She hated his words, even if they were true. No way would she admit that to him or anyone else.

"My heart, what have I done to you?" The anguish inside him unleashed metaphorical tentacles that wrapped around him, cutting him off from her, from them, destroying her.

She scooted as far away from him as possible without falling off the bed. Broken. He believed she was ruined. Everything in her screamed for her to lose it, completely break so everything would stop.

The door opened and Brie held a large stick with meat on it. Renee wanted to continue with her pity party, but her stomach had other ideas. She bolted up, snatching the stick from Brie and started chewing on the meat.

"Damn Renee, you should've told me this prick hadn't fed you. I would've made sure you weren't so hungry."

Renee didn't respond, too lost in her yummy meal. It wasn't until she'd finished and licked off her fingers that embarrassment set in. Also, the fact she had eaten recently and also attacked Zane made her feel even more like a savage. No wonder Zane thought she was ruined.

"Yeah, I think that's all that was wrong with me." Again, Renee was positive she could run a marathon or take on anyone who chose to pick a fight with her. The same euphoric sensation as before filled her. She padded to the window, peeking out from behind the curtain. It was a sunny, cloudless day. "We should head out. I think we could cover a lot of miles before the sun sets."

"No," Zane said and crossed his arms over his broad chest.

Renee turned, facing them. "It's only going to get colder."

"Where we are headed is colder," he snapped.

"True, the city is on the water," Brie commented.

"We need to do what's best for the horde," Renee said, crossing her arms, mimicking him. With her new found energy from eating, she was ready to go to battle with Zane.

"You're not in any condition to travel," he growled at her.

"I'm their queen and I can decide for myself!" She widened her stance, squaring her shoulders. Confidence fueled her, all the insecurities from moments ago had vanished.

He narrowed his eyes. "You may be their queen, but I am their king." He stalked to her until he stood towering in front of her. "You aren't thinking clearly. I won't allow them to leave."

She glared at him, jutting her chin out. "We're in Albany."

He bared his teeth. "I thought you weren't ready for the challenge?"

A nudge, an insistence inside her, assured her she was. "I won't let them starve!"

"And you think war will solve that?" he bit out.

"Yeah, it will." She swallowed, light-headed again. "Some of us will die and that will ease the burden for the others. Whoever survives will have more food and shelter until spring." Her words sounded confident, but made her sick to her stomach. Conversely, excitement made every cell inside her resonate with determination and energy.

"You're that bloodthirsty?" he asked in disbelief.

She raised her chin. "You're afraid. I'm not. If you won't lead them, *I will*." Where in the hell was all this coming from? She wasn't fit to lead the horde. Send them to war?

"Bigger picture Renny. You're doing a good job," Liam said. He stood beside Brie.

Zane's body shook with fury. The way he glared at her made her want to crawl into a hole and never come out. His irises brightened until it was like staring into the sun. The planes of his face sharpened to the edge of a razor. She wanted to take back her words, but it was too late. She used all of her willpower to stay put and not cower.

"If war is what you want, then you'll have it," he spat out in disgust. "I lead the horde, and we travel how and when I want. When we get to the city, Brie leads the charge. She's the knight commander." He backed up before turning to the door. "Since you want war, you'll do as you're told with the humans. They're part of your war, too. They aren't our allies, just another enemy." He stomped out of the room, slamming the door behind him.

Several seconds of silence passed before another door slammed, signaling that Zane had left the apartment.

"Holy fucking shit Renee!" Brie bounced on her feet before she hugged her.

Everything felt surreal, leaving Renee dazed from the interaction.

"You're so damn lucky you're... you. He'd have killed anyone else talking shit like that. I was ready to beat his ass, but I think that's the first time he actually wanted to hurt you. Your balls are bigger than any man's I've ever met."

"I need... I need to pack," Renee said, more to herself than Brie.

"You gonna be, okay? You've been off for a couple of days and I do think you're sick. Who knows with what since we're dead but" — Brie lips twisted — "I should stay here till you're done getting your things together."

"I'm fine Brie, I was weak because I was hungry," Renee lied. An odd sensation from Brie's interrogation caused her to reach up to her forehead and rub it. The motion soothed the ill feeling.

"Then Garren and I will make sure you stay full."

Hearing Garren's name made the sensation disappear. "Garren's not mad at me?"

"Hell no. He's your most loyal night guard person."

"Night Sentinel," Renee corrected Brie and checked the floor for any discarded clothes.

"Whatever, you can remind me on the way. I'll come back and check on you in fifteen, okay?" Brie headed to the door.

"Sure," Renee responded, but felt disconnected to the conversation. She waited until Brie left and flopped on the bed. The ringing in her head had returned and was louder than before. She smacked her ears, but it didn't go away.

Liam sat beside her. "It's not going to go away, Renny."

Renee stared at the slight indentation on the mattress where he perched. Her hallucinations were getting very detailed. "Is it because I'm crazy?"

"Don't say that," he scolded.

His comment reminded her of Zane, which made her chest hurt. She already missed that prick, even in her irritation, and he'd only been gone for a few minutes. Part of her wanted to leave the room, find him and make up. Compromise and figure out something that worked for both of them. He was her safe place, her other half, what made her whole.

Her eyes flicked to her brother. "Is it because I'm sick or broken or whatever?"

"It's because you're changing," he said in a low voice.

"I don't want to change. I'm afraid," she admitted.

Liam grimaced. "So is your boyfriend."

"What do you mean I'm changing, Liam?" she whispered.

"Why don't you ask *it*?" he replied.

Acknowledgements

I usually have some idea of where a story is going before I start it. Mainly because I tend to write backwards. Meaning I have the end of the book before I start chapter one. Sometimes I know the series conclusion before I dig into writing the first book, even if that series is twelve books long LOL. But with this series... not so much. I knew where the first book would end because I knew this was a unique story that wouldn't appeal to everyone and I wanted to make sure that it ended on a HEA so that if the reader didn't want to continue, they could stop there and be satisfied.

For this book I also knew where it would stop and that it would be somewhat of a cliffhanger because this book dug more into the world of the undead. What their struggles were, what their power structure looked like and what threats existed for the things that seemed unconquerable. There's always a bigger threat - even to an apex predator. Holding the top spot isn't easy and eventually something will shift the power dynamic or take their place. Sometimes it's the top species that destroy themselves from within.

Since the beginning of the Kingdom of the Dead I wanted to dig into what it meant to be human vs. a monster. I wanted to explore what happens when humanity is stripped of all its civility and taken back to our most base instincts only to rediscover themselves. Zane thinks it's evolution, and maybe it is, but perhaps it might be how an individual chooses to rebuild themselves after losing everything they were. Truly being given a new slate to start over and be a different version of themselves. They might choose to be a better version of themselves or perhaps they pick a different path, one of carnage and death.

Is there still hope for a species that only seems capable of destruction and consumption? One might ask the same question for us humans. Renee seems to think so - do you share her opinion? Or are you more of a cynic like Zane, who wants to dare to dream of a future, but can't quite let go of his doubt? I hope the final installment for the series is everything the readers want as well as Renee, Zane, Brie and Garren too.

I must acknowledge the horde of people who have helped me build the Kingdom of the Dead. Each of you has contributed to breathing life into this story in your own way. If I miss anyone, it isn't intentional.

Thea, you are such an amazing and inspiring person. Your talent and the beauty of who you are as a person shine through on everything you create. Your ability to read a book and see the depth of the story is truly remarkable, bringing insights to your reviews and your cosplays that I haven't seen elsewhere. Thank you for being a part of my journey.

Joyce, once again you elevated this story to the next level and made it something special. Your ability to ask discerning questions that made me dig into the details even deeper made this world shine. I'm so glad you're not just my editor but also a treasured friend.

Chey, thank you so much for reading this and making sure Renee was represented correctly. You pointed out so many important factors that made her a better character and her actions in the story more realistic.

I've struggled to figure out how I can put into words how much your friendship and support mean to me and once again I struggle to find the words. None seem to be enough. None capture what's in my head and heart. I can't imagine my world without you in it. You're my PA but you're more than that, Gee, you're my guiding star on a dark night. My 'dark star'. It's been theorized that dark matter stars existed early in the universe before conventional stars formed. And that's what you are - a badass dark matter star that outshines an entire galaxy.

To all of the book bloggers who took a chance on this zombie love story and all the bookstagrammers who helped this story find its readers - I appreciate your encouragement and support.

I couldn't have done this with my beta readers and ARC reviewers!! Thank you for your feedback and for loving this dark dystopian fantasy. You gave the brooding zombie king a chance and for that I'm forever grateful.

Finally, thank you to all of my readers, for sticking with me and my unique stories. I hope you enjoyed it. If you did, please consider leaving a review.

Till the night is forever,
Ryana

Other Titles by Ryana Hunter

<u>Haunted Legacies Series</u>
Savage Petal
Cruel Orchid
Cursed Soil - Val, Dev, Ren, Gideon, Bela and Madoc will return in Cursed Soil coming 2026.

<u>Kingdom of the Dead Series</u>
King of the Dead
Queen of the Dead
City of the Dead - coming soon!

<u>Shadows & Scars Series</u>
Shadowed Moon
Grim Echoes - Coming Summer of 2025!

About the Author

Ryana writes compelling dark stories to remind the world of things forgotten and challenge their perception of reality, relationships, and beyond by giving voices to characters that are not mainstream. She is a neurodivergent author working in prose and comic books. Drawn to flaws and darkness, she finds honesty and depth lurking there, believing our most interesting stories are hidden behind our protective day-to-day facade. She scratches at the surface, flips the coin over, and keeps digging until she finds the soul of a story.

Ryana lives in a small island town in the wilds of the East Coast. When she's not writing or enthralling people with oral storytelling, she can be found relaxing with a cup of coffee, designing house layouts or painting with diamonds.

Do you want to stalk me?
Instagram: https://www.instagram.com/ryanahunter23/
Website: www.ryanahunter.com

Goodreads:
https://www.goodreads.com/author/show/22954808.Ryana_Hunter

Want more? Sign up for the newsletter for announcements, exclusive content, sneak peeks, and more! To sign up visit my website or use this QR code.

The Kingdom of the Dead Series

RYANA HUNTER
KING OF THE DEAD
KINGDOM OF THE DEAD | BOOK ONE

Note from Ryana Hunter

Word-of-mouth is crucial for any author to succeed. If you enjoyed *Queen of the Dead*, please leave a review online—anywhere you are able. Even if it's just a sentence or two. It would make all the difference and would be very much appreciated.

Thanks!
Ryana Hunter

We hope you enjoyed reading this title from:

www.blackrosewriting.com

Subscribe to our mailing list – *The Rosevine* – and receive **FREE** books, daily
deals, and stay current with news about upcoming
releases and our hottest authors.
Scan the QR code below to sign up.

Already a subscriber? Please accept a sincere thank you for being a fan of
Black Rose Writing authors.

View other Black Rose Writing titles at
www.blackrosewriting.com/books and use promo code
PRINT to receive a **20% discount** when purchasing.